8th April 2008

MW01016555

Ernst W. Fox

Given to me, (EALING)
When Ernie + Honey
came to tea.

EA Dawson - Grove

Running Rain

Running Rain

Ernst W. Hanisch

VANTAGE PRESS
New York

FIRST EDITION

Published by Vantage Press, Inc.
419 Park Ave. South, New York, NY 10016

Manufactured in the United States of America
ISBN: 0-533-15487-1

Library of Congress Catalog Card No.: 2006902474

0 9 8 7 6 5 4 3 2 1

To Hanni, my wife of fifty years, the mother of our two lovely daughters, and unflinching travel companion on the dusty backroads of Kootenay Country in British Columbia.

She never complained! One day, when she saw a sign on the muddy road to Trout Lake that read, "If you keep on going you are either lost or crazy," she didn't say anything. I ignored it and we kept on driving.

It was on the hiking trails in the Shining Mountains of Alberta and British Columbia, especially on the trail to Running Rain Lake, on the steep Alberta side of the Elk Range and on the trail to the Top of the World in the East Kootenays, that she proved herself a steadfast companion.

Running Rain

First Book

1

In the beginning, when great sheets of ice still covered the land that is now known to us as British Columbia, the valleys were deserts of ice and snow, and the land was devoid of all life. Then a mighty deluge from the melting glaciers further north flowed toward the sun and toward sunset, breaking all the barriers in its path and left the valleys with sparkling lakes and rushing streams. All the rivers flowed swift and clear and found outlets to the western ocean.

Many generations later, impenetrable, evergreen forests began to cover the valleys and mountains where there was rich soil deposited by the retreating ice. Only on the tops of the mountains, where the gods lived and no man dared to go, ice and snow remained as it is today.

During the day, only the cry of the golden eagle proclaimed mastery of the air above forest and lake, while during the night the gray owl patrolled the thick forest on silent wings. Bear and wolf were sovereign masters over all the land, and they lorded it over all the animals who inhabited the forests beside them.

The few dark-haired people, who had come down from the direction of midnight on snowshoes through the valleys and across frozen lakes, pulling their sleighs behind them, had envy for neither bear nor wolf. There were enough fish in lake and stream, and in the forests there was enough game for all.

The people were content that they had their lives, and they were quite happy to stay out of the way of bear and wolf. Only when they needed bearskins for their sleeping robes and wolfskins for their parkas did the animals have anything to worry about. For their summer parkas the people preferred soft deer and caribou hides, which they made into soft, pliable leather.

2

It was early morning in the Kootenay Indian camp some-where along the lower Kootenay Lake. To the eye of the inexperienced observer, no soul stirred at this early hour of a quiet, late summer morning. Even the half dozen dogs who had roamed around the camp during the night, and who had let out angry barks when they got the scent of a timberwolf or coyote, seemed to have settled down and slept in the warm sunshine with their heads between their front paws, as if they knew their nightshift keeping prowling wolves and coyotes away from the drying fish and caribou meat on the racks was over. Secure in the knowledge that they would receive their share of offal or fish when the braves returned from a hunt or fishing-weir, they always slept through the early morning hours at this time of the year.

Only the moving ears of the oldest male dog showed any sign of life, as they scanned the edge of the nearby forest. He was watching out for a strong bitch, half wolf and half dog. He had had her enticing scent in his nose during the night. She had run away from the camp and taken up with the leading gray wolf in the area, and when they formed an alli-ance she had taken over the pack around the Indian campsite.

The old dog hated her, knowing that she was very smart and had no fear of humans. After she had given the pack a litter of strong whelps, she took charge of the pack whenever they got near the Indian camp.

After a while, the largest dog got up, stretched and yawned, and walked toward the largest teepee, where he poked his nose under the loose leather tent flap. Then he crawled on his belly over to where a boy was sleeping, bedded down under a black bear robe. At the feet of the boy, where the dog hoped he could doze away the rest of the morning, he settled down in the most comfortable position he could find and went to sleep.

Stirred up by the crawling dog, a shaft of slanting, golden sunlight played with particles of dust from the middle of the teepee. It looked as if the dust particles were lifted into space and into their own orbit by the still-warm rocks around the dead fire, like a comet coming into view and then disappearing into the total darkness of outer space. But neither boy nor dog, now sleeping soundly, paid any attention to the display of morning light that now began to warm the teepee. The boy under his bear robe only stirred now and then in order to push aside his cover, which was getting too warm for him. When he was completely uncovered, one could see that he might be fourteen or fifteen years of age. He was used to sleeping completely naked under his bear robe, which kept him warm even during the coldest nights. When he was growing up, the boy, who by this time still didn't have his final name of "Running Rain," was closely watched by the chief of the tribe, who was thought to be his father, and all of the elders of the tribe who wanted to know whether he had the necessary qualities—such as courage, generosity, and humility—to take over as chief of the nation when he came of age.

One afternoon, ten tribal elders met in a secret council in the largest teepee, which was set aside from the rest of the lodges overlooking the lake. After the elders smoked the pipe, they held a lengthy pow-wow, where everybody present could voice his opinion about the boy. To the chief's consternation, all council members expressed the opinion that the young Kootenay showed no qualities that made him fit to be groomed to become chief of the Kootenay Nation.

The boy, who was now about fifteen summers old, had so far shown no desire to leave the lodge of his mother. His mother loved the boy dearly. Everybody from the Kokanee to the lower lake knew that, and of course, the boy knew that, too. From his mother, he received the choicest morsels of food. The clothes he wore were made from the finest deer hide or chamois, which she tanned herself with fish oil. She chewed all the hides she used for his clothing, including the caribou leather for his moccasins, herself.

In short it seemed to be the unanimous opinion of all the elders of the Kootenay Nation that the boy was a spoiled brat. But then, how is a loving mother to know when she just loves a child or when she spoils him?

The boy himself, of course, didn't know the difference. He enjoyed life as it was. Even when he was sleeping or when he went fishing with his dog by his side, one could see by the way his lithe body moved that he had never done any kind of work. When the boys of the village went diving from the cliffs along the lake, he showed that he was the most fearless swimmer of the bunch, as he jumped from the highest cliffs. And when it came to swimming, he thought he could swim across the lake of the Kootenay at its widest point without any problems, even though his mother had told him not to try without a canoe to accompany him.

The Kootenay boy was like most other boys of his age; he loved fishing. The spot he loved best was not too far from where the Kootenay River flowed into the lake. The White people had now drawn an invisible line across the Land of the Kootenay.

One day many summers ago, he was laying next to the river in the dry grass, listening to the warm summer wind rustle in the dry grass. The sun felt good and hot on his naked body. In the air was the humming of bees that reminded him of the sweet smell of honey. When he turned around in order to lay on his tummy, he saw a big, black spider hanging down on this gossamer thread from a willow branch above. The spider drifted back and forth in the warm wind, supported on its invisible rope.

The Indian boy wondered in amazement at how this almost-invisible rope could carry the big spider safely. What material was it made from to be so strong, and who made it for the spider? When the spider lowered himself again to get closer to the water, it looked like the spider had all the rope inside of him. when the spider touched the crystal-clear surface of the still pool, the water made a circular pattern, which flowed all across the pool only to get lost in the ripples below.

The boy still had his eyes on the spider, when to his amazement the insect now started climbing upward toward the willow branch, where the gossamer thread was attached. At this very moment, the surface of the water opened up with a loud splash, and a huge trout with her throat wide open appeared and made the water boil. When he looked at the place where the spider had been, there was nothing; the spider was gone, and the fish disappeared with a mighty splash in her pool.

The boy hadn't known that such a big fish was in that small pool. Immediately that trout went into his inventory as one of the fish he was going to catch with his bare hands. He lay there for a while in the rustling grass, his ears listening to the humming of the bees, the warm summer wind caressing his young body.

Before he walked back to his teepee, he wanted to find out whether he could see that big fish in the pool below him. Being a boy who lived by the water, he knew that fish are very wary about anything that moves above the water. He rolled on his tummy and crawled slowly toward the pool where the riverbank drops steeply. When he got to the edge of the embankment, his head moved slowly out above the water. He first saw the mirror image of his own face in the quiet pool. Then he saw the fish. But, wait, that wasn't the fish at all; that was the shadow of a fish on the bottom of the pool, and it moved. He didn't move, but his eyes moved slowly downstream. His eyes first had to get used to the dappled effect sunlight makes on the bottom of a pool. There was the trout, almost invisible against the pebbles on the bottom of the pool in perfect camouflage. Only the moving shadow on the bottom gave away the full size of the fish. This trout was holding the best spot in the pool.

The Kootenay boy would later in his life learn from what he had observed on this day. The best spots in any pool, above or below water, are always occupied by the biggest fish. This universal rule never changes and must be applied to any living organism that struggles toward the good life and survival.

When he moved his hand to touch the water below, the fish must have seen him, and with a mighty flip of his tailfin the fish disappeared under the overhanging riverbank on the other side of the pool. Now that he knew where the fish rested, the boy knew that he could catch him with his bare hands.

It was only a few days later that four Indian boys were lying in the deep grass next to the pool where they knew the big trout was living. One of the boys was Kootenay, the other three boys had already decided that he should be the one to catch the fish. They said that since he knew where the fish was hiding, it should be him. It's true; this is what they said. But the real truth of the matter was that nobody wanted to get undressed and dive into the cold water when they could sit in the warm sunshine and watch the proceedings while Kootenay was trying to catch a fish. Since he was also the best swimmer in the group, he, too, thought that it should be him. He took off his moccasins and his deerhide leggings.

He didn't have to worry about underwear, for in those days no Indian boy owned underwear.

Slowly he lowered himself into the pool. The water felt cool at first, but after he got used to it, he thought he could stand it for a while. At first, he felt the pebbles of the riverbottom under his feet. When it got too deep, he had to swim. The cold constricted his breathing and he knew he couldn't be there for too long. A couple of powerful strokes took him to the other side. Here his feet found a slippery rock he could stand on. With only his head sticking out of the water, he took a deep, gulping breath and then disappeared.

The three boys in the meadow watched with great excitement. All three were good swimmers themselves, and they knew the time he had to stay under water was limited. They looked at each other; he was taking a long time.

Kootenay in the meantime knew exactly what he had to do. He had to move very slowly, a sudden jerking move could spook the fish, and they would all be gone. Both his hands reached under the overhanging riverbank as far as he could, the palm of his hands toward the top.

Right away, he could feel several fish in the protecting darkness under the overhanging riverbank. It was held in place by the intertwined grass and willow roots. He couldn't see anything, but he found that he could see the shape of an object through the touch of his fingers. He had the size and the shape of the fish he touched in front of him, in total darkness, with his eyes closed. It was the first time in his life that he became aware of this amazing sensation. He could see through the tips of his fingers.

The fish he touched must have thought that his hands were just another fish brushing against them. Had they known that the most deadly hunter of all hunters on earth, a hunter who could see through the tips of his fingers, was after them, they would have disappeared fast.

10

Slowly, ever so slowly, his hands moved from fish to fish. In his lungs, the pressure increased to warn him that he would have to exhale some of the used-up air he had sucked in just seconds before. That would warn the fish. He was used to this feeling of panic, and he suppressed it. He moved a little to the left until he felt the big one. Both his hands moved along the sides of the fish. This monster trout was almost two feet long. He would never be able to hold that fish; his fingers didn't even reach around her girth. But he could grab it just in front of the tail with his right hand and move his left toward the gills. That way he would be able to hold the monster.

In the meantime, his three friends watched in growing apprehension. Once in a while they watched the water boil as if there was a titanic struggle going on under the overhanging riverbank. Then the water broke, and Kootenay stood on the invisible boulder, but just for a moment. Almost at the same time, with a mighty heave, a big fish came flying out of the water and landed a few feet away from the shoreline in the grass of the meadow. The fish, now finding himself on unfamiliar, dry territory, had a strong desire to get back into the more familiar surroundings of the cool river. He flipped his tail so hard he became airborne in his futile attempt to fly.

He would have made it back into the cool, lifesaving stream, had the boys not come and hit the dragon on the head with a big rock. That in turn gave the monster a good reason to hit the boy with his tail one last time. Then it lay still. Kootenay had, in the meantime, caught his breath and was reclining in the warm sun and waiting for his amber-colored skin to dry, so he could don his leather pantaloons and walk home to his mother's teepee with his friends.

3

In the meantime, while the boy slept soundly, his fate was decided by the elders of the tribe. He would be taken out of his warm teepee where his mother had looked after him for fifteen years.

It was not very rare amongst the Indian people of the time that the many children didn't know who their father really was. All his mother had told him was that she was given in marriage to the chief of the tribe and that the little boy who was hanging on to her leather stockings was part of her, which he actually was. Since the women of the tribe owned all the property in the tribe's possession, it included all the children at the time of her marriage, and she was in fact the only person who really knew who the father of her children was. When family matters were discussed by the warm fire in her lodge during the longer winter nights, she never said anything, but her face carried a suggestive, deeply satisfied smile that ended all conversation. And it was just as well, since most of the tribe's children became well-adjusted and responsible adults. Besides, her strong pastoral instincts left her no other desires than to see her only son become leader of the strong Kootenay Nation.

She wasn't told of the fateful decision the elders had arrived at. That her son, in order that he learn humility and self-reliance, the main qualifications necessary for a leader of the Kootenay, would have to live in the wilderness by himself for a year or more. If he survived in the wilderness on his own, he would be considered as weaned-off his mother's apron strings, and he would be ready to be groomed to accept the responsibilities awaiting him as leader of the Kootenay Nation.

While the boy slept peacefully, his mother was in the forest picking berries with the women of the tribe. Now, at the middle of summer, the saskatoon berries were ripe on the hillsides, and the women would be busy all day, filling the leather bags with the ripe fruit. They wouldn't come home before late evening. Then his mother would find her lodge empty. Her son had disappeared.

All the braves involved in the abduction had to make a promise of total secrecy so that the circumstances of his disappearance and whereabouts remained unrevealed. It was a few weeks thereafter that two children of the tribe, who had watched from behind some willow bushes, admitted how the boy was taken to a canoe and blindfolded. The canoe had then disappeared toward the side of the lake where the sun rises every day.

When the boy's mother came home with her leather pouches full of sweet berries, she knew immediately that something was wrong. She found his dog, Keeno, tied to one of the teepee poles, something that her son never did. In a frenzy, she ran through the whole village asking for her boy, but nobody knew where he had gone.

She walked home, her shoulders drooping, sobbing and crying bitterly, with tears running down her cheeks. She never noticed that her boy's dog had chewed off the strong leather thong that had tied him to the empty teepee and had disappeared, too. The dog then followed his master's scent down to the beach where the braves had loaded him into their canoe and where his scent disappeared. He then lay down on the very spot that had made his master disappear and howled his agony to the uncaring sky. He bared his fangs to the children who had dared to approach him, baring his fangs he looked like a wolf. The children, who had always known the bigger boy's dog, didn't know that Keeno was half wolf and half malamute. They were frightened and ran away, thinking that Keeno had turned into a wolf. They didn't know it was the agony of the loss of his master that had removed the thin wall between wild and tame and one day he would try to join a pack of wolves again.

Keeno's painful cries were heard for days along the shoreline of the lake. During the night his mournful cries were pointed toward the cold, uncaring moon, then toward the drifting clouds, as if they could tell where his master had gone. After a few days, when he realized that his master was not returning, Keeno found his way back to the spot where his scent disappeared, and he flung himself into the lake in pursuit of his master. The last time he was seen was when a brave in a canoe saw a dog's head sticking out of the water, pointing toward the faraway shore on the other side of the lake.

The boy's mother cried until she was completely exhausted, then fell into a death-like sleep, which lasted for a few days, until she had no more tears left to shed. Then, suffering quietly, she resumed her duties within the tribe. She knew that most of the young men who were exiled into the wilderness for crimes or other reasons never returned. She had given birth to the boy when she was still a child herself. She could remember only eight summers when she carried him under her heart. He was part of her. He had grown up with her like a brother; she never had a brother. This living part of her had been torn out of her very being. In its place as a great, gaping emptiness which she knew only another boy-child would be able to fill in time.

4

As the birchbark canoe rounded a steep cliff on the morning-side of the lake, the rhythmic slapping sound of the two paddles alerted a wapiti cow and her calf. When the cow saw the canoe rounding the cliffs leading into the sheltered bay, she decided to retreat into the velvety, green dawn of the virgin forest. She used an old game trail that had been used by deer, wapiti, moose, and, during migration, by large herds of woodland caribou for eons of time. So old was that game trail that the Indian people considered it part of their secret trail system across the mountains.

One could now make out that the canoe had three occupants. One of them had his eyes covered by a swath of rawhide; the other two did the rowing at a steady rhythmic pace in a kneeling position. The canoe steered directly toward a narrow strip of sandy beach. Part of the beach was well known to them it seemed; not only did the secret trail across the mountains begin here, it also served as a hiding place for their canoe. The unloading of the canoe only took a minute. There were only three bundles, the sleeping robes for the two oarsmen, and their tomahawks. The boy's bundle consisted of his bear robe and a leather pouch, which contained a medicine bundle and a knife; that was all he was allowed to take. Everything else he needed to survive he would have to make himself; that included making a fire if he wanted to warm himself during the night. The two older braves knew all that. What the boy was up against was a do-or-die game, a game only the keenest and the strongest of his age could survive.

They took the canoe and pulled into a thicket, being careful that it couldn't be seen and no branches were broken, for that would tell everybody who saw it that something was hidden in there. No animal ever breaks a branch like a human being. This accomplished, they stood back to check. They didn't worry much about their moccasin footprints in the sand; the next storm would wash them away when the waves washed ashore.

They helped their young companion to shoulder his bundle, knowing that the one year of exile in the wilderness he would have to endure was not punishment but part of his education. If he prevailed, he would gain mastery of himself and the world around him, but above all, he would learn and experience the laws of nature. Nature is neither good nor bad, for a living creature the law of survival is the most important law. It is uppermost of all laws; therefore, it knows neither good nor bad. They knew if this young Kootenay ever walked out of the wilderness he would be humble, everybody would respect him, and his mother would be very proud. As soon as the green canopy of the branches of the trees closed behind them, they were in another world. The green, velvety dawn of the virgin forest dampened all earthly sounds; only above them in the treetops the wind sang the whispering song of the evergreen forest.

The going was difficult here. Many seasons of storm and wind had broken down old and dead trees. Some of those trees had lived for a thousand years along this lake, stretching their branches toward the sky. They had shivered when lightning and storm-driven rain walked across the land. Their roots had dug ever deeper into the rocky soil, until they reached bedrock, where their capillary roots clawed at the tiniest crevice to provide nourishment so that the giant above might live. Now the giant lay there rotting. Some dead trees were so big they had to blaze a new trail around them. Then they had to find the old, overgrown trail.

All day they travelled. They forgot how many creeks they had crossed, how many boulders they had walked around. In the clearings they found berries. They laid down their bundles and feasted on the sweet fruit until they could eat no more. Then they walked.

After a day in the forest, they had lost sight of the lake, and young Kootenay had lost all sense of direction a long time ago. Later, toward evening, the forest cleared, and they saw another lake.

It was only Kootenay who thought it was another lake he was looking at. In fact it was the same lake, but it was much wider here. The dark forest on the other shore had withdrawn into a great, hazy distance. Above the dark, jagged edge of the remote mountains stood the red fireball of the setting sun.

When they reached a river, they made a left turn toward morning, but they followed the trail on the left side of the river. Now they had the setting sun behind them. Any less-experienced traveler would have been in a rush to make camp now, before it got dark, but our three companions, being at home in northern latitudes, knew that in the summer twilight lasts for a long time, so they walked on. They knew that not too far ahead was a much better camp spot. They found the ring of stones, which was an old firepit, used by Kootenay hunting parties for generations. Leaning against a tree was a bundle of smooth lodge poles. They would have no need for them today. Tinder-dry deadwood was collected to make a fire. When the sparks from the flint rushed into the dry grass a fire was going.

The pool below a small waterfall was full of fish. Their spears, which they had carried attached to their bundles, came out, and they weighed them for proper balance.

The young Kootenay had, besides a happy-go-lucky nature, also inherited from his mother a very keen sense of observation. So it was without great effort that he watched how his two companions got their needle-sharp harpoons ready for fishing. These points were slivers of bone attached to an arrow-straight willow pole by a very thin thong of leather. He watched how his companions checked the tightness of the rawhide. Then they sharpened the point to a needle-fine consistency.

He noticed that each one of his friends carried his own wetstone. He noted that each bone-point was furnished with sharp barbs that pointed backward from the tip. While he had used a spear for fishing, he had never had the need to make one. As it turned out, in a few days he would be in a situation where he would have to make his own spear if he didn't want to go hungry.

With their spears ready, his two companions walked carefully toward the pool below the waterfall. They had to be careful not to throw a shadow across the pool; no rock should roll into the water and disturb the weary fish in the pool. Now they stood on top of a flat rock motionless. Slowly their hands reached above their heads, each armed with a deadly spear. The two hunters stood there for just a split second, then came the lightning-quick thrust of two deadly harpoons. One projectile missed its target, but the other came up with a good-sized fish that would feed the three of them. One brave had to retrieve his spear by jumping into the rushing river. While one fish was roasting skewered over the fire, another one was speared. Now they had enough food to carry them for three days, but some of the meat had to be smoked so it wouldn't spoil. The three men ate one fish by pulling tender flakes of meat from the side of the fish that was cooked. Then it was turned until the other side was ready to eat. The other fish was sliced in half down the middle and hung from a wooden tripod over a smoky fire of dry juniper root. This fire was kept going all night.

Before they crawled into their bearskins, they climbed down the steep riverbank for a drink; washing was not part of their daily routine. Young Kootenay was sound asleep as soon as he had himself rolled into his bear robe. The other two, being experienced hunters and forest runners, only allowed their eyes to sleep. On the hunter, and the hunted, the ears never sleep; they are always listening, always recording, and always warning when a dangerous sound comes too close. They heard the pack of wolves prowling on their nocturnal hunt. That didn't disturb our hunters; they knew the wolves wouldn't dare coming close to a campfire. When the wolves smell smoke, they know there are humans, and man is the most dangerous hunter of all. Wolves never attack a group of fully armed men within the golden dome of a flickering fire.

One of the barks they heard was different. It could have been the sound of a dog. No wolf would come that close to the fire, but a dog used to campfires would. They reached for their spears. The animal circled the camp. They saw his green eyes, but the animal decided not to come any closer. Then it disappeared. After they put some more wood on the fire, they went back to sleep. Had Kootenay heard the sound of the bark, he might have recognized his dog, which could have saved him some problems later.

All three slept soundly until the tangent rays of the rising sun touched their faces. Comfortable in their bear robes they rested some more until they knew the morning sun had warmed the forest around them. There was no haste. The people of the forest were never in a rush; time meant nothing to them. They knew exactly where they were going. They also knew that everything they needed was in the rivers, in the lakes, and in the forest.

After they had rolled up their robes, they ate some smoked fish and drank from the river. Then they traveled on the game trail toward midnight, until the sun stood high on their backs. At midday, when the sun had reached its zenith, they knew they had to watch for a creek that came rushing from the mountains. Here they had to make a turn toward sunrise. As it was late in the summer, they had to watch not to miss the creek, in case it had dried up during the long summer.

They knew where they had to turn when they saw a crystal-clear brook tumbling into the river below. A few moments later, our three Kootenay Indians were observed by a moose splashing around under a waterfall in paradise. Then they were seen lying on a warm rock being dried by the hot sun. They noticed the teepee rings and firepits on the flat in the willows, but they wouldn't need all that tonight. They would travel on until they came to a lake; there they would camp.

Up to now, the going had been easy for the Kootenay boy; all his life the going had been easy. Most of the things he needed his mother had carried. When he was little, his mother had carried him too. Later on, when he had Keeno, the dog had carried his bear robe. Now he had to carry everything he had himself. Everything wasn't much, but his bundle was getting heavier and heavier as he looked up toward the sharp outline of the dark forest. Beyond that, he saw steep fields of scree and, melting into the blue of the sky, the rocky crags of the mountain they had to cross. The snowy ridges of the mountain range, seemingly out of reach for him now, looked the same as the puffy, white summer clouds that drifted across the deep blue sky.

At first they followed a good game trail on the left side of the creek. When the dense forest became impenetrable, they were forced into the dry creekbed. Droppings of elk and moose told them that they were still on the trail. There was no water in the creek; it had disappeared into the gravel. They found their way around huge boulders, through steep canyons where no sunlight ever touched the slippery rocks. Where trickles of ice-cold water percolated out of a sheer wall of stone, they drank. From here on, there was no water until they arrived above timberline. Here also was the line where trees gave up the struggle against the harsh climate and the relentless wind. Only stunted trees hugging the ground and grasses survived. As the green forest retreated below them, they entered a region of barren rock and stone.

This was the most dangerous part of their journey. The steep scree and talus was unstable and shifted under their tired feet. The most dangerous spots had to be crossed one at a time. Not until they found the game trail could they feel secure. Mountain goats had built those trails and used them safely through aeons of time. In turn the Indian people had found those trails and had used them for many thousands of years. They had watched how goats and sheep cross steep avalanche slopes one by one safely; they had watched how nanny goats instructed their kids how to cross danger spots and to make no sound. They knew that sometimes the bleating cry of the young could trigger a devastating slide of rock or snow. In the valleys among the debris of rock and snow, one could find the bleaching bones of many sheep and goats.

When they arrived at the top of the sharp ridge, they entered a frozen world of ice and snow. Young Kootenay and his two companions now found the time to lift their eyes. They stood in awe for a long time, gasping at what they saw. The red fireball of the setting sun was floating above range after range of ragged mountains. The sparkling ice of the Kokanee Glacier reflected shafts of light into the darkening sky, while toward midnight, above the haze of the valleys, stood countless mountains covered in snow and ice.

For a boy who had always lived close to the water, where in the summer heat the forest steamed and very often fog shrouded the lake and mountain heights, this limitless view caused tears to run down his cheeks. He turned to his companions and said, "Is this all ours?"

His two companions didn't answer since they didn't have any perception of private ownership of land or any other property. All they knew was that everybody who lived in this country availed himself of everything there was and left everything else to everybody else. Young Kootenay didn't get an answer to his question, but he made plans that one day he would travel to the end of his world, where the mountains pierced the sky. This was Kootenay's world, the Land of the Kootenay.

It was one of his companions who gave him a gentle push that shook the boy out of his dream. He turned around, and what he saw was no less spectecular.

One of his companions said, "Shining Mountains." He repeated it, "Shining Mountains."

After they climbed over the knife-edged ridge, they had a wide valley at their feet, which was now draped in the shadowy dusk of early evening. Only the highest, snow-covered mountains bathed in the pink light of the setting sun pierced the dark sky.

His companions had discovered a patch of hard-packed snow, which pointed down toward the dark edge of the forest. Down below them, in the near distance, the silvery surface of a small lake was visible. It was indeed the snowpatch that lasted until late summer, which supplied the small lake below them with water, while in turn the lake formed the headwaters of a new river.

When they saw the slippery snow, all three jumped into it at the same time for a fast glissade downhill toward the lake. They found the well-used campsite. When they had their campfire going, they ate the last of the fish they had caught the night before. Then they fell into their bearskins dead-tired. They slept late into the next morning.

When the sun rose over the snow-covered ridges of the Shining Mountains, a big black bear came looking for food around their camps. He had the scent of the discarded fish-bones in his nose. They had left the remains of the fish they had eaten the night before on the rocks around the campfire. The bear now enjoyed the fishbones and remains of the fish for breakfast. Our three companions heard him snorting and smacking, but he paid no attention to the three Indians who were rolled up tightly in their bear robes.

Now that they were out of food, they decided to stay at the lake and fish. To keep the bear away from their camp and to smoke some of the fish they caught, they kept a smoky fire going day and night for two days. Then they traveled on for three days, having the Shining Mountains on their righthand side, stopping only to eat and to sleep.

Imperceptibly, the countryside had changed. They were now one mountain range toward sunrise, and the country was drier. At the Lake of the Kootenay, the forest came right down to the water's edge and was almost impenetrable. Only on established game trails was travel possible. Here they found open meadows along the river; there were no large lakes. On the riverbank, which was now high above the waterline, travel was easy in the dry grass.

Small patches of pine trees presented no hindrance to their travel. Kootenay watched how the white fog drifted upward against the rocky mountains, until it seemed to be one with the white snow, and then disappearing like it had been swallowed by a fog-eating giant, leaving the sky clear and the deepest blue. He wondered what the country on the other side of the Shining Mountains was like; were there monstrous giants living there, or were they people like him who could understand the words he spoke? Were there shy, slim girls with pleasant smiles who could run faster than he could when he tried to catch them?

But then how could one find out when it was impossible to climb across the mountains to see what was on the other side. Somebody had told him there was no air up there, only snow. He dropped this thought, but almost too late. He ran into a dead poplar tree, which had fallen across his trail. He shouldered his bundle and walked on. The good trails continued for one more day; then the river made a sharp turn toward sunrise and the Shining Mountains. Ahead of them was a big swamp and an impenetrable sea of dry bulrushes. In the distance they could see barren hills with scattered patches of dark pines. His two companions seemed to know their way through this treacherous bog. Many of the trails were under water in the spring and summer; now the water level was low, and most trails were dry.

They found a dry spot raised above the level of the surrounding swamp. What were they doing here? They walked on to what looked like a barren hill from where he stood, but on the other side, facing toward midnight, was a large stand of dark pines. Behind the pines, invisible from where they were now, a lush, green meadow sloped gently down to the level of a lake. That this gently sloping meadow was an ideal landing spot for canoes became clear when they rounded the thicket. There, in the middle of the familiar ring of stones, was the firepit. A stack of lodge poles, ready for use, was leaning against the trees. Outside of the visible signs, nothing indicated that the camp had been used during the last summer.

There were many droppings of deer and wapiti; they seemed to come down from the barren hills to drink here. During the rutting season, this might be the spot where the bucks met to settle who owned the cows, and to ensure that another generation of frolicking fawns may bounce across the meadows.

As the sun was setting behind billowing clouds and sharp mountain ridges, they ate their last meal of the fish they had caught a few days before. Then they rolled into their bear-skins. Nothing disturbed their well-deserved sleep. The rustling wind in the pines and the gentle slapping sound of the waves on the sandy beach below them were familiar background music, which lulled them into a dreamless sleep.

5

The Kootenay boy awoke to the gentle sound of dripping rain; in the distance was the sound of rolling thunder. He didn't even open his eyes; he went right back to sleep. He had chosen his sleeping spot carefully, under the overhanging branches, his back against the tree trunk. His mother did very well when she used fish oil for tanning bearhides. It made them soft and waterproof.

On this fateful morning he did what he had always done while traveling with his companions, he waited until he heard them rummaging around the camp. It was a comforting sound to know that other human beings were there. He had always heard the sounds his mother made in the morning when she cleaned up her lodge. He heard those sounds of comfort but he always slept through them. While she was around, he drifted in warm comfort, in drowsy half-sleep, in the certain knowledge that the world he lived in was a safe place; safe and comfortable because his mother made it so.

While he was still under his warm cover, but fully awake now, he still couldn't know that his companions had left during the night, rolled up their bundles out of earshot and walked away on him. He became fully aware of the fact that his companions had utterly forsaken him when he jumped out of his warm cover and started looking under the trees where his companions should be. There was nothing, not a sign of his companions. They had left during the night while the rain came drumming down and he could hear nothing.

As we know, Kootenay had the habit of sleeping under his bear robe completely naked, and he had done so the last night. Now, as he jumped out of his warm cover and crawled out from under the protective branches, he was hit by the stinging drops of a driving rain. As he was running around, he didn't feel anything in his feverish hysteria, trying to find his companions, the two human beings he knew he depended on to survive.

Now, a completely naked Indian boy was seen running around a patch of forest in ever-widening circles and screaming the names of his companions. He ran down to the swamp shouting their names; nothing, only the mournful sound of a raven who had settled down in the bulrushes came to his ears. He ran along the lakeshore; he ran all over the next hill not feeling the stinging rain, which whipped like needles into his body. He didn't feel the rocks that cut his feet, and finally he kept on running out of the natural need to do something when he was in distress. He ran for hours up and down the lake. It was only good luck that kept him from entering the swamp, where the rising water from the last night's downpour had risen over all visible trails. He seemed to have known instinctively that the bottomless and obliterated quagmire would have sucked him down deeper and deeper, never to let him go. He couldn't do that. He would rather die shouting his fear into the raging storm in futile agony that the world had forsaken him, or reach into the sky where the lightning came from and be split down the middle like the tallest trees in the forest. Only when it was completely dark and he couldn't see any longer did he get down on his hands and knees and crawl into the protective shelter of the trees where his bearskin lay.

Here, in prostrate agony he was overcome by the greatest pain of youthful suffering a human being can experience. He had lost everything; his mother, his playmates. He was now hungry and shivering from the cold. The world he knew had collapsed around him, and he was looking down into a bottomless pit of loneliness and perdition. When there were no more tears left in him, only the loud sobbing and wailing cries were heard in his patch of forest. He collapsed completely. Unaware of what he was doing, he crawled into the protective shelter of his bearskin, where it was completely dry. Protected from the rain, his body warmed up, and he fell into a deep, dreamless sleep.

How long he slept, nobody knows, all we know is that he slept for days.

Early in the morning when he woke up he heard the rustling of dry grass around the tree where he had bedded down. Immediately he was wide awake, and he was scared. What could it be that was walking around his camp? He still had to learn what fear was, and that it is the most important component in the game of survival. It was fear that made him wide awake when he heard the sniffing sound the beast that was walking around the camp made, and it was fear that made him lay completely still and not dare to breathe. Now he could feel the pounding of his heart. He played dead out of fear. He still had to learn how to overcome fear and do everything that he had to do to survive. He lay there for a long time after the sniffing sound and the rustling of the grass had disappeared.

What was it that came sniffing around his camp? Was it a lone wolf or a bear? No, it couldn't be a wolf. A lone wolf is a dead wolf his people had said; wolves always come in packs. A bear maybe, but he knew the sound of a rambling bear. No it couldn't have been a bear. So, as he lay there in warm comfort, he thought maybe it was a deer, or a coyote, or a porcupine, or a rabbit, or a skunk, or a squirrel, or a mouse; not realizing that in his mind he had slowly diminished the degree of danger these animals represented to him.

He clearly didn't have to worry about a mouse, or a squirrel, or a rabbit. The only animal he had second thoughts about was the skunk. To deal with a skunk, the thought alone was repulsive. All one could do is walk away.

So, as this great fear subsided, he became aware of a great pain. To a young, growing animal, the pain of hunger is the greatest pain of all. He had never known the pain of hunger. Now it stared him in the face from the inside. It wrenched his guts as if his intestines were torn apart; hunger, the mother of all invention, in the human mind. It was the fear of wild animals and the fear of the dark and the cold that made humans carry fire with them, and when they couldn't carry it, they would make it just like young Kootenay would make it when he needed it. Within the golden dome of their campfires, the people were warm and safe. Feeling his courage return to him, he pushed back the bearskin that had covered him, and he felt for his clothing. There it was, dry and warm.

First he put on his leggings his moccasins and then his parka. When he crawled out of his shelter, he found the world a changed place. A layer of fluffy white clouds billowing up from the water filled the valley on the other side of the lake; while above the clouds the Shining Mountains carried a fresh blanket of pure white snow. As the sun rose above the reflecting ridges, it sent dancing light into the blue dome of the sky. Behind him, on the branches of the tree, frozen water droplets reflected the sunlight in all the colors of the rainbow. He felt for a moment as if living in an enchanted world of color and light. The world he lived in was so beautiful he reached out and wanted to touch it. Then he felt that great hunger inside, and his eyes lost the capacity to see the beauty around him. He saw black rings dancing around him, and for a moment, he felt like he would get sick and pass out, so he sat down until he felt better. He rolled up his bearskin, slung his medicine bundle around his neck, and walked down to the lake to drink. Bending over the dark water, he saw his mirror image. His now loose hair hung down in unruly strands and touched the surface of the water. He wasn't used to that. His mother had always made his hair into a tidy braid. He now took all the strands of his hair and twisted into a single knot on the top of his head. That felt much better.

With his bear hide neatly tied into a roll over his shoulder and his medicine bundle dangling around his neck, he walked away from the lake where now a layer of gray fog sent out dragon-like arms of unctuous cloud that threatened to engulf his campsite. He walked away toward the barren hills, but he stayed on the dry-grass meadows. He didn't know where he was going; all he knew was that he wanted to get away from the wet, cold fog. Loneliness gaped in front of him like a bottomless pit that threatened to swallow him.

For almost two months, Kootenay wandered over the hills and along the creeks. He lived on berries and other wild fruit. In the forest, he found the mushrooms his mother had collected and dried. He was careful to eat only the ones he knew. He realized now how many things his mother knew. She had shown him the difference between two look-alike mushrooms; where one was deadly poison, the other delicious to eat. He made up his mind that from now on he would always listen to his mother, if he ever found his way back to her again.

When he wandered around in the forest, he was surprised to find that he could get so close to spruce-grouse, sitting on the low branches that he could kill them with a stick. They were so tame. He cut himself a sturdy willow pole. As soon as he held it in his right hand, it felt good. It was the first weapon he had fashioned himself. He himself didn't realize it, but he had armed himself. That it was indeed the hand-held weapon that had forced man to walk on his hind legs, millions of years before, he didn't know, but he could feel it. When he saw his first rabbit in the hills, he threw a rock at it, but it got away on him. The next one was not so lucky. He could now kill some of his food at a distance, and he didn't have to live on berries alone.

It was indeed a deliberate and wise decision by the elders of the Kootenay Nation to send their son into the wilderness at this time of the year when there was a great abundance of all kinds of fruit, like berries and mushrooms, in the valleys of the Shining Mountains. That would feed him for months. The first winter would be critical, but for now, he didn't think of anything like that. He enjoyed the warm, sunny days of late summer. By the time the snowline had crawled down the mountains to the valley floor, he would have to be able to make fire and to build a lodge. The elders also knew that this year's young rabbits hadn't seen a human being before. The new crop of rabbits knew how to deal with coyotes, wolves, and owls. Of those predators, the owl was the most dangerous. It patrolled forest and glade on silent wings ready to strike with lightning speed at any animal that it could carry on its powerful wings.

But a human being, what was that? Never had they seen anything like it before. It walked on two legs, but it could carry deadly projectiles with one hand and propel them with the other with great speed and accuracy and over a great distance. Many of them never lived long enough to figure it out. He never thought of taking more rabbits than he could eat, and since he didn't have a fire, he pulled the tender meat off the bones with his strong teeth and ate them raw.

At this time of the year, life was easy in the Valley of the Kootenay. There was an overbundance of all kinds of food waiting to be picked. Many of the berries that hadn't been eaten by birds had now been dehydrated by sun and wind and were sweeter and tasted better now than when fresh. He loved the dry berries of the wild, the black currants he found in great abundance.

His bivouac was usually under a rock overhang or a cave in the hills or a thicket in the forest. When his tummy was full and he didn't have the feeling of hunger, he would sometimes forget that he was alone. He would lay there on his bearskin, look into the blue sky, and watch white clouds drift across the valley. This was the fall migration of birds. He knew that every year when the sun was getting closer to the horizon great flocks of birds came from there where midnight is and cruised toward the sun. He didn't know where they came from, nor did he know where they were going, but he knew that the birds would arrive when the poplars had turned their leaves into translucent gold. For a long time, he stared into the blue sky. Where the blue of the mountains melted into the blue of the sky, there was the beginning of infinity he thought, and he wondered if he would ever be able to cross the blue mountains and descend on the other side into the land of infinity.

He had now made his bivouac for a few days under a rocky overhang. It was almost like a cave, but it was open to the midday and the afternoon sun. He had chosen this spot on purpose. When he first found it one sunny afternoon, he had touched the golden-colored sandstone. It felt warm, and at this time of the year, it kept some of the heat all during the night. After he had eaten his fill of berries, he went and cut a good pile of branches from a nearby balsam fir. They would make him a soft and sweet-smelling bed.

To think that it would be easy for a lonely and tired Indian boy to fall asleep after wandering around in the wilderness is a mistake. Only the eyes close down and need rest; only the eyes must sleep. The nose is always awake. From the nearby bushes wafts the sweet, pungent smell of fermenting berries. Out of the forests drift the myrrhic scent of gum resin. On the warm wind there is the smell of a faraway forest fire. And then there is the all-pervading perfume of dry grass.

The ears never sleep; they are always listening. They hear the complete symphony of the sounds of the night. They listen to the whispering wind in the pines above the rustling of dry grass when the porcupine ambles along on its nocturnal errand. The ears of the human being hear the bone-chilling sounds of a pack of wolves complaining to a pale moon in the black sky, and they send a warning when the sounds of the dangerous night have come too close. The human being opens its eyes. There were two green eyes staring out of the dark, but they don't come any closer. Where there are human beings, there is danger. This two-legged hunter is the most dangerous hunter of all.

As the nightly visits of the two green eyes continued, Kootenay wondered whether there was a lone wolf trying to get close to him and catch him napping. The next night Kootenay decided to stay awake to find out what animal it was that disturbed his well-deserved rest. There was no wind on that fateful night; only a pale moon floated in the dark sky like a polished metal disk, uncaring and cold.

The boy sat with his bearskin wrapped around himself, his back against the protecting rocks behind, and waited. He waited for a long time. Then there was the blood-curdling sound of a pack of wolves fighting. Kootenay was so scared that his blood ran cold. He knew he could fight one wolf, but against a pack of wolves, he was defenseless. He looked around and above and found that the rocks protected him from behind and above. That left only the open side of his cave unprotected against a wolf attack. Then it was quiet; only the pale moon illuminated the primordial scene in front of him.

His experience with wolves was limited, but he knew that wolves rarely fight amongst themselves. Only when a loner tried to join a pack would they fight to the death to expel him. Warm in his bear robe, sitting upright against the rock behind, Kootenay fell asleep. When the rustling sound of the dry grass in front woke him, he reached for his stick; with that he could deliver a deadly blow.

His eyes stared into the moonlit night. There was nothing. He looked again. Yes, there was two green eyes just barely above the dry grass. This animal, or whatever it was, seemed to be crawling toward him on its belly. When it came closer and lay still, he could hear a whimpering, moaning sound, like he had heard from badly wounded animals. This was scary.

Kootenay wanted nothing to do with a wounded wolf, so he jumped up and ran toward the animal, swinging his willow pole. He hoped to scare the animal away. It worked; the animal raised itself onto its front legs and, dragging his left hindquarter through the grass, got away.

Now, that peace and tranquility had been restored in his part of the world, the boy fell asleep. He slept late into the next day, but as soon as the tangent rays of the warm, morning sun touched his face, he was wide awake. Enjoying the warmness of the sun, he ate some of the dry saskatoon berries.

He had collected them the day before from the bushes higher up the hill. The berries had dried on the vine and were a little hard to chew, but they were very sweet. He was so absorbed with chewing sweet berries that he almost forgot all about his surroundings. That could be very dangerous with a pack of timberwolves in the vicinity.

Then he heard the rustling sound of dry grass. It seemed to be coming from all sides. Whatever it was that was trying to get close to him was very cautious in approaching. Then there was silence for a while.

Kootenay was now very alert. He didn't move. He had stopped chewing, and his mouth was slightly open, as if he could hear better with his mouth open. Then he saw it in front of him. In the dry grass, he could see an animal crawling toward him on its belly, but oddly, he could only see one ear.

It looked like a wolf, but he had the feeling it was a dog. But why only one ear? Slowly the animal kept coming closer, as if uncertain who it was looking at. Two yellow eyes stared at the young Indian boy in front of him uncertainly, yet waiting for a sign of recognition.

Kootenay now turned around. Behind him in a cavity in the rocks, covered with a flat stone, was his food cache. It contained the remains of a rabbit he had taken the day before, and he kept in the cool rock for later use.

He cut off a few pieces. Kootenay could see how the animal's nose came up sniffing the food. Now he threw a piece of meat toward the animal. The animal crawled closer and accepted the food, swallowing it whole. The animal was now close enough that Kootenay could have reached it with his stick. The animal knew that he could still get away if he had to. Two keen eyes watched Kootenay's every move, still not certain that it was his boy-master he was looking at. Even his keen, quivering nose wasn't sure; only his eyes told him that this could be the same boy who had raised him, who had thrown him the choicest morsels of food. He could remember how warm it was under the boy's bearskin when he was a puppy.

That Kootenay had the same thoughts going through his mind the dog couldn't know, or could he? Could this miserable-looking wolf in front of him be his dog Keeno? He moved a little closer. His right hand didn't carry the willow pole any longer, but a piece of rabbit meat. He didn't want to throw it. He knew if this was Keeno, he would accept it from his hand. He reached out at the same time the malamute moved a little closer on his belly. Out of this mighty wolf-hound came the small whimpering sound of a little puppy in distress.

In this magical moment of recognition, Kootenay said the dog's name, "Keeno." In this split-second, Kootenay knew his faithful dog had followed him across a lake, through impenetrable forests, across mountain ranges, down steep snowfields. He had waded a deadly swamp until he found his master's scent again. Then last night, half starved, he tried to take a little food from the kill where the local pack of wolves were feeding. He was rejected. During the ensuing fight, they tried to kill him. Bleeding from several wounds, he managed to crawl away on his three good legs. He knew that if he could make it to within the magic circle of fire, close to the human being that he knew, the pack wouldn't dare to get within the reach of the human and he would be saved. He had licked his wounds all night to stop the bleeding.

When Kootenay saw the grievous wounds the wolves had inflicted on Keeno, he said, "What have they done to you?" He touched Keeno, and this mighty dog, as a sign of total submission to his master, rolled over on his back and offered him the most vulnerable part of his body, his soft underbelly. Kootenay couldn't do anything but cry.

One of Keeno's ears had been ripped off, only tatters of skin were hanging down from it. On his right shoulder the skin had been torn off, and the bone was visible. They tried to hamstring him. That would have been equal to slow star-vation for a lame dog in the wild. He also found that Keeno had a deep cut in his upper left loin. It wasn't bleeding any more, but it would take a long time to heal.

What was he to do? He couldn't stay here in the hills; the pack would return during the night and try to kill Keeno. He couldn't let that happen. He had to get down to the lake where the abandoned fishing camp was. The old lodge poles were still there; he could make that into a warm, permanent winter camp, where he could stay and fish. Now that he had a companion, he would have to provide for him, too.

6

Now that he had made up his mind what to do Kootenay felt much better. He gave Keeno the last of the meat from the rabbit. Then he rolled up his bear robe, slung his bundle around his neck, and they were on the road.

Keeno was still hurting badly and couldn't walk fast on his three legs. Half-way down the hill, they made a detour toward the spot where the rabbit warren was. If they got lucky, they could catch a rabbit or two, for they needed food. When they got close to the warren, but were still out of sight in a creekbed, he laid down his bundle and told Keeno to lay down and stay. He knew on this hunt, a dog who couldn't run fast was of no use to him.

Kootenay was out of luck. All his rocks missed, but while he was wandering around, he found the carcass of a good-sized rabbit. It was a flock of magpies who had drawn his attention to the spot where the rabbit was laying in the grass. Without the birds he might have missed it. Only the entrails had been eaten. It looked like an owl had killed the rabbit and then found that it couldn't carry it, as it was too heavy, so it had eaten what it wanted and left the rest for the coyotes. Only Kootenay got there before the coyotes did.

When Kootenay found it, a colony of ants had already invaded it and the smell of decay was around it. That didn't matter to the boy; he knew that his dog would savor it as a delicacy. When he got back to where he had left his belongings and his dog, Keeno was wagging his tail. Kootenay had gained a companion. During the next few months and years, it was this animal that made him more human and humble than anything else.

They were approaching the old fishing camp, where Kootenay had slept for a few nights during the storm. This place would be made into a permanent camp. He found the place as he had left it. Along the lakeshore, he found a lot of deer droppings. The hunting would be good here, as many animals came down to the lake to drink.

Dropping his bundle in the dry grass, he carried his bleeding dog down to the water's edge, where Keeno drank greedily. Then he turned his head and licked his master's hand. Kootenay washed the animal's wounds. The ear was not a serious wound. He cut off a few tattered pieces of skin and left it serrated as it was. It would heal within a few days. The left hind leg was a very serious wound. The sharp fang of a wolf had sliced through skin and muscle, which had left a deep gash that opened and bled every time when Keeno tried to put weight on his leg. Around his neck were bite wounds, not bleeding any more. He washed the punctures and left them. On his right shoulder, the skin was peeled back; that would have to heal by itself as the boy couldn't do anything about it. Now he went and fetched the rank-smelling rabbit, which he had left dangling from a tree. Keeno loved it.

Setting up the lodge poles was the most difficult part of setting up his teepee. The old leather thongs had dried out; birds and squirrels had chewed on them. Kootenay had to go down to lake to soften the leather in the water. When he came back, his newfound dog was asleep. At first he thought he didn't know how much blood the dog had lost, Kootenay would have to stay close to the camp. If the wolves found Keeno in this condition they would kill him. As it turned out, Keeno had found the most comfortable position to rest his tortured body and heal his wounds. When Kootenay looked closer, he noticed that Keeno's good ear was moving. It was a good sign. He was still alert, and any unusual sound would alarm him and wake him up.

When the poles were standing, Kootenay spaced them evenly around the old firepit. The rest of the afternoon he spent collecting pine branches and transporting them to the teepee. When the red fireball of the setting sun dipped down behind the mountains, Kootenay had built himself and his dog a temporary shelter. As the lodge wasn't complete yet, it was still open to the sky. He would think about that to-morrow.

The following weeks brought warm, sunny weather to the Valley of the Kootenay. It was what the White man called "Indian Summer." The boy completed his teepee and nursed his dog back to health. Down by the swamp, he found tall, dry bulrushes. He thought they would make a better roof for his teepee than pine branches. He found plenty of dry reed-grass, which made a fine bed for himself and the dog. He also found cool moss, which he carried home to dress Keeno's wounds. His foraging for the things he needed took him deeper and deeper into the swamp. Water levels were lower now.

At first he followed what he thought to be game trails. The droppings he found told him that deer, wapiti, and wolves were using the trails, too. Far off from the regular trail, he found the tallest bulrushes for the roof of his teepee.

Every time he got back to his camp, there was his dog waiting for him and wagging his tail. That was a great comfort for Kootenay.

One fine, sunny morning, the boy had jumped from lump to lump of dry bulrushes. He was almost at the water's edge when he saw what looked like the bow of a canoe sticking out of the vegetation. He jumped across some open water; there was higher, dry ground there for him to stand on. The canoe had been turned upside down, obviously to keep snow and rain out. He tried to pull it out from its hiding place but couldn't budge it. He tried to turn it right-side up, but it wouldn't move. Storm and rain had bent the tall bulrushes over the canoe and held it fast. Not until he had removed several layers of them could he turn the boat. Once he had it on its keel, he could pull the craft easily out of its place of concealment. He found two paddles laying under the hull in good shape.

Kootenay realized that he had found something of great value to him. This canoe, if he could get it floating, could take him to the best fishing spots on the lake and beyond. Of course, at this time, he couldn't know that the same boat would one day take him to the furthest reaches of his domain after he had traveled for years in the land of the Shining Mountains and he had become a famous hunter.

First Kootenay had to make certain the canoe didn't leak. He had a look at the outside of the hull. It looked fine. The layers of birchbark had been sealed with pinetar, which had become brittle in time.

He wondered if it would float. He pushed it toward open water, where the water was deeper. First he threw the two paddles in; he would need them. As soon as the canoe was afloat, he jumped in and grabbed a paddle. On his knees, he paddled furiously to get to the shore. He noticed several leaks, which he would have to repair, but the canoe carried him as far as the sandy beach before it was completely swamped. When he pulled the boat onto the beach, his dog came running and wagging his tail. He now had a dog and a boat to repair.

The next few days were full of feverish activity in Kootenay's camp. As soon as the sun rose over the silvery ridges of the Shining Mountains and it was warm enough, boy and dog were out picking berries and hunting rabbits. Kootenay found out that his dog Keeno was a formidable hunting companion. Even with only one ear scanning their surroundings, he could hear more than Kootenay with two.

In time the two made the most efficient hunting team by complementing each other. Kootenay found that Keeno's nose was their most valuable asset. When they were close enough to a rabbit for Kootenay to throw a rock, the dog would point his nose and freeze for a moment, just long enough for Kootenay to get a fist-sized rock ready and see where the rabbit was hiding. Then he would get himself into a position where he could cut off the rabbit's retreat into a warren. It seemed to Kootenay as if the dog knew that if they didn't catch a rabbit he would go hungry. As it quite often happened, when the boy hit a bunny with a rock, he didn't kill the cottontail. He just knocked him out for a moment. That gave Keeno enough time to catch the bunny before he disappeared into his warren.

Many golden days in sun and wind and healthy exercise helped to heal Keeno's wounds completely, and in time, he became the best rabbit hunter a hungry boy could own. The dog's system was very simple. He had found out that he had to rely completely on his nose and not on barking. That just scared the bunnies into their warren. Later on, when Kootenay got busy repairing his canoe, Keeno would go hunting by himself. Very rarely did he ever come home without a rabbit or a bird. The big, ugly scar on his hind leg seemed to have slowed him down a bit for now, but what he had lost in speed was more than made up by the experience he had gained hunting beside his boy.

He had found out that speed wasn't the only thing that counted; one had to walk quietly and always work a straight line, and always zero in on one single rabbit. If you thought you could catch two, you got confused and lost them both. All you got was two cottontails bobbing up and down, and that made one very hungry. Another thing Keeno had learned from Kootenay was that you always carried your catch home. So when he came down from the hills with a fat hare hanging from his muzzle, he would put it down in front of the boy's feet in the knowledge that he would get more than his share.

Kootenay had collected enough pine resin to repair his canoe. He had noticed that a pine tree would bleed resin when the outer bark was peeled off the wood, so he made incisions and pulling the bark down on several trees. It was like a wound on the body of the tree. The sap would run out like a clear liquid but solidified into a golden, honey-like consistancy, which could then be applied and kept malleable for a long time.

To caulk all defective seams took him a long time. Since he had also collected a good amount of hard resin, he needed heat to melt it. Now he had to make a fire. He had watched how people made fire, but as he found out, watching some-body making a fire with two sticks of wood was one thing and making a fire was another. No matter how hard he tried, he couldn't twirl the sticks he held between his hands fast enough to catch fire, but he could feel that it got hot by friction.

Keeno was watching him with great interest, with his head turned sideways, trying to figure out what Kootenay was up to. Finally he said, "Keeno, making a fire is the one thing you can't help me with. You know nothing about it." As it was, the dog didn't care if he ate his rabbits raw, but Kootenay was tired of raw meat. He thought that it would be nice to have some cooked meat for a change.

Down by the water's edge lay his canoe, repaired, upside down, calling to be launched for a trip of exploration into the wild, blue yonder, where the silver of the mountains melts into the blue of the sky. There, where it was always night, where no sunray ever penetrated, was the country of midnight.

One day the canoe was launched and tested to see if it was seaworthy. They cruised along a swampy part of the lake. Keeno on the bottom of the canoe, head between his paws, watched Kootenay.

Another day, late in the afternoon, they came upon a gold mine of fish that would keep hunger away from their camp for days. In those days, Kootenay lived in the wilderness, the lake they were on was still a spawning area for salmon, as the rivers still ran free without dams. In a shallow pool of water, several large salmon were trapped when the waterlevel dropped quickly overnight and left the fish stranded without an escape channel open to the lake. The sandy pool was so shallow one could see the dorsal fins of the fish sticking out of the water. Kootenay and his dog now went on a fish hunt that was a lot of fun to watch. Kootenay, using his willow pole, clubbed some salmon, and Keeno chased and caught the rest.

The canoe trip toward midnight on the lake was delayed for a few days while fish filets dried on the racks. During the night, a pack of coyotes was heard howling around the teepee, attracted by the smell of drying fish, but when Keeno bared his fangs and went growling after them, they disappeared in a hurry. He had developed an intense hatred toward anything that looked like a wolf or a coyote since his cruel mauling by that pack of wolves.

7

During the next few days, a canoe with a man and a dog in it was observed cruising toward midnight, in beautiful fall weather, by an old Indian trapper who was living as a recluse somewhere in the Shining Mountains. As a matter of fact, he had several semi-permanent camps established, and depending on the time of the year and what activity he was presently engaged in, whether it be fishing or hunting or looking after his traplines, he would occupy the camp most conveniently located in relation to his present activity. By far, the most important part of his daily activities was doing nothing outside of contemplating the world around him.

The old man, besides being desirous of maintaining this most satisfactory state of affairs, preferred to live in paradise by himself. At the time, he was heading for his winter camp, which he called "the place where the warm waters flow." He didn't give a signal that he had seen the canoe cruising north. Since the craft was cruising north, toward midnight, he reckoned that the canoe was heading toward Nlak-Pamux country. A few days' travel toward sunset and he would never see them again.

In the meantime, Kootenay and his dog were enjoying their stay in paradise, too. On some days, when they weren't fishing or hunting, they could be found reclining in some secluded poplar grove along the lakeshore, where the last golden leaves of the year were whispering in the mild autumn wind. The green leaves of summer had turned into a translucent curtain of warm, flowing, autumn-gold, which made the hearts of our two travelers glad and carefree. They forgot the precarious state of their present mode of existence.

Keeno had completely recovered from his injuries; to Kootenay it seemed as if his dog was stronger and more confident now than he had ever been. By his master, Keeno was treated as an equal, and toward his lupine cousins, he felt and showed an irreconcilable hatred. On some days, he would steal away when the boy was fishing and go on a hunt by himself, and it was a rare day when he came home with an empty bag. When it rained, they would sleep under their upturned canoe.

Some star-filled nights they would sleep on a dry spot in the reeds. For hours, they listened to the wind in the dry bulrushes and stared at the black sky with its countless stars, a pale harvest moon, and shooting stars. They didn't know what this display of extraterrestrial fireworks were all about. Kootenay would reach over and touch his companion to console himself, and the dog. He didn't say anything because he didn't know any more than his dog did about what it was. Only that magic ribbon of comfort remained tying them ever closer together on this lonely journey through space.

On one warm morning, the lake narrowed down and became a fast-flowing river. Kootenay was confused. How was it possible that this river was flowing toward midnight, where no sun ever touched the earth with its warming rays; where the cold wind came from that turned water into ice so hard that one could walk on it, when the river of the Kootenay was flowing toward where the sun was at midday? Was this another river? Was this the river of no return that flowed to the everlasting ice? The boy had cold shivers running down his back. He didn't want to go where there was only ice and where the sun never shone. He got scared.

With a few fast paddle strokes, he turned his canoe around until he had the light of the warm sun in his face.

Then the rhythmic splashing sound of his paddle was heard all day. He wanted to get away from the river of no return as fast as he could. Rowing against the current of the fast-flowing river was hard work. Progress was slow. They camped in the reeds behind a beaver dam. That night, when they lay still, Kootenay could hear the sound of silence. Just above his head was the hissing sound of birds' wings, flocks of low flying geese trying to find a spot on the lake to settle down for a night's rest on their migration south in this uncertain world of total darkness. The boy knew that he had to make choices; that some of the choices could mean life or death to him and his dog became clear to him in the morning.

All night they listened to the hissing sound of birds' wings. Then there was the eerie sound of silence after the birds had stopped flying. Not a ripple was heard on the beaver dam behind them. It felt like the world was holding its breath to prepare for the oncoming winter storm. They both fell into a troubled sleep, short and restless.

When Kootenay awoke, Keeno stood above him licking his face to wake him. They both looked into a changed world. Angry, billowing, gray clouds were there where the Shining Mountains had been. From midnight, a black roll of clouds came thundering toward them, sending stinging snow pellets into their watering eyes.

Kootenay knew what they had to do. He rolled up his bearskin, threw it into the canoe, then jumped into the canoe, and Keeno jumped after him. From a pile of dried fish, he threw a piece to Keeno, and he chewed on one.

As soon as they left the calm waters of the beaver pond, they were in the open water of the lake. For a while the full fury of the winter storm hit them and tossed them about, but the wind now hit them from behind. Kootenay knew he was cruising toward noon. He held the boat close to the shore. The lakeshore was now on his right, where he could see it in the driving snow. He had to be close in case the boat got swamped and they had to swim for their lives. With the wind hitting them from behind, Kootenay didn't have to paddle very hard to keep the canoe moving as fast as the waves. There was no need for steering, as the wind kept the canoe on course. Once, when the snow squalls cleared, he had the shoreline just on his right side and he was traveling fast.

Still it took them hours before the shoreline looked familiar. Then he pushed against the familiar, sandy beach below his old camp. In the driving snow, he could hardly see his teepee as he ran up the hill with Keeno by his side, but there it was; his home standing in the gloom. There was no damage from the wind, only the reed-mat he had made to cover the door opening had blown into the branches of a tree.

Kootenay now moved fast. He pushed his bearskin through the small opening of his teepee. A handful of dry and now-frozen fish was the only food they had left. It, too, went into the teepee. Then he pulled his canoe on the beach and turned it upside down to keep it dry in case he had to use it. Only then did he notice that his hands were almost frozen. There was no feeling in his fingertips. He swung his arms wildly around his body so that his hands hit his back; that brought circulation back into his fingertips but also excruciating pain. He knew that his hands weren't frozen.

In the dark inside his teepee, he rearranged the pile of reed grass. He pushed a pile against the outer wall of his teepee to keep the draft away from his back. Then dog and boy were chewing on a piece of dried fish. He pushed the reed-mat against the opening so no snow could blow in.

Outside, the fury of the winter storm increased, but inside of the teepee he had built himself, boy and dog were warm. The dog had crawled in with Kootenay under his bearskin, so they fell asleep, while through the opening on the top a fine, powdery snow drifted down to them. The howling of the blizzard outside and the feeling of safe shelter lulled them into a torpid state of hibernation, and they both slept. They slept for days.

Kootenay didn't notice that his dog crawled out of the teepee and went hunting on his own. His malamute-wolf was in his element. He could lay in the snow all day as long as he had food. In the deep snow, he would walk up the hill where the rabbits were. He would then dig himself into the deep snow not too far from where the bunny had to appear. Then, when the bunny was out far enough, he would cut off his retreat and a quick bite would make it hang from his muzzle. He carried the rabbit home and laid it at the teepee door, where it froze stiff. After the snow covered his tracks, there was no sign of life around their camp. Unctuous cold, ice fog over the lake held all life in an icy grip. The marauding wolf pack gave a wide berth to Kootenay's teepee, since they had found out their archenemy had not succumbed to the grievous wounds they had inflicted upon him.

With the vast experience of their kind, they knew that a wolf-dog who forms an alliance with a human being receives from that man the strength and the cunning of the human hunter, which they could not overcome. They also knew that such an alliance would form a durable bond, which would last for the lifetime of the wolf-dog. After a few days, the ice fog lifted from the lake. The sun, drifting through the icy haze in the sky, hanging low over the valley, had no warmth. When he got down to the lake, Kootenay found that the spot where he had fished was now a sheet of ice. Only toward the deeper part there was still some open water. The valley had become quiet now that all the birds had gone.

When, on the following day, the sky cleared completely, it got very cold. The sun had lost all its warmth. He noticed a plume of smoke rising from the forest toward the Shining Mountains, exactly at the spot where the sun appeared late in the morning. Had he not rowed away from where the cold wind came from? Would it not be warmer if he walked toward the sun? The next day, the same wisp of white smoke appeared, but it stood there in the ice cold air. It didn't drift like smoke. He knew that smoke from a fire would disperse in the air. This white plume didn't move, it remained in the same spot. Once the white wisp of smoke had aroused his curiosity, it wasn't too far for the idea to go there and investigate.

He was cold, and where there was smoke, there had to be fire. That his decision to go there and see would be the key for his survival he couldn't know at the time. His desire to investigate would change his life. It actually saved his life because without fire he was destined to perish.

After he made the decision to abandon the relative safety of his present camp, he went into feverish activity. First he had to winterproof his moccasins. He found the dry material he needed for that in the pile of reed-grass, which he had used to sleep on. All he had to do was cut it to the proper length and shove it into the bottom part of his moccasins. Then he put his foot in and pressed them together.

He did that twice. Right away he felt how warm his feet stayed in the snow. He tied the two largest rabbit pelts around his ankles. He could walk in deep snow without getting his feet frozen. Then he went about hiding his canoe. He chose the same spot where he had found it; there it would be safe in case he needed it again. Then he swung the bearhide around his shoulders. It was held in place in the front by a wooden clasp that would leave his hands free to carry his willow pole and the dead rabbit, which was the only food they had besides some dry berries in his pouch. They were then off.

Kootenay left his teepee as it was. He had secured the upright poles with rocks so that even a strong wind couldn't blow them down. From a distance, he looked back. In the bright winter sun, he saw his teepee standing there. It had become home for himself and his dog. He felt no sadness for leaving this place. What he felt was more a sense of adventure, the riskiest adventure of all, the great game of survival.

In the deep snow, he found his way through the swamp. It was a lot easier to walk here now that all the waterholes were frozen. All day long, he had the cold, crunching snow crying under his feet. The plume of white smoke hadn't come any closer. In the afternoon, they came to a river. It seemed familiar to Kootenay. For a stretch, he remained on the sunset side, his dog at his side. Most of the river was frozen now, but in fast-flowing stretches, it was still open. He noticed that the river of Kootenay was flowing toward the sun.

In the afternoon, when the sun was nearing the horizon, he knew he had to make camp somewhere fast. He decided to first cross the river and enter the virgin forest on the other side. In the forest, it would be warmer than out in the open. He found the spot he was looking for in a dry creekbed. The storm of the last few days had piled up a huge snowdrift, filling the low areas of the creekbed. The top was so hard it carried him. When he stuck in his willow pole, he found the lower layers of the snow soft.

He dug out a cave in the soft snow with his willow pole and his bare hands, large enough for himself and the dog. When his hands were cold, he warmed them in the heavy winter coat of his dog. Then he prepared his snow bed carefully. His bearskin was laid out with the fur inside. Then he gave his dog part of the rabbit Keeno had laid in front of the teepee. Kootenay chewed on the frozen hindquarter and a handful of dry berries until he fell asleep, leaving the rest for the next day.

Keeno had found a spot on the open side of the snow cave, at the end of the boy's bearskin, out of the wind, his feet under his warm belly. Sound asleep, Kootenay's feet found the same warm spot, under the dog's belly. They slept soundly through the long winter night. Only once during the night Kootenay heard the snarl of his dog, but nothing happened, so he fell asleep again. Only when the two continued their travel late the next morning did Kootenay find out that a huge mountain lion had approached their camp, attracted by the smell of the rabbit. That was when Keeno let out the angry snarl, which convinced the cat that there would be no easy pickings there. The two traveled on through the thick forest, with Kootenay making tracks and Keeno right behind.

Kootenay couldn't see the white smoke any longer, so he traveled toward the morning sun. It wasn't long until he arrived at the edge of a canyon. The fast-flowing river was deep down in a rocky gorge. Kootenay knew that crossing this fast-flowing stream would get his feet wet, so he stayed on the sunny side of the canyon. There the going got difficult. He had to watch not to slide into the river. Higher up, the river squeezed through a tight canyon, ending in a waterfall below. Above him, on his side, a steep cliff blocked his advance into the hills. Looking across the river, he saw a wall of trackless rock. The spray from the waterfall had pulled a thin layer of sheer ice across rock and vegetation. To walk through this wall of rock armored by a sheet of ice would be impossible. This bastion of sheer rock started on the other side of the river and continued on Kootenay's side.

It seemed as if his effort to advance up the river, toward where the smoke from the fire came from, which was burning up there, had come to naught. On a little spot of dry grass where the sun shone warmly, the dog and Kootenay sat down and consumed the last raw pieces of meat from the rabbit. When Kootenay had eaten the last shreds of meat from the bones, he threw the bones to Keeno. Their hunger stilled, and they rested for a while.

For the first time in Kootenay's short life, he became aware that hunger and starvation stared him in the face. But then there was the dog; he could eat his dog if he had to. The dog, crunching a bone to get at the marrow, looked at Kootenay with big, trusting eyes. That thought had made Kootenay feel guilty, and he pushed it out of his mind.

He said, "I'm not going to eat you!" Then he fondled his dog with loving hands to reassure Keeno that he would not eat him. Deep down within him, he became aware of a deep conflict, a conflict between right and wrong, which he had to bridge. The feeling of trust in those eyes was so deep and so absolute that Kootenay was ashamed of himself for being capable of carrying such a thought. For the first time in his life, he became aware that he carried within him a moral sense between right and wrong.

They walked along the steep escarpment on loose scree, which rolled away under their feet. Then they found a spot where gravel rolled out of an opening in the rocks. It was the opening they were looking for. It was the only opening in that rockband which would allow a dog to walk through. Kootenay had to push Keeno ahead of himself while he held on to the rocks on the side with one hand. When Keeno reached over a ledge above with his front paws and jumped out of sight, Kootenay knew they were over the top.

Now they stood on a grass-covered ledge. Kootenay enjoyed the amazing view, that opened up in front of him. In the blue haze of the cold winter day, he could see the lake they had left two days before.

Right below his feet was the waterfall, which had barred their advance through the canyon. When he turned around, he could see the white smoke rising not too far in front of him. He noticed there was something different about this smoke. Smoke is visible but it also smells. This smoke didn't smell. The air was perfectly clear there; only the white plume of smoke stood in the cold air.

In the few months Kootenay had spent in the wilderness, he had learned to be cautious with anything he didn't know. Caution is the mother of wisdom. He decided to walk around the spot where the fire was burning. He gave it a wide berth, and he thought he would approach from a spot up top where the canyon was not so steep. Hugging the ground, where on some spots the snow had melted, he found bushes of juniper. They carried dark blue berries. He ate them to still his hunger. They tasted like the resin from pine trees. He didn't like the taste, but the berries stilled his hunger. Then he found shrivelled rosehips. He ate them, too, and his mouth felt better. When they went down a steep incline, Keeno stopped and let out a short, angry growl. The boy reached down and touched the dog to calm him. Keeno was quiet, but he shivered with exitement. There was somebody within the dog's nose whom Kootenay couldn't see or hear. The boy knew his dog by now, so he knew what was bothering him wasn't a wolf; he was hard to restrain when there was a wolf or a grizzly bear in the vicinity. This was different; the dog was excited but there was no fear.

They had to walk around some large boulders to get down to the river for a drink. Now there was the smell from a campfire. It was the familiar harmony of smells from a cold campfire curing meat over juniper smoke. To Kootenay, it smelled like all the places where human beings made their home. When he turned around, he saw that the plume of white smoke was now behind him. His people had no word for steam, so he called it smoke.

They were now walking on what felt like a well-used trail. Again Keeno shivered with exitement; the boy could feel it when he touched him. When they rounded a large boulder, they both saw an old man sitting on the trunk of a fallen tree. The last golden rays of the setting sun flooded the whole scene and gilded the man's unkept hair, but it gave the man, and his whole figure, the unreal radiance of a golden halo. Kootenay was taken by surprise and stood transfixed for a long time. Keeno watched, only his wet nose quivering with exitement, not knowing what to make of the scene.

It was only now that Kootenay found the concentration to study the whole appearance of the man. His shoulders and back were covered by a gray wolfskin, which hung in tatters from his bent shoulders, mixing with the man's long, white hair. Both fell, down to his moccasins, where all ended in the dust with fallen leaves, dry grass and pine needles. Despite the haggard and unkept outside appearance of his humble attire, the man's countenance was very composed and almost regal. During all this time, the man's eyes remained fixed on some imaginary spot in the distance in front of him. There was no discernible movement of limbs or eyes of the man. Only a wisp of breath in front of the face of the figure indicated in the cold air that this human being was alive.

So they stood there for a long time waiting for what was to transpire.

8

When the man decided to speak after the long silence, his greeting sounded like a revelation, like a disclosure of divine knowledge by some supernatural agency. During the months of his imposed exile, Kootenay had heard no voice other than his own and the bark of his dog. On his long wanderings through forest and mountains, he had taken to talking to himself because he felt there was always somebody listening, and sometimes he felt that someone else was talking while he was listening. And then he had learned to talk to his dog. He knew that Keeno was listening when his one ear swivelled back and forth, and his eyes always indicated full agreement with what Kootenay had to say. Now when this old man spoke, he spoke in words Kootenay could understand. Of course, Kootenay had never given it any thought that there might be people in the world who spoke in different tongues than he did. He was surprised how beautiful human words sounded. And he was very amused by the old-fashioned words the old man chose while speaking to him.

He said, "Be welcome in the humble abode of an old man! Whence didst thou come from, and what might be the purpose of your visit? What is your destination, and if you have a name, what might that be?"

Kootenay explained that he had been exiled from the Kootenay Nation for reasons not within his ken. As the old man was hard of hearing, Kootenay didn't realize that he had to speak very loudly so the old man would hear. Since the old man had understood the word Kootenay, on his wizened face appeared a sign of recognition and a smile. He said, "Kootenay," pointing at himself. From this moment on, Kootenay's name would still be Kootenay as long as he stayed with the old man, and the old man became Old Kootenay until Kootenay changed it back to old man.

The real truth is that in the Kootenay Nation, a child was not given a name at birth. The child had to earn a name by some act of heroism or for some other act of distinction. It was for this reason that Kootenay didn't earn his permanent name of "Running Rain" until his return from the odyssey into the land of the Shining Mountains and the sea of grass.

After a while without saying anything, the old man arose and walked to a rock overhang where he stored his dry firewood against the rock wall. He carried a few pieces to his firepit. There he pushed aside a pile of ashes. Under the insulating layer of ashes, Kootenay could see glowing embers of charcoal. The old man blew into them, and at the same time, he lit a few twigs of kindling and the flames flared up. This way he kept his campfire going day and night.

"It's the fire that keeps the wolves away from my lodge when I sleep," he said.

Kootenay watched with great interest. "*So that's the way it is done,* he said to himself. *You dig a hole in the middle of the firepit which fills with glowing embers, then when you don't need the fire you cover the whole thing with ashes that way, the embers keep hot!*

The old man waved Kootenay to come. "I will show you where the white smoke comes from." He walked ahead of Kootenay. Soon they were deep inside of a canyon. With his right hand, he could touch the canyon wall, while he was walking on a good trail. On his left, steep scree fell right down to the rushing river.

The old man looked back, knowing that Kootenay was getting worried, as it was getting dark. He said, "Don't worry. Stay right behind me. You'll be safe."

It wasn't long before Kootenay could see steam rising from a pool of hot water. The old man looked back at Kootenay and said, "This is the place where the hot waters flow!"

Kootenay stared at the phenomenon with his eyes full of wonder. "How is it possible the earth I walked on is covered with snow. It gives me cold feet. Everything is frozen, even lakes and rivers, but here hot water flows?" He bent down to put his hand into the water. It was warm. It was warm, almost hot. "Can we swim here? Yes, we will." He continued, "The earth we live in is alive. Inside of the earth are huge fires, and everything that is alive now, like plants and all animals, including you and myself, will eventually be recycled. Everything that you and I are made of will undergo this change where all substances will be subject to metamorphosis into different substances. Nothing will be lost.

"Maybe one day you and I will be fertilizer and we will make beautiful, sweet-smelling flowers grow. So it is with this purified water. It may have been a chunk of ice like the blue Kokanee ice. This water, which came from the sky, purified and then was heated by the very core of the earth. It will purify, soothe, and pamper your tired body, and you will emerge clean and strong, even your food will taste better." After they took their clothing off, they stored it under some rocks where it was dry. With snow and ice all around, they descended into the pool of earthly delights. It was now completely dark under the rock overhang where the pool was located, Kootenay had to feel his way around the rocks to discover how large the pool was. It wasn't very large; there was barely room for more than three people, but when he moved his feet along the sandy bottom, he could feel the spot where the hot water bubbled out of the earth. He couldn't hold his feet over the hot water very long, so he floated back to the open side where the black sky appeared above.

As it was the time of the year when the earth moves through showers of meteorites, Kootenay wallowed in the hot pool in unrestrained delight while watching shooting stars appear and disappear in trackless space. He watched in awe but didn't know what to make of it.

The old man had stepped out of the water and dried himself with the tanned hide of a white rabbit. He stood there now waiting for Kootenay. They went back to the man's camp in complete silence.

The old man began thinking whether it might be possible to persuade Kootenay to spend the winter with him. He was getting on in summers, and hunting wasn't getting any easier. Then there were the traplines. For the last few years, he had found it very tempting during the cold winter to lay in front of the warm fire in his cave on mats of soft grass. He had neglected his traplines; for that reason, there were very few pelts for trading. When the Nlak-Pamux came, he had nothing to pay them for the things he needed. On the other side, he could see that Kootenay and his dog would make a potent hunting team. He could supply them with the necessary equipment and teach them what they needed to know.

Behind the old man Kootenay walked quietly, and behind Kootenay was Keeno. The old man, of course, couldn't know that Kootenay was thinking along the same lines. Kootenay was wondering what he had to say to convince the old man that it would be to his advantage to keep him for the winter. The boy had quick eyes and a strong right arm with spear and stone, and what he couldn't hit, Keeno would run down. Together the two could easily earn their keep. In the meantime, Keeno himself was thinking along the same lines; all he wanted was one piece of meat a day and a dry spot to sleep, but if he could crawl under the bearskin with

Kootenay, all the better. He wouldn't say no. Keeno, of course kept all this to himself.

While all three were thinking, they arrived back at the camp. The fire had died down, but there were enough glowing coals. The old man got an armful of wood and piled it on; then he went toward the vertical rockface and removed two dry pine trees, which in turn revealed a reed-mat hanging down from the rocks. He now pushed the mat, which had concealed the entrance to a roomy cave, aside.

It was pitch dark now. Kootenay couldn't see anything inside, but the old man knew everything inside his lodge blindfolded. He now grabbed a crackling chunk of burning wood with two flat pieces of cedar-wood, which he only used for this purpose, and carried it inside of the cave. Soon he had a crackling fire going, throwing light around the small cavern. Then the old man took two pieces of venison from the ceiling above the firepit and handed one to Kootenay. He dropped a dried fish to the dog. Then they ate. While they were eating in complete silence, the old man got up only once to fetch a wooden bowl with chunks of salt in it. He handed that to Kootenay. It made the meat taste "sweet." Then there was a long silence while they ate. Kootenay ate like a hungry wolf. They had been on the trail with very little food for two days, and now, after the hot pool, he was tired, too.

When Kootenay looked up, he noticed that the old man had fallen asleep in a leaning position, with his back and sides supported by warm, dry grass, his tattered wolfskin covering him up to his shoulders. His eyes were closed, but that part of the face which he could see showed a great smile. Kootenay had the impression that the old man hadn't slept so soundly in a long time, in the knowledge that the world was a safe place, it was good to be alive with a young man and a dog around.

Kootenay himself, considering his situation, thought that everything had changed for the better for him. He had had a warm bath; he had a full tummy; he felt like a new man. The golden warmth of the flickering campfire spread a peaceful comfort throughout the cave. When he now stretched his legs, his feet touched the warm fur of his dog; he could feel the exhaustion of the last few days flowing out of his body. He was completely at peace. He hadn't felt like that since the last day in his mother's lodge.

He got up and pulled the reed-mat across the cave entrance to cut out any draft that might come up during the night. Then, as he rolled into his bearskin, he could still feel his dog crawling up to him and lying down at his feet. Then he was asleep. Kootenay slept the sleep of the just until the old man pulled back the mat from the entrance and the slanting rays of the sun, which floated barely above the stark outline of the mountains beyond, touched his face. It warmed the gray fur of Keeno, and he stirred, got up, and licked the boy's bare shoulder as if to check if his master was still alive. That woke Kootenay out of his deep sleep. For a short moment, he didn't quite know where he was, but as soon as the warm sun touched his naked body, he had the most wonderful feeling. For the first time in his life, he had the feeling as if he had been reborn. All the strain and exertion of the last few days and months were wiped from his memory. He thought, *Isn't it wonderful that every day the sun rises a new day dawns and man and beast get a new start.*

The old man was sitting on his log by the fire. Early in the morning, a warm wind had sprung up from sunset. Kootenay walked out of the cave and sat down next to the old man. After a while, the old man said, "Chinook." As Kootenay had never heard the word and didn't seem to know what it meant, the old man added, "The Na-Koda across the Shining Mountains call it the wind that eats the snow."

The boy noticed that most of the snow around the camp had disappeared. It was dripping from the trees from the rocks, and small rivulets of water were rushing toward the river. Then there was a long silence; neither of the two wanted to say what he had on his mind, the old man for fear that the young man would run away and try to find his way home. He remembered the previous winter when the deep snow came and he couldn't go out and hunt. He had almost died of hunger.

Kootenay himself thought the old man might want to be rid of him because he wanted to be by himself. So the two sat there by the fire in the warm wind and looked across the valley where in the blue haze of the afternoon the glaciers sparkled like polished silver in their unapproachable remoteness. As it was up to the elder of the two to speak, the old man finally asked, "How many summers are you old?"

"I can count ten summers not counting the last one."

"That would make you about fifteen summers old."

Kootenay nodded.

"You are still too young to go out into the world on your own; you will perish."

"Yes, but it wasn't my own desire to be here. It was the elders of the Kootenay who banished me here to become humble!"

The old man nodded. "Yes, I know. I was banished for different reasons so many years ago I stopped counting. It was hard on me. There were many times when I thought I would die of hunger, but I lived. The passage into manhood is never easy. Then, slowly, I got used to living in the wilderness on my own. After I found this place here, 'where the warm waters flow.' I learned to make fire, spears, and fishnets. Later on, after many summers, I liked life here so much that I didn't want to return. You will love it, too, but you will have to learn much before you are ready. I can teach you many things if you are willing to listen.

"I can show you many more places where warm water flows out of the earth. But any time, if you would like to go away, I will not stop you. I think I still have a few summers left to teach you."

He rested for a while, and then he continued. "I have spoken too much. I have spoken more to you than I have spoken in the last ten summers. It is not good to speak too much!"

Kootenay, knowing that it was the custom among his people to leave an expellee in the wilderness for at least one year before they came looking for him, gladly said yes. "I will stay with you as your son, if you will have me as your son."

The old man nodded his head as a sign of approval.

To Kootenay the two long winters and the one short summer he stayed with the old man would be the most important period in his life. Of course he couldn't understand that now in his young years, but when he was an old man himself, when all the world around him was changing so fast that he couldn't follow any longer, he realized that without the great knowledge of the way of his people, which was handed down to him by the humble man who became the only father he had ever known, he could not have survived.

9

The old man laid a large piece of wood in the firepit. Then he walked toward the cave. After a while, he reappeared with a long-stemmed Indian pipe and a wad of tobacco. He then cut a piece of tobacco and rubbed it into small flakes in the palm of his hand, taking care that nothing of the precious herb was lost. From his left hand, he stuffed the sweet-smelling smoke into the bowl of his pipe. He then found a small, glowing ember in his fire and laid that on the tobacco in his pipe with his bare hand.

Seated next to Kootenay, he inhaled deeply. Then he handed the pipe to the boy. In the meantime, the old man held the smoke in his lungs waiting for the euphoric effect of the tobacco. Kootenay did the same. When the blue smoke from their pipe drifted into the treetops and mingled with the smell of pine resin, a communion of the two minds took place that would last as long as the two lived and hunted together.

The last snowstorm had dumped a heavy load of snow on valleys and mountains. Then the warm chinook had roared through the pines and cedars. Up over the high ridges stood while plumes of drifting snow, reaching into the blue of space. The trees shed their burden and the branches reached up into the deep blue of the sky again. The old man said, "Today, you will fashion yourself a spear for hunting!" Walking around his campsite, he picked a perfectly straight willow pole about twice as tall as the boy.

Like all people of his time, he collected everything that he thought he might be able to use at some later date. Then he picked the longest legbone of a mule deer, which he had laying around. Talking to Kootenay, he said, "If you would like to get the best spear point, you have to split the bone of a deer lengthwise. The ideal way is to split the bone in half. One end will then be sharpened to a needlepoint; the other remains as it is, a half circle. It will then be lashed to the shaft of willow with a thin rawhide thong."

After days of work, the spear was ready to use. Kootenay took it and balanced it in his hand. The old man stood back and watched with keen interest, knowing that every boy of his people was born with the desire to carry a weapon in his right hand.

The old man had noticed that if you gave a boy a rock he would throw it. This has been so ever since the first human being had raised himself on his hind legs. He could now look out over the high grass of the savannah. He held a rock in his right hand. The rock was a weapon, and the weapon felt good in his hand. He could now kill his next meal without having to touch it with his hands, and more important, as long as he had to carry a weapon, never again could he afford to walk on four legs. Man has never looked back. When a wolf exposes his soft underbelly to his enemy, he does it as a sign of submission. When man first did that, he had to carry his weapon, and he had no other choice.

While the warm weather continued, they walked through forests and hills, and they hunted. Kootenay learned where the wapiti and the deer congregated during the rutting season. Keeno became a very valuable hunting companion to Kootenay. The dog learned fast. To Kootenay it looked as if Keeno understood the desperate food situation the three were in. Where the old man would have had food for months, the three had eaten most of the meat the old man had stored in one week.

One day Keeno disappeared. He was gone all day. Kootenay thought that maybe Keeno had reverted to his old wolf ways and struck out on his own. When Keeno didn't return the following night, Kootenay got worried. He couldn't sleep. He felt as lonesome as he had felt before he found his dog wounded not far from his camp. Then, on the following morning, Keeno was there. He had reappeared silently, carrying a big, fat, white rabbit. The rabbit's early, white coat had become his undoing. Soon the rabbit roasted on a skewer. Keeno received a generous portion raw. More than once, it was Keeno who would bring down a wounded deer, which otherwise might have escaped and been lost had it not been for Keeno.

This animal had the amazing capacity to read Kootenay's mind by first pointing the game. Then he would slink away in order to position himself to cut off the game's retreat and bring it down or hold it while Kootenay moved in to deliver the final blow. He would then stand back and wag his tail until he received the entrails, with the exception of the liver. That would be shared between the old man and Kootenay, and eaten raw.

Sometimes the trip home was long and arduous. At home, Kootenay was glad to leave the rest of the work to the old man. He was an expert at that. He would slice the meat into thin strips and hang it on pegs he had attached in the rocks above the fire. That way the meat was safe from the coyotes and wolves who frequented the area.

One trick Keeno never learned was dealing with a porcupine. He did so badly he looked pathetic. When he ran into his first porcupine, it was obvious he didn't know what to do. He had never seen anything like it. This thing was supposed to turn and run away. Everybody else ran as fast as they could when they saw him coming. This thing didn't move; instead it turned around and faced him squarely with big, black, confident eyes. The only other animal who had ever done that, and got away with it, was a bull moose. But then there is a big difference between a bull moose and a porcupine. That this little fellow, who had no respect for him at all, had all kinds of tricks up his sleeves Keeno would have to learn at his peril.

Kootenay looked at him, and to make certain he was seeing right, he turned his head sideways both ways. Then he danced around him in circles to see if this thing would lose his nerve and he could attack, but this thing hardly moved, just enough so he faced Keeno squarely. This was too much, he attacked. The porcupine was waiting for that. He rolled into a ball. By that time Keeno's nose was close enough. With a jerky motion he stabbed ten needle-sharp quills into Keeno's delicate nose. The dog retreated from his quarry with a painful cry. That was enough for Keeno; from then on, he made a wide circle around anything that looked like a porcupine. As far as Kootenay was concerned, it took him days to remove the irritant spines from Keeno's tender nose.

Kootenay, of course, had no problem with porky, and for the old man, who was a connoisseur in such delicacies, it was a welcome change in the boring menu of venison, moose meat, and fish, especially since he prepared this game himself in the spit with the various herbs he collected during the summer. His piquant sorrel and wild onion dressing was his favorite. Even Keeno received his share of the savory meal, mostly bones, but that was fine, since at last he got the satisfaction of finally having the upper hand over the critter.

Kootenay wandered through forest and glade in warm sunshine and chinook wind. On the lower elevations, all the snow had melted. On the Shining Mountains, the snowline had retreated past timberline. Kootenay learned how to find the game trails. From the droppings on the trails, he found

out what kind of game used the trails. He found the droppings of rabbit, deer, elk, moose, and bear. He learned to tell
the difference between fresh and old droppings.

Keeno knew the difference by sniffing. Nothing changed
Keeno's behavior more, and faster, than fresh wolf droppings. When his hackles rose and he bared his fangs, Kootenay knew that he was ready to fight.

On a warm autumn day, Kootenay and his dog were
sitting on a windswept, rocky ridge far above the valley bottom. On a clear day like this, Kootenay had the impression
that one could see forever. The river he could see clearly had
to be the River of the Kootenay. Beyond the river, he could
see a lake sparkling in ice and snow. That must be the lake
where his old camp was. Then there was the swamp where
his canoe was hidden. It didn't look like a swamp from where
he sat; it looked more like a plain meadow. The river seemed
to empty into the lake, but when he looked again, he found
that the river made a turn just before it reached the lake and
continued on toward midday. There had to be a ridge of
higher ground separating the river from the lake, but the
waters from the lake flowed toward midnight. Kootenay
made plans to ask the old man.

Short, satisfying days in sun and wind, in the evening a
long luxurious bath in the hot pool under the appearing stars
added much comfort to the newfound life of Kootenay. Only
half of the sun was visible over the ridge at midday for a few
weeks, but then as the sun started rising it became much
colder, and it started to snow. From the direction of midnight, an angry black cloud had engulfed the mountains on
the other side of the valley. This was the weather change the
old man had been talking about, which he, with the age-
old experience of his kind, had felt in his bones long before
Kootenay had seen it.

Now he could feel it, too. All movement of air had ceased. It felt like all life held its breath for a moment to prepare for the coming winter storm. He felt a shiver run through the earth and the trees. When he touched his wet hair there was the crackle of electricity. He walked faster.

It started snowing before the first wind gusts hit the tree-tops, even though down here, protected by the steep canyon walls, there was no wind. The snow sifted silently through the branches as he rushed toward the camp.

The old man had prepared very well for this winter storm. It happened every winter. There was enough firewood to last for months, and if they ate only one meal a day, their food would last for a long time.

It stormed and snowed for many nights and many days. They slept during most of the storm, getting up only to keep the fire going and to eat a small meal. During one night, a small snowslide came down from the south-facing wall of the canyon. All they heard was the hissing sound as powdery snow piled up in the canyon. Luckily for them, the river found an outlet. Otherwise it might have flooded the camp where they lay dreaming. They went back to sleep.

In his dreams, Kootenay listened to the sound of the falling snowflakes. They made a sound like tiny glass bells. He had often wondered about the source of the blue-green color of glaciers and lakes. During one of those long, snowy nights, it came to him in a dream. As the snowflakes drifted slowly down from high above each one rubbed against the sky. A little bit got stuck on the flake, but they always left enough for the sky to turn blue again. Later when the snow-flakes turned to ice on the glacier, the ice turned to jade, and much later, when the ice melted, it flowed into lakes and rivers as liquid jade.

The old man had chosen the location of his winter camp very carefully. Even during the darkest winter days, at midday, the slanting rays of the sun managed to reach the entrance of the cave.

After the deep snow had settled down, Kootenay was on the trail of deer and rabbits. He had been equipped with a pair of the old man's snowshoes and a pair of mukluks. In his snowshoes, he could travel faster than Keeno, who had a hard time in the deep snow. Often the old man would sit at the entrance of the cave in the warming sun with a crackling fire behind him and hope that Kootenay would bring home a rabbit or a spruce grouse.

During those long winter nights, warmed by the crackling fire, they would sit in great comfort with Kootenay listening as the old man told stories of the Indian people as they had been handed down through the generations. One night Kootenay asked why the waters from the lake, where he had his camp, were flowing toward midnight when the water from the River of the Kootenays flowed toward the sun.

The old man was sitting there with his eyes closed as if he was asleep, but he had a smile on his face. Kootenay was staring into the flickering fire, waiting for the old man to speak if he knew anything. He waited patiently because he knew that the old man would speak only if he wanted to, but then, once he had started, he would speak for hours.

Kootenay went to push a fresh log on the fire, while outside a fierce winter storm was blowing snowdrifts around the camp. He pulled the reed-mats in front of the cave so no snow would drift in during the stormy night.

When he turned around, the old man was sitting there wide awake. He spoke thus. "It was many, many summers ago, many more summers than I can remember, when a White trader arrived at my camp. He was traveling with an Indian guide, a Na-Koda from across the Shining Mountains.

They came from a place called Yaha-Tinda. This White man, I forgot his name, had long, yellow hair, and his eyes were the color of the Kokanee ice. Those eyes are what I remember most about him; they looked right through me. His eyes were only interested in how far it was to the next mountain range, and if he might be able to see a spot that would allow him to travel through.

"He carried contrivances made from shiny metals, the likes of which I have never seen before. These instruments had markings of a very mysterious nature on them, which I couldn't understand. On one side, there was a round button which the White man used to adjust the instrument. The Na-Koda man told me that the White man said that he could tell exactly on what spot of the world he was if he aimed his instrument at the sun. What amazed me the most was, this White man carried a book with empty pages, and with a pointed lead pencil, he made secret markings in this book.

"I looked at it but it didn't mean anything to me. A White man who can decipher his markings will be able to tell where he had been. He also measured all the mountains and rivers and wrote them down in his book. Can you imagine that a man ten or a hundred summers from now can tell exactly where this White man had been, even if this man died in the meantime and couldn't tell anybody himself. I think this is pure magic. I think the people who have this magic will take over the world.

"It was this White man who had traveled by canoe on the river you asked me about, all the way to the great ocean. It was him who called that river the river of the big bend. It flows through Nlak-Pamux and Issan-ka country. From there it flows into the great ocean. That ocean is so big that one can not look across it and see the other side. Just think, this White man can write down his thoughts, and one hundred summers from now, somebody will decipher his writing and he will know exactly what this man thought.

"He told me there is a man in his country who has no hearing but he can see the markings of music on a piece of paper, and through his eyes, he can hear what the music sounds like; he can hear through his eyes. This same White man told me that from the markings in his book, he will make a sketch on a large piece of paper of the exact shape of Kootenay country and all the rivers and lakes and mountains in it. You see, Kootenay, a thought that you or I have is only a thought. When you forget what you have been thinking, it's lost. But when you speak it, I can hear it, and when you write it down, I can hold the sound and the meaning of your words in my hand. Your words have become tangible and can be discussed by anybody who can read it. The power of thought increases by the number of people who read the thought.

"When we smoked the pipe, this White man said there are now many more White people coming. They come on big canoes, out of the mist of the ocean, where the sun rises. Their ships are so big they can hold a hundred people or more. These ships are pushed across the water by white clouds above them. They are using the power of the wind to sail across the ocean as fast as the wind. And now, he said, they come across the land in noisy wagons on wheels. Do you know what a wheel is, Kootenay?"

"No, I don't. I have never seen one."

"Nor have I. I know how to walk on snowshoes, but walking on wheels?

"These White men bring everything with them. Their women have long, golden hair. Their have thunder sticks. When they point their sticks at a wapiti, the thunder will kill it from a hundred paces. Their wagons are pulled by horses or oxen. They have horses like the Sa-haptin. They can run fast and carry a big load, much more than a dog. They now come by the thousands from across the sea of grass, where the sun rises, behind the Shining Mountains."

When Kootenay heard that, he thought that he must go there, where one can see forever, not just to the next mountain. Kootenay lay there in great comfort under his bearskin. His dog was at his feet sleeping, his only ear moving, listening to the winter storm howling outside. For a while, Kootenay was watching the grotesque shapes the flickering firelight was painting on the rock walls. When he looked up, he noticed that the old man had fallen asleep. He had a big contented smile on his face.

It was the first time Kootenay had the opportunity to look at the old man's face. It seemed to him as if the man's cheeks had filled out a little, and when the boy saw him walking, his walk was more elastic, as if some of the spring of his youth had returned to him. When Kootenay looked at him now, he even thought that the old man might not be quite as old as he had first thought, and he got the idea that he might even like this old man and his didactic ways. With that thought, his head rolled slowly to the side, and he was asleep, too.

Those long, dreamy winter nights in the warm, cozy cave with the storm and the coyotes howling outside he would remember for the rest of his life. Even when, in his later years, he stayed in the comfortable homes of White people, he would never have that same feeling of shelter he had felt in his teepee and now in the cave when the snowslides hissed down from the steep canyon walls toward the river. Nor was there a greater feeling of well-being when he, after a day of pursuing wounded game, would soak himself in the hot pool and then cool himself off in the icy river below.

The Kootenay people didn't have a word for paradise, but deep down, without thinking about it, Kootenay knew that things didn't come much better than what he had now. It never occurred to Kootenay that the reason his people didn't have a need for the word paradise was the fact that they lived in it.

Both man and boy spent weeks in torpid inactivity, eating only once a day in order to stretch their food supply. Quite often, Keeno would come in the morning and lick Kootenay's face to remind him that it was time to get up and eat.

Only when it was absolutely necessary would they go out in the pursuit of game. Kootenay had discovered that the grassy ridges above timberline were blown clear of snow, and it was easier for him to walk there without his snowshoes. Keeno seemed to like it better, too.

One warm day, when the chinook was blowing, they climbed up there. By accident, he made another discovery. In order to get the wind in his favor, he had climbed into a rock wall above a rocky ridge. He had told Keeno to sit. Keeno seemed to know exactly when the hunt was on; he lay perfectly still until he heard the boy's scream. By the droppings he found on the trails, the boy knew that not only sheep were up there, also deer and wapiti, and the huge paw marks of a mountain lion. The puma was after the same game he was after. He would have to watch!

It felt good to have Keeno watching, too. Up there in the rocks, Kootenay made an amazing discovery, for which he never found an explanation. He had noticed that rams seemed to think no other animal was capable of climbing higher in the rocks than themselves. They had never seen anything like Kootenay climbing in the rocks and, quite unexpectedly, showing up above them. All the animals had had to watch for up to now were wolves when they came out of the forest. Then they would climb a little higher in the rocks and watch the wolves in their frustration.

They never saw or heard Kootenay above them, nor did they hear the deadly sound of his spear. It penetrated deep behind the shoulder of the nearest ram, who, being delicately balanced on the narrow ledge he was resting on, fell down the cliff. Down below, Keeno was waiting. He dug his fangs into the hindquarter of the ram and held fast until Kootenay arrived to dispatch the quarry.

Kootenay eviscerated the game on the spot, with Keeno receiving the entrails still warm. Kootenay himself ate part of the liver raw. When satiated, he left the rest for the old man. That evening they arrived home late. Only after Kootenay found out that he could drag the carcass of the ram behind in the deep snow on the forest trail was it possible to get the game home in one piece.

When Kootenay and Keeno came scooting down the steep hill behind the cave, the old man came out to watch. He was happy. He took over immediately to skin the animal and prepare the meat. They would be feasting on mutton, and the precious winter coat of the ram would be the old man's new cloak, replacing the tattered wolf skin he was wearing now. He did all the work quietly by the flickering movement of light from the fire. Some choice cuts of meat were hung in the smoke of the campfire. The rest of the meat hung out overnight to freeze.

Kootenay, in the meantime, was lying in the hot spring. He had come home splattered with blood from butchering and carrying the ram. Now after he had cooled off in the snow next to the hot pool, he felt clean. When he came back to the cave, pieces of mutton were roasting on skewers, enticing Kootenay to eat of the meat, which was dripping with fat. He spiked a piece with his knife and ate. For Keeno there was offal by the fire.

During the night, a pack of wolves was heard howling around the camp, attracted by the scent of the meat. They came so close that Kootenay had to restrain Keeno. After that the rest of the night remained quiet.

For a long time, the boy and the old man thought that it might never be spring again. Then a chinook wind, lasting for weeks, shook the heavy burden of snow out of the trees. It rushed through the forests and up the mountains, heavy with snow. It jumped over the ridges and pulled long flags of powdery snow into the blue of the sky. Then they heard the thunder of avalanches going down in the valleys. Now they knew that the Shining Mountains were trying to shed the cold burden of winter into the valleys. They heard the thunder of the slides as long as the warm chinook blew.

One day, Kootenay had seen a group of mountains sparkling in the bright midday sun, resplendent in their crown of ice and snow, so far and yet seemingly so close he thought he could touch them with his hands. He mentioned those mountains to the old man, who said, "Top of the World. We will go there in the summer. We will fish there all summer. Then we will go to another place where the hot water flows. We will swim there."

Slowly, but unrelentingly, spring marched north through the valleys. Rivers and lakes shed their shackles of ice and snow. Countless rivulets rushed down into the valleys and rivers, already swollen with runoff water, below.

Down below the chasm, the waterfall, the same one that had stopped Kootenay's advances the previous fall, freed now from the ice of winter, was heard with fresh thunder. While on the steep hills facing the sun, vails of fresh green began to appear. Herds of deer and elk were seen grazing on the new grass.

One day Kootenay was lying in one of the fresh, green meadows looking into the blue sky when he noticed a flock of birds appearing out of the sun. For as long as he could remember, he had known that in the spring, when the ice had melted, the birds returned to the valley, but he had never paid attention.

Today was different. He was practicing what the old man had told him. "Always listen to the sounds of the earth and the sky, and be aware if you have in mind to survive. You must be aware of and obey the laws of nature. There are no other laws. Remember there are no laws of god in the real world. In the real world, only the laws of nature count. Without observing them you will perish."

He watched in awe as bird after bird melted out of the golden sun. He started counting, but soon he had to give up. He couldn't count any further. There were to many. The bright light forced him to close his eyes. As his eyes were watering, he had to look away and keep them closed for a moment. During that short moment, while his eyes were closed, he could hear the birds talking to each other, and what happened next was so close to a miracle he thought it was one.

He could understand what the birds were saying to each other. He could understand the language of geese. First he heard the lead bird saying that he was getting tired and that somebody who had cruised through this region before should take the lead. It would have to be somebody who knew thermal updrift. Since they still had to cross the Shining Mountains they would have to gain altitude. Then it was quiet. After that there was the voice of an older bird who told somebody to take the lead.

Then he heard instructions given by an older bird who had flown this route before, "Don't break formation; your safety depends on the group. By yourself you will never find the lake where we are going, on the other side of the Shining Mountains."

Kootenay watched with a sparkle of wonder in his eyes as this endless line of birds on the wing moved in elastic motion, stretching like magic back and forth. Of course, Kootenay didn't know where this lake in the promised land behind the Shining Mountains was. The last few words he heard were from a young bird asking, "How far are we still going today?" Somebody just said, "Minne-wanka. If that is still frozen we will go as far as Yaha-Tinda." Then he watched the birds cruise higher and higher over the ragged snowy ridges of the Shining Mountains and finally disappear into the blue.

Kootenay was not aware that he had watched one of the great miracles of nature. He would be an old man before he recognized it as such. What he had gained was a little bit of humility from a flock of geese. This simple animal could fly thousands of miles and find the exact spot where it was born and where it had spent the first glorious summer of its life, and where the coming summer the same young birds would find mates and raise a clutch of goslings, just like countless generations had done before them, keeping the cycle of life going.

What was he compared to a goose? A goose could fly, walk, and swim. All he could do was walk. Even his wolf-hound Keeno was wondering what was wrong with Kootenay. He was so quiet. He thought that Kootenay could do just about everything except fly.

The inside of the cave where they slept now received the rays of the warm midday sun long enough so that it heated the rocks. The heated stones kept the cave warm all night.

10

Kootenay had now been with the old man for the duration of a long, complete winter. His appearance had changed considerably. Of course, he himself was not aware of that. It was the old man who watched when he climbed out of the rocky hot pool. When he thought of the lanky, half-starved kid traveling with a wolf-hound, who had appeared at the entrance of his camp, and compared the boy's appearance to what he saw now, he didn't see a boy any longer. The boy had grown. Where his shoulder bones had stuck out when the old man first saw him at the pool, there was now well-rounded muscle. His outward appearance was that of a well-adjusted young man, and above all, he was devoid of all pretence.

The old man was well aware that Kootenay had, without being told, taken over all the more strenuous tasks around the camp. All winter long he had carried water from the river. He had collected all the firewood they needed. When they sat there in the evening and watched the red fireball of the sun dip down behind the mountains, they just sat there silently. They had become so used to each other they didn't have to speak to understand each other.

The old man was worried. There were so many things he wanted to show Kootenay. There were days when he thought he was running out of time, that his end was near. But with Kootenay as a companion, this was different. He knew that with the boy he could still live for many summers.

Even the winters in the warm cave held no fear. On his thick cushion of warm grass and with his new sheep pelt as a cover, he would be very comfortable. He knew that Kootenay liked listening to his stories during the long winter nights when the snowstorm howled around the cave and the trees crackled outside in the hard frost.

He also knew that a posse of braves would be sent from the Kootenay Nation into the wilderness to see if the boy had survived. If they found him, they would take him back and he would be lost to the old man, too.

The close relationship which had developed between the two was that of grandfather and grandson. It even entered the old man's mind that the boy was his grandson, but he kept that to himself. Since the Indian people kept no written records, nothing could be proven, and only his grandmother would know. However, the thought alone made his heart feel warm toward the boy. He noticed so many traits in his character and his appearance that it reminded him of himself when he was a boy of Kootenay's age. That couldn't be only coincidence.

As soon as the thought came to his mind, he pushed it aside. In the meantime, the least he could do was treat the boy as his grandson and, above all, try to keep him out of the hands of the tribal elders when the braves came looking for him. One thing the old man was certain about was the fact that when the boy got itchy feet, he couldn't hold him. He knew Kootenay would disappear one day just like he had arrived in the camp, quietly and without good-bye. One wet morning, when the thunder rolled through the valley and the rain dripped from the trees, he would take his bundle and his dog and he would be gone. So irresistible was the call of the Shining Mountains.

One day when he thought about these things, the old man had tears in his eyes. Kootenay noticed and asked the old man, "Are you hurting? You are crying!"

The old man pushed the question aside and said, "No, my boy, I was sad, but now I'm happy. I'm crying the tears of happiness!"

Kootenay looked at him confused. He didn't know yet that one could cry out of happiness. He could only cry when he hurt his toes. Then there was silence, a long silence.

The old man finally exclaimed into the silence, "No man receives manhood ready-made. You will have to work on that yourself. I can help you with that.

"Tomorrow we will do sweetgrass and the sweat lodge, and the day after we leave this place. For the summer, we will go to the Top of the World. We will stay up there at my camp at Fish Lake. Nobody will find us there."

Early the following morning, just as the sun sent the first rays into the cave, the old man said, "Come."

The old man had his bundle. They walked down the steep incline toward the river. There they followed the well-worn game trail upriver to a spot where the river bent. There the river left deposits of gravel and clean, white sand during the runoff, when the snow melted. A sandspit, which ended in a gravelbar, left a sparkling pool of water separated from the river. It was inviting to go for a swim, but still too cold. The old man paid no attention to all that as he walked to a small clearing in the forest, Kootenay behind him.

The old man said, "My sweat lodge." Now Kootenay noticed it, too. It looked like a small teepee. The floor was covered with flat stones of black slate. The roof, which was covered with reeds, needed some repair. The old man told Kootenay to get firewood. They had to heat some stones. A pile of round, clean stones was laying around a firepit. It only took a few minutes to build a fire around the stones.

While Kootenay kept the fire going, the old man repaired the sweat lodge. It was the roof that needed most of the work. He rearranged some of the reeds on the top to seal the roof.

Next he placed a few branches of balsam fir over the top. Then he walked down into the warm, soft sand next to the river. In the middle of the sand, he placed a flat stone large enough to build a small fire upon.

Kootenay watched with great interest. He knew that all the elders and all the braves took part in the sweat lodge and sweetgrass ceremonies, but he himself had been too young. Here, with the old man, he was, for the first time in his life, privileged to take part in these secret proceedings of his people.

The old man took his bundle and carried it down to the patch of white sand by the river's edge. The sun was shining brightly. It was a warm spring day, and the soft sand was warm under their bare feet. Around them the virgin evergreen forest provided a sheltered recess around the small cove. The old man now sat down in the warm sand, leaning forward slightly. Beside him lay his bundle.

He pointed down across from himself for Kootenay to sit down. He opened his pouch, which contained all the necessary herbs. He spoke very quietly now, almost like a prayer. "I collect all these herbs and mushrooms myself. I will show you what plants to pick, and where you can find the purest ones. You must know that this sweetgrass ceremony was brought to the Kootenay from across the Shining Mountains generations ago, when the Kootenay were pushed across the Shining Mountain passes from there where the sun rises. The Tsuut'ina, the Sik-sika and Na-Koda people use only sweetgrass for their ceremonies. This grass does not grow here, so we have to use various herbs and mushrooms. I will show you where they grow. I only use the best from the highest mountains. They have to be prepared properly, and they must be dried fast in the sun and no flies be allowed to sit on them.

"This is especially important with the mushrooms. I store them in a secret place in the cave with my tobacco. Good mushrooms are good for trading. You can get lots of tobacco for them. Mushrooms grow during the night, and they have to be picked early in the morning, when the dew is still on them, before the sun rises, so no fly can spoil them. And when you pick them, take the freshest ones, the smallest ones. In them, the magic power is the most concentrated, the way the earth put it there. Go put some more wood on the fire so the rocks are hot when we need them."

When Kootenay came back, he sat down again in the same position as the old man, who now began separating the various herbs into small piles. The mushrooms he ground into a fine powder with his thumb. Then he pushed about half of the mushroom powder into the middle of the rock. Over the top of that, he placed the various herbs in a certain order. Then two small bundles of dry grass were placed over the top in the shape of a cross.

"Now," he said, "this is not allowed to burn in a bright flame. It has to smolder. Only that way do you get the proper effect."

The old man now got up and fetched two large pieces of glowing embers from the fire and placed them carefully between the piles of condiments. Soon puffs of curling, fragrant smoke rose from the altar.

Kootenay watched the old man with great interest as the upper part of his body swayed back and forth. Now he reached out with both hands fanning the smoke toward his face. Kootenay could hear the old man inhaling deeply, and did the same, reaching out and fanning the fragrant smoke toward his face and inhaling at the same time. Soon the upper part of his body fell into the same rhythmic swaying motion as the old man's. The old man interrupted only to move the remnants of herbs and mushroom dust on top of the smoldering embers. Then they sat there inhaling the mixture of herbal and fungoid fumes.

Kootenay, having no previous experience with the procedure, soon felt the euphoria, as a wave of well-being rushed through his body. All his senses became sharp and clear. Everything he looked at had a sharper, crisper outline than before. All colors were brighter. Never had the forest been so green, the clouds so white, and the sky so blue.

His hearing became so keen he could hear all the birds in the forest. The chatter of the magpies in a nearby tree became a symphony of words he could understand. He felt a prickling sensation from the warm sun on his back. Then he relaxed completely as he slowly rolled back into the soft, warm sand with his eyes closed. Now, utterly relaxed, a powerful surge of energy concentrated in his body. This power was so great is body felt as light as a feather, and he had the feeling he could fly. He was floating on a soft, white cloud. Without effort he could go higher or lower. He could steer the cloud he was reclining upon with the greatest ease. There were moments when he thought he got a glimpse of heaven.

How long this state of euphoria lasted he couldn't know. The next thing he could remember was when the old man touched him and handed him a leather pouch and said, "Go down to the river and get water."

Kootenay jumped up, not knowing where he had been, and ran down to the river. He filled the leather bag with water and returned to the sweat lodge.

It was warm inside where the old man was sitting on a cushion of moss. In front of him were the hot stones. The old man sprinkled water on the hot stones so that steam filled the narrow confines of the lodge. He repeated the procedure whenever new steam was required and the stones were hot enough to make it. Then they both got up, walked down to the river, and took a short dip in the ice-cold water. They rubbed each other down with clean, white sand. To wash the sand off, they had to take another dip. Then they sat there drying in the hot sun.

This punctilious procedure had taken the better part of the day. On their way back to the cave, Kootenay had a feeling of cleanliness and lightness such as he had never experienced before, but there was also a feeling of ravenous hunger. Now he realized that they had fasted all day.

From the old man he found out that fasting was a necessary part of the sweetgrass experience. After they had eaten, they sat by the crackling fire watching the sunset behind the mountains. The old man spoke, "Only with an empty body and mind is it possible to come out of the sweetgrass ceremony clean. It is the sweetgrass and the mushroom that cleanse your mind and your soul and your body of all accumulated thoughts, fears and worries. Our mind is like a trash-heap of discarded thoughts and dreams and ideas, and unnecessary worries. This trash has to be flushed out and washed away. There is never a need to worry. The grass grows by itself, and when the grass grows, everything else will have food.

"Your soul? I know you wanted to ask me about that. All animals, including human beings, have an immortal soul. Your soul is a minute part of the total energy of the universe, which is given to you for safekeeping at the time of conception. And if, as I know the universe to be, the total energy of the universe to be the creator of all things and beings, at the moment of conception you become part of the universe, and with that you, as an individual, became part of the whole.

"At the moment of termination of your life, your soul, your life energy, flows back to the total pool of energy, comprising the whole of the universe. Your body will segregate into the chemical components it was made from and will transfer back to the dust from whence it came, only to be recycled at a later date into a different form. So, when you as an individual cease to exist, your energy and all the components your body was made from remain part of the universe because nothing, no energy or matter, can escape the whole."

The old man's pipe had gone out. He went to the fire and picked a hot ember and placed it on top of the tobacco. Blowing smoke he continued, "You might have noticed the unusual power you imagine you have, such as the power to fly; don't let that fool you. It's a glorious illusion. You are not a bird; you can not fly. Your body is still vulnerable. Only your mind has taken wings to conquer the infinity of space. So, when you take part in the sweetgrass ceremony, make certain you are in a safe spot where you can not hurt yourself.

"Let this be a lesson to you to be humble."

11

The following morning found the old man and Kootenay descending down from the mountains. Going down turned out to be easier than Kootenay had thought. The old man, during his many summers of living in the area, had found an easy way of walking through the cliff that had given Kootenay problems on the way up. The easy stairway was visible only from the top. Only the lower part had a short funnel of steep gravel with good handholds in solid rock. Only Keeno had problems; he was not a good rock climber. What made it even worse for the dog was the fact that this time he was carrying a load, too.

The old man had made a harness for him from rawhide straps. It was fitted to him around his shoulders and the neck instead of a collar. Keeno had, of course, at first rejected the idea of being fettered down by an unwieldy, heavy load, which restricted his personal freedom, as undignified and therefore unacceptable. Later, after he got used to the idea of carrying part of the gear, he actually seemed to enjoy it. As a matter of fact, every time after the harness with the load was taken off him, he jumped around like a puppy. But at the moment, the load he carried became unbalanced, and Kootenay had to help him through the steepest part.

Further down on the trail, when Kootenay didn't have to watch his footing, he found time to enjoy the surroundings. As they were still walking high in the hills, they were high above a layer of snow-white fog. Often this kind of fog forms during the night in spring and fall in the Valley of the Kootenay. On this morning, it covered the lake, the swamp below them, and the entire valley as far as the eye could see. His eyes followed the billowing carpet of pure white to the ice-clad mountains that reared from the sea of fog. It seemed to him as if it was possible to step out on this pure-white surface and walk as far as the silvery mountains. Slowly, the noon-time haze had moved the hills into their proper distance; only the pure snow on the Top of the World sparkled undiminished in the clear mountain air.

While he was daydreaming Kootenay had fallen behind the old man. Now he tried to catch up. When the old man turned around, he said, "Top of the World. We will go there later in summer, but first we will harvest duck eggs in the swamp and young rabbits in the hills."

They crossed the River of the Kootenay, not far from where Kootenay had crossed after the snowstorm the year before. It was a difficult crossing, as the snow in the high mountains was melting. A week later it would have been impossible to cross there. The water in the swampy downs was still low, but it would rise as the water in the lake rose. The trail through the swamp was easily found. Winter snows had flattened most swamp grass.

In the afternoon of the second day, they arrived at Kootenay's old camp. On the way across, they scared up huge flocks of ducks and geese. Up in the sky, they observed myriads of birds cruising toward midnight and their summer nesting grounds behind the Shining Mountains. The boy noticed that the local birds were building nests on spots raised above water level to make certain that their nests wouldn't be flooded when water levels rose during summer storms.

The old man was pleased when he saw the repair work Kootenay had done to the lodge. As soon as they arrived in the afternoon, they commenced a feverish activity. The old man was rebuilding the roof on the teepee, which had been damaged during a winter storm. Then he carried in more reed-straw for them to sleep on.

Kootenay first took off the harness his dog had carried. Relieved of his burden, he jumped around like a puppy for a while. Then, when he realized that this was his old hunting ground, he was gone. The old man noticed that Kootenay was gone, too. During the winter months, the old man and Kootenay had developed a working relationship in which each one knew exactly what to do. No orders were necessary by the old man; he simply let Kootenay go about his business. Sometimes when Kootenay was playing with his dog, he let that go, too. He knew that a close bonding between a half-wild animal and a young human being was of greatest importance if they were to live successfully in close contact with the natural world for any length of time and survive.

Kootenay was gone for a long time, but when the old man saw him rowing toward the sandy beach, he knew what the boy had been up to. He walked down to the lakeshore to inspect the canoe. He said, "Nlak-Pamux. That's the way they build their canoes." They turned it upside down and inspected it carefully. It needed caulking, but outside of that, it was in good repair. It was large enough to carry both of them. Nothing would be better than a canoe for collecting duck eggs.

The following weeks were a scene of pastoral peace and easy living for the old man and Kootenay. Kootenay learned how to make baskets from the pliable shoots of willows. Then he learned how to make fishing nets. As the willows grew in profusion along the lakeshore, they cruised along the water's edge and collected only the longest shoots in spring sap. Kootenay also learned that the old man used the inner bark of willows to make a preparation he used to treat rheumatic pain in his old bones. For days, Kootenay was out collecting pine resin. Keeno in the meantime was out hunting rabbits.

One evening they were sitting in front of their tepee when the old man said without preamble. "I'm worried about you, Kootenay!"

Kootenay looked up from the basket he was working on and replied, "What did I do wrong?"

"Oh, it's not you, Kootenay!" he exclaimed. "I had a dream about you. The braves from the Kootenay Nation showed up in our camp looking for you. It's the custom of the people to exile a young man into the wilderness to put him to a test, to see if he can survive on his own for one winter. In your case, they did it to see if you had the necessary qualifications to become chief of the Kootenay Nation.

"It isn't easy for an inexperienced young man to survive the winter in our country on his own. You got lucky; you found an old man who could show you many things you needed to know in the game of survival. But the old man was even luckier. You came to me like you were a gift sent from heaven; without you I might not have lived to see the world renew itself once more. I know that you still think to be immortal. You still can not imagine that one day you will be old like myself. For an old man to experience the miracle of spring once more is a gift of such proportions that I can not possibly thank you for that.

"It's a gift of life! I am!

"You see I firmly believe that the Kootenay braves will coerce you to go home with them when they find out that you have survived without the help of the tribe. But I would like to prevent them from taking you away from me. For that reason we will leave your camp sooner that I had planned."

Heavy rains fell for a few days. The grass in the swamp grew very fast. Kootenay thought sometimes he could watch it grow. When he looked out from his teepee, he looked at a sea of grass waving in the wind.

When the old man saw that he said, "Let's go. There will be eggs now!" Ducks build their nests on islands of high ground to make certain that the water level stays below their nest. These islands of high ground consist mostly of floating vegetation which stays dry all year, and is held in place by new growth. The birds are careful to leave the new growth in place as protection from wind and sun. All our two egg collectors had to do was float along in their canoe and watch where the ducks were sitting. When they got too close, the birds would leave their nest and swim away. Most nests had some eggs in them.

At first Kootenay wanted to take all of them, but the old man stopped him and explained, "If you leave one egg the bird will come back and keep on laying until she has a full clutch of eggs in the nest, but if you take all the eggs she will move on and build another nest somewhere else, which you might not find."

Food in the form of eggs became plentiful. Sometimes they found goose eggs. That's when Kootenay found out that a pair of nesting geese made a formidable fighting team, and he learned to approach them with great respect. A fully grown gander in a diving attack was a frightening opponent. He preferred to leave them alone since he had learned to understand their language, and of course, the geese had found out that he was afraid of them. As a result a truce for permanent cessation of hostilities between the two opposing parties existed, to which Keeno agreed fully since he had no desire getting involved in territorial disputes with a mad gander, particularly due to the fact that the gander could fly and he couldn't.

For many days, Kootenay and Keeno would lie on the bottom of their canoe and listen to the fluting of the yellow-headed blackbirds in the bulrushes, or they would fall asleep to the whispering of the wind in the swaying reeds. Every time they came home, the old man had cooked some eggs. He had developed a way of cooking eggs in the hot ashes of their firepit. He didn't like eating eggs raw, so he built up a good fire, then when the fire died down, he put a layer of eggs in the hot ashes and covered all with a thick layer of hot embers. In a few minutes, they had hardboiled eggs. They were delicious. They had so many eggs they couldn't eat them all.

The old man had stored pemmican and other foods in underground caches before, why not eggs? He found a good spot that was never touched by the hot noon sun. Digging a pit deep enough wasn't easy, but he managed to get deep enough that there was still some frost in the ground; that's what he wanted. Layers of reed-grass would help to insulate from the top.

First he cooled his eggs in the cold lake water for days. Then he placed them carefully into his cache between layers of dry grass. He sealed the cache off with packed layers of soil, and finally, he rolled heavy rocks so that wolves wouldn't be tempted to dig out his food. Only a very determined bear would be strong enough to dig down far enough into the soil to get at the eggs.

During the following days, the old man was getting very nervous. Every day when Kootenay got into his boat to go fishing, the old man came to him before he left and said, "If you see smoke from a campfire, no matter how far away it is, you come home right away, you hear! It might be them. We can't take any chances. We will have to move on."

On a beautiful day in late spring it happened. Kootenay was fishing a shallow spawning bed for lake trout on the other side of the lake when he saw the blue plume of smoke just below the midday sun. He called Keeno, who was hunting rabbits. Then he placed the few trout he had in the basket he had brought for that purpose. He placed spear and net on the bottom of the canoe, but where was Keeno?

He ran up the hill as fast as he could. There was Keeno busy trying to dig up a rabbit warren. He didn't stop; he was sure he could get his rabbit. Kootenay said, "Not today," and pulled him away from his excavation.

12

To paddle across the lake took a while. The old man saw the smoke when Kootenay was halfway across.

He jumped into action immediately. First, he put his fire out, hoping that nobody had seen it. He had a full basket of cooked eggs. He carried them all down to the beach. Then he went and pulled a tree trunk in front of the teepee. Everything else he left as it was. There was firewood and a good teepee. He hoped that the braves, if they came, would find the camp inviting and would be tempted to stay and not try to follow them too soon.

When Kootenay pushed his canoe onto the beach, he noticed the energy the old man displayed. All their gear and food was ready to be loaded. "We will cross the lake by boat. That way we are not leaving any tracks. If we cross the swamp, they will know which way we have gone. Then there will be a short portage before we cross the river of the Kootenay by canoe. On the sunrise side of the river, we will hide your canoe somewhere in the hills where nobody will find it."

13

After the river crossing, they found themselves in tall timber, on a good game trail pointing toward sunrise. Keeno was out front in his harness carrying a good load, followed by the old man and Kootenay. The river crossing had been difficult. As it was early summer, the river was a muddy torrent from the melting snow in the high mountains.

After they had stored their provisions in the bottom of the boat, Keeno jumped on the top in great excitement in anticipation of running the rapid below. Both Kootenay and the old man were more apprehensive about getting into the fast, cold water then Keeno. They knew very well if their light lake canoe hit a rock in this torrent of rushing icewater it would surely spring a leak, and as a result they could lose all their possessions. Kootenay thought of his bear robe that made sleeping so warm and comfortable. No they couldn't afford to see their skins floating down the river. He was in the stern with his only paddle, the old man with a long pole in the bow. Kootenay had jumped in last and let himself fall on his knees exactly where he wanted to be. He knew from experience that his canoe was steadiest when his weight was at the lowest point in the boat.

As soon as he shoved off, the bow of the canoe swung around by the force of the current, and he found himself in midstream traveling fast, and getting faster in water deep enough to avoid rocks. Now things happened so fast he had no time to settle down. Already the next bend in the river came into view much faster than he had anticipated. All Kootenay could see from where they now were was a rocky cliff, which was now, late in the afternoon, in deep shade. What he couldn't see was that the water, in thousands of years, had washed out the rocks and the cliff formed an over-hang. Their fragile craft began picking up speed as the torrent of water was funnelled into the narrow sluice where it formed a huge crestwave. All Kootenay could think of was *If the mighty force of this water smashes us into the rocks we're finished.* There was no time to talk now. The only sound was the roar of the river.

Like one frozen in time, the old man stood with his long steering pole ready to cushion the unavoidable collision with the rocks, while Keeno was looking at his master, full confi-dent that he knew exactly what to do in such a situation. But Kootenay was afraid. The best they could expect was to come out alive if the canoe broke up in the rapids. This endless moment of horror lasted only a split-second, as it was washed off his mind by the instinct to survive. He saw the old man pulling his pole out of the water and stemming it against the rockwall to keep the bow of the canoe from being crushed by the force of the current. While he had started paddling against the current, he watched the old man's body bend under the strain like a tree in a storm.

Without realizing it the two oarsmen now worked in perfect unison. The bow of the canoe swung around enough to clear the rocks, when Kootenay pulled his paddle out of the water and stemmed it against the rocks to avoid the crush-ing blow that would have taken the stern off the boat. At this moment, the crestwave washed over the bow, and the old man disappeared in front of his eyes into the foam of the wave. His dog was gone in the same instant the foam of the wave washed over his naked body.

Kootenay was blinded for a moment by the water. He couldn't see that the old man had lost his pole, but as he saved the canoe, he was thrown back into the boat and his pole was floating down the river. Now luck stepped in, in favor of the canoe, as it was now almost rudderless in the middle of a compressed flow of water between walls of rock. The speed of the water increased as it was squeezed through the narrow funnel. Kootenay saw the old man as he was hanging on for dear life. He saw his dog wet in a puddle on the bottom of the canoe. He saw the whirlpool ahead and below the bow of the canoe. In his hands, he clutched his paddle as the only thing that could save them now. At this moment, the bow of the canoe was pointing to the center of the swirling cauldron where the water was sucked down into the fathomless depth of the pool below.

Without thinking, he knew if he could hold his ship toward the outside of the water flowing in a circle, the strong current of that circular flow would force them toward the shore where they could grasp the overhanging branches of the willows and be safe before the power of the river pushed them back into the rushing stream stern first, and out of control.

The hull of the canoe hit the water with a thud when his paddle sprang into action. He dug it in as far as he could. He felt the paddle bend under the exertion of his muscles. For a moment, the fragile ship sat there on the top of the boiling cauldron uncertain where to go, while Kootenay paddled with the power of despair, just holding his own. Then he took a foot of water away from the raging torrent, then he felt how the current helped to carry the boat to the protection of the overhanging willows.

The old man had turned around to find the bow of the canoe above the surface of the water below, and then he heard the thud of the hull on the water. He watched how a young god saved them from a watery grave by the sheer power of his will. The old man held fast to the sturdy branches of the overhanging willows. When Kootenay stepped onto the grassy shore, he found that the keel of the boat was touching a shallow sandbar, which the river had deposited against the shore. It made the unloading of the canoe a lot easier.

After they had pulled their canoe ashore, the old man gave Kootenay a hug and looked into his eyes. No words were spoken as they stood there, Kootenay naked, his wet body glistening in the golden, afternoon sun.

14

The old man was satisfied of the way things had turned out. They had all their gear; their canoe was well hidden in a thick stand of trees. Best of all, nobody in his right mind would dare cross that raging river for weeks. By that time they would have disappeared on the "Top of the World."

Keeno, at first, shirked against the harness. He would have preferred cruising down the river in a canoe. In the end, he accepted what couldn't be changed. When the old man sat down for a rest, he was silent. Kootenay finally said, "I have been wondering about fear. Do I have to be ashamed of it?"

The old man said, "No, fear is a completely normal reaction, the everybody experiences when he faces the unknown. Every time you take a step into the unknown, there is fear following behind you, like your shadow. You can't walk away from your shadow. But you will have to overcome fear, as long as you don't let it get the better of you. The process to overcome fear is called courage.

"While you are young, you don't know what you are capable of; that's why there is fear. You will lose that fear when you know. Freedom from fear is very important; you will only understand that after you overcome the fear of dying. At that point, you will gain a much larger dimension of freedom.

"Total freedom from the material world is impossible. But freedom from fear is not only possible, it is necessary if you intend to live in peace with nature. Everything you need and use for your material well-being comes from the ground you walk upon. Every constituent part of your body came from the ground you are standing on now, and as such it is and will, like you, remain part of the whole from which it came in the first place.

"As part of the whole you are no more important to the universe than the dog who walks beside you, or the animals who sacrifice themselves so that you might appease your hunger. The next time you lie on your back and look at the stars at night, think that the myriad of stars out there, uncountable as they are, are part of you, and you are part of them. It might humble you to realize that some building blocks of you may have arrived on this earth by a shooting star, as intergalactic projectiles from outer space."

Kootenay listened intently but couldn't really understand until many years later when his own grandchildren were dancing around the campfire on the shore of the Lake of the Kootenay. Now that they knew that nobody was behind them, what had started out as a frantic pace to put away what they thought to be pursuers behind them, their travel turned out to be more like a pleasant walk.

Most of the game trails were in virgin evergreen forest. The foothills there were forested almost to the top, only the very top, consisted of barren, rocky ridges. From the old man, Kootenay learned about all the edible herbs that grew in the clearings and on the hills. The man showed him how to pick wild onions and dry them. When they found sorrel leaves in the rich soil next to a waterfall, he explained the thirst-quenching properties of that plant.

"We will collect and dry sorrel from the Top of the World. It is better from up there than from anywhere else." He showed Kootenay how to pick the most tender sprouts of dandelions. One day when they saw a patch of twin flowers the old man made him kneel down and inhale the heavenly scent of those tiny flowers. Kootenay had never paid any attention to those little pink flowers, until the old man stopped him as he almost stepped on them. After he found out how beautiful they smelled and how they made the world smell better, he never stepped on these plants again.

During the first night after their hazardous river crossing, no fire was made, for fear that somebody might see the smoke and get ideas. For food they still had plenty of cooked duck eggs. As it was a warm night, they bedded down in cool, soft grass behind a rock outcrop to break the wind.

When they woke up the next morning, the sun was perched on top of the silvery rim of the Shining Mountains. Toward midday, and how much closer, stood the snowy peaks of the Top of the World. In the valley below them was the green carpet of rich forests. They got moving as soon as they rolled up their gear. This morning they were plagued by thirst. There had been no water on top of the rocky ridge.

At the next creek they rested and stilled their thirst. Down in the haze of the valley was another river they had to cross. The old man explained, "This is the same river as the one below our winter camp, where the warm waters flow. It makes a big bend, and further toward noon, it joins the river of the Kootenay. Where it joins is not far from here, no more than two days' travel."

In the valley below, spring had broken out in extravagant profusion, with flowers everywhere. The valley bottom was drained by a meandering stream. Birds whose songs Kootenay hadn't heard since the previous fall had returned, and their songs were in the air.

They too had no problem crossing the creek. Only their moccasins got wet. In the afternoon as they were climbing up a steep meadow, the old man suddenly stopped and sniffed the air. At the same time Keeno pointed, having his nose high in the air, and then he made an attempt to run toward the scent. Kootenay had to call him back.

The old man said, "Carrion, probably a bear kill. We will have to be careful. Hold your dog!"

Kootenay grabbed Keeno by his harness to make certain that he didn't run away.

The old man continued, "Never challenge a bear when he is feeding on his own kill. Sometimes a bear will hang around near his kill until it's putrid. He will only go away after the best meat is gone and leaves the rest to the coyotes and the birds. To risk your dog's life would be foolish. A grizzly can kill an inexperienced dog with one blow."

So they left the trail they were on and walked up a steep scree chute, since they had to get over the ridge anyway. Before they angled back toward the trail, which was easier walking, they saw a thick clump of trees where they hoped to sit down in the shade. They had hardly settled down to rest when they heard a snorting and growling sound coming from the thick of the trees.

Kootenay had taken the heavy load off Keeno's back, so had Kootenay and the old man dropped their loads for a rest. They had hoped to sit down in the shade.

At this point, a huge black bear came charging out of the clump of trees, where he had been resting in the cool shade after feeding on the carcass. Seeing that they were the same guys who had scared him away from his dinner, this was the second time they had disturbed him, he decided that it was too much; once was enough. Now he came charging out of the forest, breaking branches and trees in his path.

But at this moment something happened that changed the situation in favor of Kootenay and the old man. The bear got wind of Keeno. He turned around and charged after Keeno. Keeno, who had the scent of the bear in his nose long before the old man, was prepared for this. He had positioned himself in the center of the steep meadow where he could outmaneuver the bear at will.

The big black now charged downhill with a full head of steam. Keeno was ready. When the bear was almost close enough to pounce on him, he side-stepped the monster. That got him away from the avalanche of muscle and fur, but also got him out of reach of the gigantic paws.

The bear, now out of balance, rolled downhill. That really got him mad. He came charging uphill again. Keeno, now aware of the fact that he could outmaneuver the brute, just danced around him while the bear just sat there waiting for an opportune moment to strike a deadly blow. While the bear figured out that this game was at a stalemate and Keeno sat there watching him, the old man and Kootenay carried their gear away to a safer location.

The bear, in the meantime, remembering that there might still be some meat left on the carcass he had been feeding on, ambled away downhill, while Keeno, now realizing this was a face-saving moment, disengaged himself from the duel fully convinced that he was the winner. All he had to do is run back to where his two companions were waiting. Never mind that chunk of venison. It didn't smell that good anyway.

They continued their steep uphill climb for hours. When they stepped across the rocky ridge night overtook them. Night came late in early summer. Even after sunset a warm, golden twilight lingered until midnight.

Since it was almost dark, they decided to make their camp out of the wind on the east side of the ridge. They made a fire this time. Nobody would see the smoke at night, but it might help to keep the bear at a safe distance, just in case he still carried a grudge against Keeno and had decided to follow them up the mountain. Their meal was frugal, just a cooked duck egg from the camp of plenty by the lake. The leather pouch, which had contained their supply of water, was almost empty, hardly a sip for each of them.

Once they lay down between the rocks, there was no view, except for the dark, almost black, sky, where slowly the stars appeared. They both, Kootenay and the old man, observed the world around them, since every free living being must, out of necessity and for its own safety, understand the world. The accumulating of the daily details of all experiences becomes a stock of permanent data in man and beast necessary for survival.

As it turned out, the bear's accumulated knowledge of man and his dog proved quite sufficient to keep him away from their camp, even though the fire had gone out. They used their sleeping robes like a ground sheet, one side to the ground, the other side folded over the back. Kootenay had the advantage that his dog kept his feet warm.

One would think that it would have been easy to fall asleep after traveling all day in some of the most dangerous terrain in the world, but that was not so. The night, in unfamiliar surroundings, was full of mysterious sounds. If anyone dared to open his eyes he would see the most incongruous shapes of imaginary monsters, all seemingly unfriendly and dangerous. And yet the night pulled a protective blanket over the hunters as well as the hunted. Right next to them, a mouse or some other rodent went noisily about its nocturnal errand.

From behind the dark outline of a large boulder, a few steps away, two green eyes stared in their direction but didn't dare to come any closer. Man was a dangerous animal, and all other animals knew it.

Is it a wolf? Keeno shivered with excitement. Kootenay could feel it, but when he touched the dog with his steady hand, he quieted down but remained poised until the eyes disappeared.

The warm wind played its music in the cracks and fissures behind which they rested. Kootenay couldn't sleep. He ended up counting shooting stars. He felt like he was suspended on the highest point in space and the universe revolved around him. The black sky opened up with a mighty bombardment of shooting stars of extraterrestrial origin. He thought of the possibility of being hit by an astral projectile from deep outer space, propelled by the mysterious forces of the universe. Feeling the nearness of his watchful dog next to him relaxed him, and the boy fell asleep.

But on the hunter and the hunted only the eyes need sleep. The ears are always open and need no sleep, and the nose never sleeps. The ears of the hunter are always in close contact with the world around him, always listening to all sounds around; listening, recording, storing away information, analyzing, and warning.

Riding on the wind came the smoky scent of a faraway forest fire, with a symphony of spring and alpine flowers wefting in between. The familiar, now pleasant, odor of sheep and elk-dung mixed with the fermenting smell of rotting vegetation tantalized his nostrils.

When the pink, tangent rays of the early morning sun touched the serrated ridges of the mountains toward sunrise, Kootenay was up. Had he slept at all? Not much but he felt refreshed. The packing of their gear took mere minutes. A trickle of moisture in the rocks from a snowpatch higher up stilled their thirst. Then they stumbled down the steep, grassy meadows into the fog-filled valley below.

Around midday, they arrived at the valley bottom. The thick fog was beginning to burn off, but where it was still thick, all sounds were muffled. Above their heads, the sun drifted like a polished metal disk in the milky white. The silence in the fog was eerie. Nothing moved; no bird sung there. Then, as if by giants' hands, the fog was pushed aside and drifted high along the rocky crags. As the white fog receded higher up the mountains, an awesome sight revealed itself to Kootenay's wondering eyes.

As far as the eye could see up the valley, there was no green tree visible. Only the dead trunks of fire-blackened trees reached without hope into the intense blue of the sky. When he looked closer, he saw that all the dead trees had burn marks on them. He looked at the old man as if to ask what happened there.

"What is the reason for this devastation?"

"It was many years ago that a violent thunderstorm started many fires up the dry valley. There had been a long drought in the Land of the Kootenay; many rivers dried out. Only rivers like this one, which are fed by glaciers melting in the high mountains, had a flow of water. Even in this river, the fish, who come up to spawn every year, stayed away as the ashes from the fires choked the river.

"After the fires started burning, a hot wind came roaring down the valley out of the searing sun, stoking the flames and intensifying the heat. As the sky darkened from the roaring inferno, the increasing heat sucked more hot air down the valley and the storm became a rippling gale that fanned the flames. The heat in this valley became so intense that everything living that couldn't escape was burned to a crisp, and the water in the river started to boil.

"At the time, I was at Fish Lake at the Top of the World; there was no fire there. When I went down to my winter camp, I found dead animals like sheep. They were choked by the smoke and the heat. Further down the valley, where the heat was more intense, I found the skeletons of a whole herd of deer picked clean by wolves and coyotes and birds. When I walked down to my winter camp that fall, I was still a young man, but I became humble when I saw the awesome destruction done by the forces of nature. But later I found out that while nature destroys, it also prepares to rejuvenate itself, as you will see tonight."

Later in the day Kootenay found out what the old man had meant when he said that nature rejuvenates itself. They walked into a great field of flowering fireweed waving in the wind. There, under the pink flowers, they set up their camp. The menace of the day before was long forgotten when their campfire crackled and they ate their eggs. A sparkling pool in the river invited Kootenay for a swim, and his dog joined him. In the last few days they had become more playmates than hunting companions.

When the two came back to their camp, they found the old man sound asleep, rolled up in his sheepskin robe. It had been a long day for an old man. When Kootenay looked at the sleeping man, he found that he had a smile on his face. Kootenay had by now known for some time that when the old man slept like that there was peace in the world around them. This kind of mood was contagious to a tired young man, so he rolled up in his bear robe and lay down. Before he fell asleep, he had enough time to watch the golden evening sun set fire to the Shining Mountains.

Kootenay slept late the following morning. A warm sun stood high in the sky. As he lay there enjoying the warmth of his bearskin, he still had his eyes closed. It seemed to him that the rest of his senses were keener, and he had a much sharper edge of perception without looking at the world through his eyes.

At first, he felt like he was enveloped in the sweet smell of the flowering fireweed. Next came the sweet smell of honey. Then he became aware of many sounds that he might have heard before but hadn't paid attention to. He already knew that he could hear things that the old man couldn't. At this moment, with his eyes still closed, he could distinguish at first the sound of bees. It reminded him of the sweet taste of honey. Then there was the whispering sound of the summer wind as it brushed the pink field of fireweed into waves around him. Then there was a more distinctive sound; he couldn't be certain he had heard it before. He knew that it was part of that symphony of sounds of the forests and mountains and waves of the lake of his childhood home. He still couldn't tell what it was that made that minute whirring sound; he had to open his eyes to see what it was. When he finally opened his eyes, there it was; a hummingbird was dipping its beak into the pink flowers of the fireweed in order to sip its nectar and rushing from flower to flower in a frenzy, as if there was somebody around who would take the sweet stuff away from him. As soon as he moved, the bird was gone. He had flown away so fast Kootenay's eyes couldn't follow.

When Kootenay heard Keeno barking, he jumped up and ran toward the river. He was still in the nude when he saw the old man coming through the fireweed carrying a string of fish. Keeno was by his side, excited that finally there was some decent food coming up. The old man had been fishing with his dipnet, but first he had to attach a longer handle to reach into the shallow pool.

The fire from the day before was stirred up, and soon there were fresh kokanee and trout roasting on skewers. It was a feast for the three; this was much better than the stale eggs they had been eating for days. Keeno even ate the fishbones. The fishing was so good in the shallow pool they stayed for several days just fishing and eating and smelling the sweet blossoms of the flowering fireweed.

Then one morning, they moved on, the snowcaps of the top of the world in front of them like a guiding beacon. The warm and sunny weather left them in an equable mood as they came to the spot where the fire had stopped. Now they had to cross the river, which had narrowed to a creek, and was easy to cross. On the other side, they had to find the game trail first if they wanted to make any progress in this tangled chaos of broken and rotting trees. They found the trail, but it looked like it had never been trodden by moccasins. After the fire, much of the game might have stayed away, since much of the valley remained barren for years. Now many of the original grasses had returned, and the valley looked as green as ever.

That night they camped under the overhanging branches of a gigantic fir tree. There was no counting of shooting stars that night, only the murmuring music of the brook lulled them to sleep.

They were up early the next morning, since they had a long day's march ahead of them. In the thick forest, only the sound of squirrels, high in the trees above, betrayed the silence on the gloomy forest floor. There was life here, too.

Late in the afternoon, the old man stopped suddenly and said, "That's what I have been hoping for. Listen!"

Kootenay couldn't hear anything, and he couldn't see anything. The dense undergrowth made it very difficult to make headway. They arrived at a logjam which consisted of a tangled mass of fallen trees. It formed a natural dam to the lake above, and, at the same time, functioned to regulate the water level of the lake and the outflow of water to the headwaters of the river below.

They pushed on until they reached higher ground on the grassy shore of the lake. Now Kootenay could hear a splashing sound, and looking down toward the water, he saw what made that sound. For a long stretch at the outlet, the lake was very shallow, with a sandy bottom. Every spring countless fish from the deeper part of the lake came to spawn. So many fish were there they covered the bottom of the spawning ground as far as the eye could see. At the more shallow spots the dorsal fins and the tail fins of the fish were sticking out of the water and making that splashing sound.

Young Kootenay stood in awe, watching this wonder of abundance in nature. Keeno his dog had different ideas. He jumped in the lake with his harness still on when he saw all the fish, and, in no time at all, came up with a big trout.

The old man turned around and smiled, for he knew that they would spend the summer here, and they would never go hungry. "Come," he said, "first we make camp."

They went to a clearing in the forest. There were several firepits there. They didn't look used. Many lodge poles were laying around. It looked like a fierce storm had tossed them about.

15

The old man went around the camp looking at everything. "The Issan-ka came here, a large hunting party, but they didn't stay long. There is no garbage. Before the fire, the Issan-ka came here for fire-making stones and for hunting. Now they trade with the Haida for iron arrow points, which they get from White people."

Now they got busy. First the old man made a fire. "That will keep the bear away," he said.

He had seen signs of a bear on the trail and around the camp. At the same time Kootenay was busy setting up poles for a lodge. This would be a large lodge, as they were planning to stay all summer and into late fall. In the middle of the lodge, there would be a fireplace. Up here it could snow any time, even in summer. After he had the poles up, he secured them with rocks. Then he got busy cutting branches for the roof; that took some time.

In the meantime, the fat trout Keeno had caught was roasting on skewers over the smoking fire. Now the old man got busy roofing the lodge while Kootenay was cutting more branches to keep the old man going.

On the day of their arrival, they never finished the roof, but what they had for that night gave them shelter from the wind. The roof was finished the following morning. On the top they left an opening large enough for the smoke from the fire to escape. The old man's insistence to finish the roof on the teepee before doing anything else turned out to be a very wise decision when the next day the rains started.

111

Late in the afternoon, they walked down to the spawning bed. There were more fish here, it seemed, than the day before. The shallow pool was a mass of wiggling, splashing fish. When Kootenay first saw this, he was tempted to jump in and hit the fish with a club and catch them that way.

The old man held him back and said, "If you try that, you won't catch many that way. They get away on you. If you use the dipnet I have made, you catch more. Watch!" Now he took the net and eased it into the water and let it settle on the bottom.

"Now, watch," he said. "The fish I scared away come back after a while. You have to be patient. Now you take the handle and raise the net slowly. When you get to the point when you lift the fish out of the water, the fish don't like that. They seem to like it better in the water."

Kootenay turned around and looked at the old man but didn't say anything. "As I was saying, now you have to move fast. Set the net out of the water and dump the fish on the shore. If you don't get them out far enough, they will try to jump back in."

It took Kootenay a little while to get the hang of things, but he found that it was fun catching fish that way. That evening they were feasting on fresh trout. The rest was smoked and dried for later use.

They slept well with full tummies that night, until early in the morning, when a violent thunderstorm rumbled through the valley. It came from the direction of midnight. At first, they heard the rumble of thunder in the distance, far enough they didn't have to pay attention. The next lightning bolt hit a tree in the forest so close that lightning and thunder arrived at the same time. When they heard the crashing of the falling tree not far from them, it was time for Keeno to be scared. He crawled all the way under Kootenay's bearskin.

There he felt safe. His master would know what to do about this thunder and lightning.

Kootenay couldn't do anything about this thunder. It rumbled on between the mountains. Then, when the thunder eased off, there was a tremendous downpour, and the heavens opened up. Inside of their teepee, they were protected from the full force of the monsoon, but due to the nature of their roof, a fine spray of water, almost like a mist, came through. They would have to improve their roof if they had in mind staying there all summer.

The rain lasted for a few days, which forced them into a few days of leisure. All the old man did was build a fire in their teepee. In the gentle rain that was coming down, things inside of the teepee dried out slowly, and life became very comfortable.

One morning they heard the thunder of avalanches. In the nearby mountains, what had been a downpour at the camp had fallen as heavy, wet snow. As soon as the sun hit, it became even heavier, and it thundered into the valleys as monstrous slides that tore everything in their way toward the valley bottom.

When the weather improved they continued their leisurely pace of fishing, eating, and sleeping. Kootenay learned fishing with a harpoon. He found a spot where a fallen tree trunk reached out into the lake. From this vantage point he could hover over the best pool in the lake without being seen by the fish below, as long as he and his dog didn't move. In time, he became so proficient in the art of harpooning fish that he carried more fish to their camp than they could eat.

One sunny afternoon, Kootenay was reminded of the fact that other denizens of this neighborhood liked to eat fresh fish now and then. It all started with a crashing sound on the steep hillside on the other side of the lake. The distance to the other shore was considerable. Somebody was coming down a scree chute with a load of gravel and an enormous racket. Then out of the bushes that lined the lakeshore, a huge black bear appeared.

At first, Kootenay didn't pay any attention. The distance to the other side of the lake was too great for the bear to swim, so there was nothing to worry about. But then that bear, after playing around in the water a bit, started swimming across the lake, and it looked as if he were heading for the spot where the tree trunk on which he and Keeno were sitting was located.

Now this was getting serious. If that bear got to the spot where Kootenay and Keeno had to jump to the shore, they would be cut off from their retreat. They would have to jump in the lake and swim for their lives, and from what Kootenay had seen, neither Kootenay nor Keeno could outswim that bear.

Now they had to get off that tree trunk fast. When they jumped from the tree trunk to the shore, Kootenay had the idea that saved the day. As we know, Kootenay already had a string of fish laying in the cold water. He now pulled the fish from the water and laid them across the trail where the bear would come.

While they both ran away, the bear charged after them. What Kootenay had hoped for then indeed happened. When the bear smelled those fish, he stopped so suddenly that he almost fell on his face. When Kootenay didn't hear anything behind him, he took time out to look back. There was the bear sitting on his hunches devouring his fish.

Kootenay felt good about that. He had avoided a confrontation he couldn't win. The bear got what he wanted, fresh fish, without having to catch them first. This was the fine solution for the bear, too, since he had no interest in eating a human being.

At camp the old man had built himself another scaffold. He said it was actually nothing more than a tripod, the same as the frame for a teepee, only it consisted of three poles. This way the fish got smoked and dried at the same time. Fish cured that way could be kept for a long time.

16

When life is good time passes fast. Summer in the Valley of the Kootenay is a time of plenty for man and beast. The herds of elk and deer had moved into the higher regions of the mountains, where lush alpine meadows were rich in succulent herbs and grasses, and cool winds kept flies and mosquitoes away. Only a pack of timber wolves who had laid claim and annexed the territory for the season had to be watched. The breeding bitch, who controlled the pack and had given birth to six whelps in her den in an impenetrable grove of stunted trees, demanded fresh meat for herself and her fast-growing litter every day. The males of the pack could be seen herding deer and elk in their territory and taking what they could. Everybody had to watch that no young calf or fawn strayed away from its mother.

Just below the zone of everlasting ice and snow, in the rocky crags, bighorn sheep and white goats had taken up summer residence. There they spent the all too short summer in amiable harmony. Only when the snow-white billies felt like introducing their offspring in the dangerous sport of rock climbing did the eagle see them drifting across the most exposed ridges, where no other animal dared to traverse. Their pure white coats shined in the sun like spun gold, a great temptation for the eagle, who glided in a thermal updrift. But the old billy watched. Many ambitious kids had been dropped down a cliff by the eagle in the sky.

This was the time when Kootenay learned about all the edible berries on the hillsides and in the forest. The first berries to ripen were the strawberries. From then on, there was no end to the earthly delights that Mother Earth put on their table. One day Kootenay was sitting in a blueberry patch gorging himself, when not far from him, on the other side of the patch, was a young bear doing the same. Luckily for Kootenay, the bear didn't know yet the difference between human and bear.

The long, warm summer evenings by the fire were the best time for our two companions. This had always been the time for story-telling for the Kootenay people. By the safety of the golden dome of their fire generations told the history of their people to their children for aeons of time. So it was with Kootenay and the old man. They sat there and talked and watched the golden glow of the sun, just below the horizon, wander across the North Pole and send flaming sheets of Northern Lights into the dark sky. One night Kootenay told the old man he was more and more convinced that he had to find the secret trails of the Kootenay across the Shining Mountains, where the Na-Koda and the Sik-Sika, a Canadian tribe, lived, and where at one time the Kootenay people were at home, too.

The old man took a deep breath and started talking. "I myself have traveled all the trails. I will tell you about the best trails. Some of those trails are covered with snow all summer long, and from the mountain passes the avalanches come down and cover you. If you travel by yourself, you might perish. But still by just knowing about a trail that doesn't mean that you know the trail. In order to know the trail, you will have to walk every step of the way and wear out many moccasins. You might be on the trail for many summers. No path can be traveled by just knowing about it. You might find that after many summers on the trail the trail has become your destination. You may, like I did, get to like that kind of life.

"I's not saying that you should do that. I think it is better to be with your people and raise families, and above all accept the responsibilities that come with that. To see your own children grow makes your heart glad. There is great joy in that. There is also great joy in being with women of your own kind. They will look after you when you get old."

17

One full year had now passed since the two braves from the Kootenay Nation had dropped young Kootenay off in the wilderness to fend for himself or perish. He had to assume that the Kootenay people, after one year had passed, would send a bailiff out to find him and, if he had survived, return and restore him to his old standing within the nation.

In this one year, a great metamorphosis had taken place in young Kootenay. He had grown; he had gained weight. But above all, he had gained in confidence and speed. One had to see him move to realize that. The old man, who had watched him on the hunt, had noticed that the boy moved like a mountain lion when he was after game. But most importantly, and only known to Kootenay himself, he was now beginning to like this life of great freedom. The old man, since he was fully aware that Kootenay looked after most of the more demanding tasks, left Kootenay all the freedom that he could wish for. In other words, the old man gave Kootenay what he himself had demanded and never received.

So now that high summer was in the valley, Kootenay got itchy feet. He had observed a herd of bighorn sheep just below the snowline on the high meadows. Since he knew the old man wouldn't be able to climb with him up the steep scree, into the lofty heights of soaring rock and stone, he decided not to tell the old man that he might be gone for a few weeks to hunt the Kootenay ram.

Without the old man's knowledge he had cached a good stock of smoked fish that would feed him for more than a week. If he stayed away longer, he would have to hunt his own game. He would travel in his old moccasins, the new mukluks the old man had made for him he left in the camp at Fish Lake.

His hunting gear consisted of his knife and a spear with a hardened steel blade attached to a perfectly straight shaft of mountain ash. The old man had traded the steel blade for a few beaver pelts. To Kootenay, this iron spear blade was a priceless possession.

At first Kootenay had thought that he might tell the old man where he was going. Then there was a night when he couldn't sleep, and it came to him. If that posse, which was sure to arrive, found their trail, they might force the old man to tell where he had gone. He thought that it might be wise not to tell the old man where he was going.

Kootenay had watched sheep and goats in their rocky domain. The warmer it got in the valley, the higher they moved into the rocks. One day, he had observed a herd in a lush meadow barely below where the last snow of summer was melting off. He had seen them first as they came down steep slabs of rock, then crossing a snowpatch one by one. He was amazed that these simple animals had figured out that this was the safest way to minimize danger to the whole herd in case of slides.

Further down, meltwater from snow higher up had washed a deep ravine out of the gravel. They stopped for a moment to survey the situation. Finally, an old ewe took the lead with a snow-white lamb right behind her. He counted them one by one as they climbed safely out of the deep ravine on the other side. The only member of the herd still to come was the largest ram, the same ram he had given the name Kootenay ram.

At this moment, it looked like the animal was hesitating before the crossing. Actually the Kootenay ram was covering the rear of the herd. He was watching a pack of wolves at the edge of the thick forest below. They had in mind scattering the herd and then cutting stragglers from their retreat into the rock wall behind them. Then there was the lone puma, a female with a pair of kittens to feed. Over the years the Kootenay ram had watched many an innocent lamb disappear. The cat was invisible in the golden-yellow rocks. Her leap out of her perch in the steep rocks above was lightning fast and totally unexpected, and as a result, usually a fresh, naïve lamb was lost. Then there was the pair of eagles in the sky he had to watch out for. The ram knew they wouldn't tackle him, but the lambs were always in danger.

Kootenay was watching. He expected that the ram would crawl into the ravine like the rest of the herd. But no, not the Kootenay ram. With one mighty leap, he jumped across the ravine. Then, after he had secured his footing, he stood there in the meadow, his mighty horns pointed toward the sky as a challenge to every other ram on the mountain. The most impressive sight on the ram was his set of mighty horns. Those horns were a full curl with the sharp ends flaring out like daggers. Anybody who saw him knew that he was the master of the range.

For the time being, the rams were still with the herd, but pretty soon they would drift apart. The Kootenay ram would look for a more solitary existence to contemplate his mastery over the range.

That night, Kootenay and his dog slept under a quickly built lean-to. The logs from their shelter reflected the heat from their fire. From the inside of the golden circle of their fire, they could see four green eyes moving back and forth, two wolves. The wolves knew where there was a fire there were human beings. They circled around the camp a few times. Then their frustrated howls faded into the lonely night.

When the first rays of the rising sun colored the tops of the surrounding mountains with a golden hue, they were up and on the move. They ate dried fish and drank from a rivulet that came out of the rocks. So early in the morning, it was only a trickle, but it was enough to slake their thirst.

In the first harsh light of the new day, Kootenay was looking for his herd of sheep and the Kootenay ram. They were gone. His eyes scanned the surrounding meadows, the steep rock-face above, and finally a field of gravel and boulders. Could they have gone into the high rocks and from there into the ice and snowfields of the mountain? If that's what they had done, Kootenay's attempt to bag the Kootenay ram ended right there. He would turn around, and he could be home at the old man's camp in one day.

In the shifting gravel, above timberline, the herd left no visible tracks. But Keeno had his nose to the ground, something that Kootenay hadn't noticed.

Since Kootenay had to assume that the ram had taken his herd into the inaccessible realm of ice and snow, where he couldn't follow, he now decided to turn around and walk back to the old man's camp. Tonight they would be talking by the warm fire, and he would sleep in the comfort of their lodge.

In the meantime, Keeno had picked up another trail. It was following a visible trail in the gravel. Now Kootenay found the fresh dung of several animals. That confirmed what he had suspected all along. The herd was heading up the mountain into remote rocks where he couldn't follow. But then Keeno stopped. He sniffed up into the scree, came back to the spot where he had stopped before, but now walked down the hill, toward the green valley below. His nose was still on the ground. When he stopped, he had his nose in the air, and he let out a whimpering sound.

Now Kootenay was confused, too. When his dog let out that whimpering sound that meant that he was confused and hoped that his master knew a way out of the dilemma. There was only one choice. If the ram had split the herd and sent one part with the ewes into the high rocks, where Kootenay couldn't follow, he would have to follow the trail downhill into the valley, where he was going anyway on the way home.

It wasn't too long before the situation changed drastically. As soon as they were out of the gravel and into softer ground, he found the fresh tracks of a mountain sheep. It was a large animal, so big that it could only be the footmark of the Kootenay ram. Now it became all clear to Kootenay. In order to confuse his pursuers, and hoping that they would follow the rest of the herd, the ram had split himself from the herd so that he could find the solitude he was craving. The ram was traveling in great haste through dark, evergreen forest. He didn't like it in there; one could tell that he was out of his element in the confined surroundings of the thick forest.

They traveled all day and lost the trail again, with Keeno standing above a meandering creek not knowing where to go and the ram nowhere to be seen. When it was getting dark, they settled down behind sheltering rocks, and they ate their last food. Kootenay didn't make a fire since he didn't want to tell the ram that they were still on his trail.

To get his camp ready, all Kootenay had to do was fold his bearskin on the dry ground, lay down one side, and fold the other side over the top of himself. When Keeno came and curled up in front, they were quite comfortable. They lay there and watched the darkening sky, where slowly the stars appeared. Kootenay had the impression that he and his dog were at the center of the universe, and the limitless sky was revolving around them when Keeno let out that whimpering sound. This time it ended like the doleful cry of a wolf. Kootenay knew that they both had the same problem; they were both looking at a universe of which they were part but didn't know what it was all about.

The following morning they were scooting down a steep scree chute into the still dark valley below. They were going there not because they knew where they were going but because it was easy going. In the early morning light, they found that they had descended into an almost barren valley that contained three small lakes. They were strung out like shining pearls on a string, now sparkling in the early morning sun. Three Lakes Valley Kootenay would later call it. It was one of those valleys which had been formed by glacial ice during times long past. Now Kootenay and his dog were about to find out that they had descended from high above into a valley of plenty.

The highest of the lakes was very shallow and contained no fish. There they both lay down and stilled their thirst. Keeno looked at Kootenay with great anticipation in the hope that his master would now find some food, as he always did. The outlet from the upper lake to the middle lake formed a beautiful waterfall, which they hadn't been able to see from above. Now, as they walked toward the next lake, they found that the outlet from the lake also irrigated beautiful, terraced meadows filled with late-summer flowers.

At the very bottom of the waterfall, where the last winter snow had just melted, they found a patch of exuberantly thriving glacier lilies. But our two companions had no eyes for such beauty, as they were now very hungry. Only Kootenay picked a handfull of sorrel leaves and chewed them. While the sour taste of the leaves refreshed him, it didn't still his hunger. Keeno looked at Kootenay with disgust. He couldn't see how anybody could eat such stuff.

The shoreline of the middle lake showed signs that avalanches had swept the lake during winter, but no sign of fish. It was the third lake that gave them some hope. As they approached the shallow upper part of the water, they saw schools of rainbow trout. The far side of the lakeshore held a stand of stunted poplars. At this high elevation, their leaves had already turned into the translucent gold of early fall.

As they walked along the shoreline, Kootenay found a rock protruding into the lake. He put down his bundle, and on his hands and knees, he crawled across the rock for a careful look into the lake. He had to be careful there, as trout in these crystal-clear water were wary of anything that approached from above.

Slowly his head moved over the edge. First he got to see his own mirror image. Then his eyes adjusted and he could see the rainbow trout, big, fat rainbow trout. Each one would make a meal for both of them. Slowly, he moved backward. He didn't want to disturb the fish.

Keeno was laying on the shore watching the proceedings. Out of Kootenay's bundle came the harpoon, the same one the old man had made for him. Kootenay knew from watching braves fishing in streams that this kind of fishing was the ultimate test of patience. One had to move ever so slowly; any kind of jerky movement would scare the fish, and they would disappear in deep water.

Keeno was still watching with great interest. Slowly, Kootenay stood up with his right arm extended, in his hand the deadly harpoon, waiting until a fish moved to within his reach. In the meantime, a fly crawled across his face and tickled his nose, but he couldn't move. He was hungry; he needed food.

Then came the lightning-fast thrust. At the end of his harpoon was a fine rainbow trout, wiggling and trying to get off the hook, but the barbs on the harpoon held fast. With his bare hands, Kootenay pulled the fish apart and ate most of it raw. The rest went to his dog.

The next few days Kootenay spent fishing and eating fish and succulent blueberries, which he had discovered on the sunny hillside. He had built a lean-to from poplar branches. His firepit was made from rocks he found on the shoreline of the lake. For his fire there were dry juniper roots, which made a fragrant fire and were best for roasting fish. Their afternoons they spent in idle recline in the shade of the golden leaves of a poplar. The whispering wind in the golden dome above made life easy.

Kootenay forgot that he was on the trail of the Kootenay ram until one afternoon when they walked to the end of the lake. In the muddy shoreline, they found the ram's footprints. Not too far into the high grass were his droppings. Then there was the spot where he had rested and chewed his cud. In the very same spot where the ram had stilled his thirst and rested for the night; they drank the same water as the ram. Then they rolled around in his putrid-smelling dung until they carried the same rank smell as the ram; only now the foul smell had lost its offensiveness. It had taken on something pleasant, something like kinship. He now knew there was a mysterious thread connecting him to his quarry. He felt that he could never go back to his people until he had been face to face with the ram. Not until he could walk on rock and stone, across treacherous ridges of snow and glacier ice like the ram, would he be satisfied.

Early in the morning, still in the cool of the early dawn, when the grass was still heavy with melting frost, they headed up into the sliding scree of the next mountain range. Kootenay watched the slanting sunrays as they danced across the dark sky, reflected from the ridges of the Shining Mountains, while they were still climbing in the cool shade on the trail of the ram. It would be a hot day.

Still the ram climbed on. Kootenay now had the feeling the ram was guiding him. Only on well-established goat trails could a human being travel through this mass of stone and rock in perpetual downhill motion. When they got into steep slabs polished by sliding snow, wind, and rain, Kootenay heard his dog whimpering behind him. When he looked back, he found his dog far below himself unable to climb the slabs of polished rock.

He climbed back down to the animal. Keeno was still whimpering. It sounded like an apology, as if the dog felt like a failure because he couldn't follow where his master was going. Now Kootenay noticed he was licking the underside of his paws. When Kootenay looked at his dog's feet, he was shocked; the soles of his feet were a bloody mess of shredded skin. On the sharp rocks he had worn the tough skin on his feet right off, until all four feet were bleeding. He couldn't walk any longer. Kootenay now carried his dog to a sheltering rock, where he knew there would be shade from the blistering, high-altitude sun until late afternoon, when he would return there he bedded down his faithful companion behind his pack and ordered him to stay.

He himself took his spear, knife, and bedroll and followed the faint track of the ram into the most impenetrable cliffs. He saw the horns of the ram above him, where he couldn't follow. The animal always stayed ahead of him at a certain distance, as if he knew how far the effective range of Kootenay's projectile extended. When Kootenay found a narrow ledge to take him up to where he had seen the ram, he hoped that he had him cornered, only to watch the ram scramble down to the next rock wall over a cliff so steep he froze in fear of falling.

For the first time in his life, young Kootenay had the feeling that he had come to the end of his capabilities. He was scared. For the first time in his life, he had come to experience humility. There was an animal who could do things he couldn't do.

For a long time, he sat there shaking and shivering in the cold air. He had no eyes for the beauty that surrounded him. He crawled behind a rock to be out of the wind to rest, since he was completely exhausted from the steep climb. Most of all there was something that Kootenay didn't know about; he had climbed into a region where thinner air was beginning to have an effect on him.

Under the warmth of his robe, he fell asleep. It was a short fitful sleep of exhaustion. Without realizing it, he had done exactly the right thing. When he awoke, he was completely refreshed. He decided to climb up the next rock pile, which looked like it was the highest point on the mountain, in the hope that he might be able to see his quarry. He didn't see the ram, but what he saw was so beautiful that he forgot all about the ram. Toward the direction of midnight, in the golden light of early evening, mountain range after mountain range reared into the dark blue sky. This must be what the old man had called Kana-Naskis. There was no path through those mountains that his moccasins could travel. All valleys were filled with ice and snow, and where the ice melted, waterfalls cascaded over precipices so steep that no human foot could purchase a hold.

But still, the old man had told him through these mountains, upon which the heavens rested, the secret trail of the Kootenay would bring him into the land of the Kai-nai, Picani, and Nenii-Yawak people. It was here, on top of a mountain, that Kootenay decided that one day he must travel the trail of the Kootenays, and only then return to the gentle shores of the lake where he had spent his childhood.

When the light faded on the Kana-Naskis Mountains, he climbed down to the spot where his sleeping robe was hidden to spend the night. He ate a little bit of smoked fish to still his hunger. In a rock crevice he found a patch of melting snow to quench his thirst.

He was surprised to find there was no disappointment about the fact that the ram got far away on him. The more he thought about it, the more he felt a sense of relief. *Why would I want to kill such a magnificent animal? Why would I want to kill my brother? How could it be that I discovered a sense of kinship with a big horn ram?* With that happy thought, Kootenay fell asleep without having seen the most dramatic celestial display of shooting stars in the black sky above.

He slept until the hissing sound of the morning wind, which was now rushing down from the cool mountaintops into the valley, woke him up. While his side of the mountain was still in deep shade, the tangent rays of the sun were illuminating the snow fields on the other side of the valley. He lay there for a while, enjoying the warmth of his bearskin while he watched the dancing light of the morning sun on the faraway mountains. Then he realized his dog, Keeno, was waiting for him.

He jumped up, swung his roll over his shoulder, and looked down the cliff where he had climbed up the day before. He got scared and found out that sometimes it is more difficult to come down a mountain than go up. He also found that every time he stepped across the threshold of the known into the unknown there was that curtain of fear. He was now gripped by fear. No matter how much he looked for the diagonal ledge that he had used to come up the mountain the day before, he couldn't find it. He walked the full length of the rockwall on both slides. There were sheer walls so steep he couldn't see the bottom. A fall there would be deadly.

With the courage of desperation, he started descending the sheer rock face where he thought that he had to cross the narrow ledge which had given him access to the top of the mountain. Below him he couldn't see. His toes had to feel for even the slightest foothold. His hands moved across the rock in the hope of finding the slightest crack to dig in his fingernails.

When one hand got tired and started shaking, his other hand needed a solid grip to suspend his tired body, while his toes were searching for even the most minute toehold to rest his fast-tiring arms. Kootenay knew that if he slipped on this rock wall he would perish. He fought a battle of desperation for his life.

When he thought things couldn't get any worse, he became aware of another problem. A stabbing pain ran through one of his feet. The harsh rock had worn through the soles of his moccasins, which in his excitement he hadn't noticed. Now the skin on his toes had worn through on the abrasive rock when his bare toes clawed into the unfeeling stone. His feet were bleeding, and he still hadn't found the life-saving ledge. He had passed it by a few feet, but when he looked up, he saw it. To get to it, he had to cross a narrow field of unstable scree.

To put all his weight on the soles of his feet gave some relief to the pain on his bleeding toes. As soon as he started crossing a loose gravel, the whole mass of stones moved downhill. It felt like the complete mountainside was in downhill motion. Realizing that he had started a rock slide, he knew he had to get out of this mass of moving stone. He jumped on top of a large rock, but as soon as his weight was on the rock, the rock moved downhill, too.

Soon the whole talus slope below the cliff started moving. On a protruding piece of bedrock, large enough to hold his feet, he gained enough time to rest while he watched the landslide thunder down the mountain in a plume of dust. He didn't know how long he sat there and watched. Only after he gained the ledge that he had been looking for in the first place did he know he was safe.

Climbing down the rest of the cliff to a grassy slope was easy. He found his dog Keeno where he had left him, not too far from where the slide had come down. Not even while the slide thundered past him did he move. His trust in his master was so absolute that he would have rather died than move away from the spot where he knew his master would re-appear.

The meeting of the two was a sight to behold as they rolled around on the steep grass slope until they were exhausted. Then Kootenay looked at the dog's feet. His hind feet had healed almost completely in the short time Kootenay was gone. Of course, Keeno had licked his feet and that way had kept the wounds clean, which had helped the healing.

They were both hungry. They both knew where there was lots of food. It was about one day's travel; with their sore feet it would take them two. How resourceful Kootenay was now became evident. He took the harness the old man had made for Keeno and cut the longest straps off the bottom. Then he tied the straps around Keeno's front paws, leaving the claws sticking out. The hind legs he left as they were. Then he filled the bottom of his moccasins with tough mountain grass to save the soles of his own feet. He could replace the grass as often as he had to. Now Kootenay swung his pack over his shoulders and they were on the move, Kootenay carrying his own pack plus the load Keeno had carried to give the animal a chance to heal his feet.

Hunger plagued Kootenay and the dog. The animal hadn't eaten in two days. Hunger is the most potent driving force behind all living things; it is the mother of invention. Since all food grows on the ground we walk on, it is also the father of aggression.

They traveled all day. On the way, Kootenay ate everything he knew was edible, like dry berries, wild onions, and mushrooms. When he found sorrel leaves, he ate them, too.

131

From the same trickle of water, they drank and were refreshed. Keeno went hungry, since he refused to eat berries.

They traveled all day and late into the night, finding restful sleep under a tree on soft pine needles, kept warm under Kootenay's bearskin. They slept until early dawn, when the noisy chatter of a flock of magpies woke them. Kootenay could understand the language of magpies, and he knew that magpies didn't argue except about food.

But Keeno knew more than his master. First, his one complete ear swivelled in the direction of the sound. Then Kootenay could hear the sniffing sound his dog's nose made, and Keeno knew that there was food somewhere close by. That knowledge increased his hunger tenfold, and his determination to get some of that food grew into desperation.

When he jumped up, Keeno felt no pain in his front paws as he ran toward the enticing smell of carrion. Kootenay had known since he was a papoose that a single brave can not claim part of a bear-kill when the bear is around, and that it was the better part of valor to stay clear. Kootenay tried to call his dog back. For the first time in as long as he could remember, his dog didn't listen. So he stayed where he was, under his bearskin. He made certain that his spear was handy.

In the meantime, Keeno proceeded toward the enticing smell of rotten food, unaware that his sore feet were a decisive handicap if he had to outmaneuver a bear. It wasn't long before he arrived at the clearing. He chased away the feeding magpies, then circled around the kill in order to determine who it was who had killed the deer. When he was certain that it was a bear and not a pack of wolves, his archenemies, he took what he thought was rightfully his and started feeding. While above in the trees, the magpies complained loudly about the interruption of their meal, not too far away in a thicket in the forest a big black bear slept soundly with full guts.

After Keeno had stilled his hunger, he tore away a piece of the hindquarter of the animal, which was still attached the rest of the carcass by skin and bones and dragged it toward the resting place where Kootenay had gone back to sleep. After a while, Keeno dug a hole in the ground and dropped the putred carrion in the hollow and covered it with leaves and soil. Then he walked back to Kootenay as if nothing had happened. Only the bad smell of rotten flesh gave him away.

They arrived at the campsite at Third Lake when the sun was high in the sky. Kootenay found his harpoon where he had hidden it. It wasn't long until several trout were hanging from a skewer roasting.

18

This scene of tranquility, an Indian boy, stark naked, spear-fishing from a rock next to him his dog, Keeno licking his paws so they would heal faster, was observed by a black bear with two cubs. The she-bear and her two cubs were feeding on a patch of berries higher up on the hillside. Her cubs, when not eating berries, were chasing butterflies, even though they knew that they would never catch one.

The reason Kootenay was naked was a most unusual one. He had washed his leather leggings and his deerhide shirt. When he and his dog were after the Kootenay ram, he had thought if he took on the rank smell of the ram the animal would allow him to get close enough for his spear to be effective. Now that the hunt was over, he found the smell of the ram offensive.

For an Indian boy to wash his clothing was a most un-usual, activity. When he was still at home, he had watched his mother do it. She had spread out the garments at the water's edge and rubbed them with fine sand. Then they were rinsed in clean water and hung up to dry. While his clothing was hanging on the branch of a tree, Kootenay was running around naked.

The next few days, while their sore feet healed, they spent in a virtual Garden of Eden. They swam in a crystal-clear pool below the waterfall. Kootenay picked honey-sweet berries on the hillside: Days of leisure and recuperation and playing in the sun. The nights on the hard ground covered by an animal skin under their lean-to were peaceful and quiet.

But young animals heal fast. Kootenay knew the old man would be waiting for him at Fish Lake, and he also had to expect the bailiff to be there waiting for him. He had to approach with great caution. He also realized that it was a good thing that he had taken Keeno, as they would have recognized the animal as Kootenay's dog.

One morning Kootenay looked at Keeno's feet and found that they had healed, so had his own feet. For the first time in days, Kootenay wore his leather stockings, deerhide shirt, and moccasins, and they were on the trail to Fish Lake. Since the harness had been cut for bandages, he had to carry his own bundle, including a string of smoked fish.

Keeno enjoyed his freedom of not having to carry a load, and forgetting his feet, he jumped around the trail like a puppy. Through the thick forest he roamed far ahead of Kootenay, and just before they arrived at Fish Lake, he reported back to Kootenay with a fat spruce grouse. There would be a treat waiting for them when they arrived back at the camp, since the old man would by now be tired of eating fish.

At this spot, Kootenay decided to take an extra precaution. He left the main trail and angled toward the direction of midnight. If he now crossed the steep scree slide, which he had seen from their camp, he would meet the trail which approached the lake from the other side.

Travel in the virgin forest was difficult. The evergreen canopy of the trees allowed no direct sunlight through to the moss-covered ground. In this tangled mass of growing, broken-down, and rotting trees he sometimes had to walk around fallen giants. He had to find his way around trees so big they may have lived for a thousand years, and then when they got old a storm had toppled them. Now he walked around the rotting remains and he saw fresh, green saplings pushing toward the light above.

They crossed the steep slide fairly high on the mountain, and as Kootenay had hoped, the Promontory where their camp was located could be seen from where he was sitting, well-concealed behind bushes. There was no sign of life in the camp, only a thin strand of smoke curling into the sky. It indicated to Kootenay that the old man had lain down for his afternoon nap, and that he was smoking fish. Kootenay watched for a long time. When nothing moved, he was satisfied that there was nobody at the camp and all was safe. They moved on, dropping down to the trail that followed the shoreline around the lake as far as the campsite.

Long before Kootenay could see the teepee, Keeno must have gotten a smell of curing fish and ran ahead barking loudly, alerting the old man. The reception Kootenay got from the old man was that of a long lost son, even though he had only been gone for a few days. The old man had a few things to tell. There had been no braves from the Kootenay looking for him, but two braves from the Sa-Haptin people came, and they talked after smoking the pipe. They were from an advance party of scouts from the Sa-Haptin.

What they told was not good. First they met two White men who told that they came in the name of the great White father who lives in a big city far away. They also told that they came up a river which flows into a sea many thousands of miles away toward the midday sun. The old man said he couldn't believe that because as far as he knew all rivers flowed into the great ocean toward sunset. The two Sa-Haptin scouts told him that the two White men were looking for a pass across the mountains in the direction of the great ocean. When they found out that the Sa-Haptin had horses, they traded and paid well for them with blankets and tobacco.

"The White people have so many things that we have never known. They had cooking-pots made from shiny metal and all kinds of knives." While the old man talked, he prepared the bird Keeno had caught and put it over the fire on a skewer.

Many months after the two men and their porters had left, many more White people arrived in wagon trains. They even had a man with black skin, who they say came with the White people. The Sa-Haptin scratched the black man's skin to see if they could get the black paint off him, but they couldn't.

"These White people bring everything with them. Their women have long yellow hair, their children, too. They say they all came from a land from across the sea where the sun rises out of the ocean, and the fog never leaves the land. That's why they are so pale.

"They came and asked the chief of the Sa-Haptin to trade their worn-out horses for fresh horses. They needed them to pull their wagons across the snowy mountains. The chief declined, but the White men took all the horses anyway and left them their worn-out beasts. The Sa-Haptin say that many more White people will come from across the sea, and they will take our land.

"I'm too old to wait for that to happen, but it will be up to you to prevent that. This is your land. For as long as people remember, this has been the land we have fished and hunted and taken care of. We take no more from the land than we need, and all we need is more than enough for everybody.

"They say the White people think differently. They were told by their gods to go forth and multiply and subjugate the earth. I was told that behind the Shining Mountains, across the sea of grass, the White people put up fences so nobody can walk there. That will make you a slave. I think that you should be free to go wherever you please and share every blade of grass, share every tree, share the wind and the sun and the rain with everybody else.

"They told me where they pass their wagon wheels, with rims made of iron, the grass will not grow any more. Our moccasins leave no mark on the land where we pass. That's the way we should keep it."

The old man turned the roasting bird and sprinkled some salt on it. Then there was a great silence about him, while he looked at the faraway mountains. Just as abruptly as he had fallen silent he spoke again.

"Kootenay, you will have to learn much about these people so you may confer with them in order to keep them out of our land."

They ate their meal in silence. Then they ate from a pouch of blueberries and drank the sweet water from the lake. The old man put more wood on the fire to smoke the fish he had caught.

There was more silence of late summer, when all the animals have much food and don't move around much. Elk and deer stay in the forest where there is shade. The fish in the lake go into deep water where it is cool. Even the eagle catches his fish in the morning when the fish rise to the surface to feed on insects. It is the splashing sound of the eagle's talon that wakes them, but they don't stir.

All day, the old man sat in the shade repairing Kootenay's moccasins. He didn't need any more fish. They had enough to last them for a long time. Kootenay swam in the crystal pool below the waterfall. He picked berries completely naked on the hillsides until he could eat no more. These were the days of easy living, of restful nights and days filled with tranquility, enjoyed by all to the fullest.

In the evenings the old man sat and watched the sunset, but his eyes didn't see the great distance any longer. Instead

138

he seemed to be looking inside of himself, counting his waning years.

Early the next morning, they were on the trail through the silent forest, a trail which led toward midnight. The land was ripe with wild cherries and mushrooms and berries of all sorts, and there was no want for anything.

The passing of their moccasins left no marks on the forest trails. In three days of easy travel, they arrived at the Lake of the White Swans. The old man knew where to find his old campsite, even though he hadn't used it for many summers. They found the lodge poles for two lodges, the main teepee and the sweat-lodge.

The old man spoke very quietly but with great emphasis when he gave orders, and he always explained why he gave orders. "We will stay here until the snow flies, but first come the big rains. We will need a warm teepee to sleep in. We will make the roof watertight with birchbark. You go and collect birchbark while I prepare our teepee and the sweat lodge."

The next few days were days of hard work. The grass in the fireplace had to be removed, and a store of firewood collected. With every load of birchbark Kootenay brought home, the main teepee took shape. The opening in the top was for the smoke from the fire to escape; one shingle was attached conveniently so it could be moved to cover the opening. To protect the birchbark roof, branches of spruce and pine were piled against it.

How important it was to get a good roof on a teepee they found out when the rains came. It rained day and night; it rained for several days without interruption. The old man, when asked how he knew the rains were coming, said, it was his rheumatism that told him, when his bones ached there would be rain.

Kootenay didn't understand since he had never experienced rheumatic pain. But he enjoyed the long, restful nights when the storm shook the teepee and the golden shine of the crackling fire warmed his feet and his dog Keeno crawled under his bearskin. After the rains stopped, trees and grasses carried sparkling beads of frost in the morning.

One day, when Kootenay looked out of their teepee, the hard frost had turned the green leaves of birches and poplars into sun-warmed, translucent gold. On the rocky hillsides, the leaves of dwarf maples turned into flames, like hot, burning iron glowing in the sun.

While Kootenay and his dog roamed the hillsides, the old man was working on a strange contrivance, the likes of which Kootenay had never seen before. He had watched the old man collecting willow shoots. "Only the longest and most flexible will do," he had said.

Then he peeled the soft bark off and stored them in the lake to keep them soft and pliable. When Kootenay came home after a day in the sun, he saw a contraption like a basket. But it wasn't a basket, it was almost square and had two or three openings on one side.

When Kootenay asked the old man what this strange contrivance was for, the old man said, "Pretty soon the fish will be running. They come up from the river of the Kootenay to spawn in the lake. I use this to catch fish. We will feast on fresh fish for weeks." One day after the sweat lodge was finished, they did the sweetgrass and mushroom ceremony. The old man had collected the best mushrooms on the Top of the World. He had dried them on flat stones while he watched that no flies came and laid their eggs in them. Now he ground them into a powder. When the mild euphoria of the mushroom smoke overcame them, they crawled down to the sandy lakeshore and slept in the mild sun for the rest of the day.

When the fish started running, they had their hands full. At the end of the lake, just above where the lake emptied into the river, the old man had set up his trap. Then there was shallow water and above that the logjam. Kootenay had found himself a spot on the logjam to stand on. As he stood there, he watched in awe as masses of fish jumped over the waterfall to get to the spawning grounds in the lake. For days, there were so many fish they covered the ground at the shallow end of the lake. The stick which Kootenay had used to balance himself on the logs he now used as a club to harvest the fish. Even Keeno got in on the act, trying to catch fish unsuccessfully as he never mastered the trick of getting his nose underwater and biting into the fish and hanging on to it at the same time.

Their fish harvest was enormous. It would ensure their basic food supply for the winter. As usual the old man had prepared for the catch. He had his smoking rack and drying rack ready. They worked day and night to conserve their main food supply for the coming winter. After a few days, they began transporting food to their winter camp. They could do one roundtrip in one day. After two days, they had most of their winter food stored away cool and dry. They thought they would make one more trip. After weeks of warm fall weather, they knew that a change had to come.

On that day, they had slept late. The weather was warm, but overcast, and there was no wind. The old man was complaining that his rheumatism was bothering him, a sure sign that a change in the weather was in the offing. Since there was no wind, the last golden leaves hung limp on the branches, as if they were waiting for the storm to come and send them drifting to the ground. A silent shiver went through the evergreen trees, as if down deep in the bowels of the earth some primordial beast was stirring and coming to life, or an earthquake had taken place. Even the dog Keeno, with the age-old experience of his wolf ancestry, knew that some momentous event was going to take place, but he didn't know what. All life, man and beast and plant, took a deep silent breath to prepare for the coming winter storm.

They were still about an hour from the safety of their camp at the lake when an angry, black cloud with bluish edges rolled across the rocky crags on the other side of the valley. Sheets of lightning tore the edges of the clouds apart and began dumping their heavy loads of snow over mountains and valleys. When this phalanx of lightning and thunder reached them, one lightning bolt ripped the dark cloud ahead of them apart in one serrated, white sheet of flame, which blinded them for a moment. The thunderclap that followed hit them so hard they almost fell to the ground. Keeno, frightened now by the thunder, ended up between the legs of Kootenay. The animal was scared by the forces of nature.

They pushed on in the hope that they might make it to the safe shelter of their teepee before the full force of the storm hit them. To make things worse, they ran into an unexpected obstacle in the form of a giant fallen tree. The force of the lightning had split the tree trunk in two. One part of the tree trunk was still sticking one splintered finger boldly into the black sky. It smelled of smoke and sulphur from the enormous heat of the lightning. They had to find their way around the fallen giant through the virgin forest.

The chaos of broken-down trees and splintered wood was almost impossible to negotiate. A wide detour and a new trail had to be found, which took them a long time. While they were busy blasting a new trail, they hadn't had any time to pay attention to what was going on in the treetops above them. There the storm was howling with undiminished fury. Only after they had reached their old trail did they look up and find the treetops shaking above them. Then, silently, the snow began to fall. There in the forest, protected by the trees, the snow came drifting down silently.

As soon as they got out in the open along the lake, they were hit by the full force of the winter storm. Needle-sharp snow pellets hit their faces and made their eyes water. Only due to the fact that the old man and Kootenay were experienced pathfinders could they survive the struggle against the forces of nature and not get lost. They found their teepee in the gloom of a wall of snow that was now descending upon them.

The habit of the old man leaving a store of firewood for those who came after him had paid off again; this time for himself. Only once did they go outside during the next few days, to find their food cache. While the storm howled and the snow piled up waist-high, they easily fell into a state of semi-hibernation; their slumber interrupted only when the storm shook the teepee.

One morning, Kootenay noticed a slanting shaft of sunlight at the top of their teepee. Then he noticed the absence of Keeno. The fire in the firepit had gone out. He touched one of the stones with his foot; they were still warm, kept warm by the thick layer of ashes and the warm earth below. His old companion was still sleeping.

Quietly Kootenay dressed; he was still in the habit of sleeping naked. Then he took some of the dry grass from his resting place, cut it to the proper length, and placed a thick layer of it into his mukluks so that his feet would stay warm in the deep snow outside. He took a big chunk of firewood and pushed it deep into the ashes; this way the log would catch fire from the still-glowing embers and the fire would keep the teepee warm while he was gone.

Outside he felt an icy wind that blew from midnight. It had replaced the snowstorm of the last few days. The wintery world was a sparkling wonderland of crystals of ice drifting in the clear but cold air. As he tried to get to the peninsula from which he had fished before, he thought that he might be able to spear some fish for their supper. He pushed his way through the deep snow toward the rocky shoreline, which jutted out into the lake to form the protected bay where he could see their teepee, where the old man still slept.

As he was standing there, he was looking into the dark water from the overhanging rocks. The waters of this mountain lake were very dark. That morning it seemed almost black in contrast to the bright shoreline. All he could see was his own familiar mirror image and the cold, blue sky above.

But then, while staring into the water, he saw two graceful white birds appear in the picture. For a moment he was perplexed, he was looking for fish down in the dark water, but what he saw was two white swans cruising in gracefully wide circles in the cold blue. To Kootenay, it looked as if the birds were cruising in a bottomless lake deep underwater.

What Kootenay didn't know was that these graceful birds were the vanguard of a huge flock of white swans who had been forced to leave their summer breeding grounds on the lakes above the arctic circle, where they had raised many chicks, early. Since the old birds, who had made the long flight to the midnight sun before, knew if the lakes, where they spent the summer, froze, they wouldn't be able to take off. All the young birds would perish.

Thousands of them had taken off into the freezing winds and hitched a ride on the fast-moving arctic storm above the low snow clouds. Many of the young birds perished in the attempt to gain enough altitude to get above the clouds, where they could cruise through the night while navigating by the stars and by the knowledge they had gained through aeons of time.

Many of the birds had cleared the precipitous rocky crags of the Shining Mountains in elastic V-formation when Kootenay first saw the reflection of two lead birds above in the water below. Now he heard a honking sound coming from the sky above.

We know that Kootenay had learned to understand the language of geese, so if those two stately birds had been geese, he would have known what it meant and he could have prepared himself for one of the greatest miracles of the natural world. But he didn't understand the language of swans. We know now that nobody has watched this great wonder of the natural world since Kootenay walked the sacred trails of the Kootenay Nation.

So he stood there in awe and wonderment. The two birds had separated, and they were now flying in separate circles, one much lower than the other, each one making different sounds. Of course, Kootenay couldn't see from where he was standing what the two birds in the sky could see, and they were now preparing to direct one of the most difficult landing operations they had ever seen.

As the first flock came in over the rocky ridge in V-formation, flying with the wind, and much too fast for a safe landing, they now had to make a tight turn so they would face into the wind for the difficult landing. At the same time, they had to form a single line while they made the turn. As this maneuver was completed right above Kootenay's head, the birds never saw him, and of course, it wouldn't have made a difference anyway, as they were now committed to land. It would have caused a terrific pile-up of tired birds had the lead birds panicked.

Kootenay now watched flock after flock as they changed from a V-formation to a straight line, one bird stacked above the other for a landing. As each flock approached, he heard the rasping sound as the birds changed the angle of their wings to maximum lift. Then there was a splashing sound as they skidded across the lifesaving surface of the water.

For hours they came in numberless legions, one flock after another, to settle down on White Swan lake and feed for a few days. They would restore their strength before they continued their flight to the shores of the great ocean to spend the winter, each one on his own, until that mysterious, primordial call went out again to assemble in the old formation and rise into the misty sky and cruise toward their northland home and find the very spot where they were born and where they saw the Northern Lights playing above the horizon all the short nights.

In the meantime it was getting dark, and Kootenay and his dog were still sitting and watching. They were getting cold sitting and listening to the sound of birds' wings. It was this mysterious sound that brought the stories of Northern Lights, and faraway places, where during the short summer the sun would never set, where in one cold night, a lake could freeze to solid ice, something that never happened at the Lake of the Kootenay.

How long he sat there and listened to the stragglers coming in by the dim light of the moon he didn't know. It was that hissing sound of the wings that mesmerized him and he wondered how the birds could make a safe landing in almost total darkness and survive the crashing impact on the water.

When he woke the following day, it was late into a cold, sunny morning. The old man had kept the fire going, but he was not there. Kootenay saw him sitting on a rock looking out over the lake, which was now covered with white swans. When Kootenay came up to him, the old man said, "This is why this lake is called White Swan Lake, and that is why I brought you here. I was hoping that the birds would come here this year when it got cold. It doesn't happen every year, in some years the birds, for some unknown reason, take a different flight path and only very few show up."

For a few days, the birds kept the lake from freezing by moving around and churning up the warmer water. Every night, however, the choking collar of ice around the shoreline of the lake tightened.

Then one day, in the early light of dawn, there was a flapping sound of a thousand mighty wings. It had to be this morning while there was still enough open water to get the necessary speed to get them airborne. Kootenay looked out of the teepee, and he watched the birds treading water to accelerate their foreward motion for liftoff. Toward the end of the lake, they formed the familiar V-formation. All morning, flock after flock rose toward the golden disk of the sun, and then disappeared on the horizon.

There was silence now at White Swan Lake. Only a few white swan feathers drifted on the deserted waters toward the shoreline.

On the following morning, the lake was frozen solid. The sheet of ice covering the lake was as clear as a sheet of glass. When Kootenay took small pebbles of rock and cast them across the ice, they made tinkling sounds like silver bells. The pebbles kept on going far into the lake.

White Swan Lake would be asleep until the sun rose far enough above the horizon to melt the ice and bring life back to its shores.

19

Kootenay, the old man, and Keeno, loaded down heavy with dried fish, returned to their permanent winter quarters. They found all their winter food intact. Only mice had taken their share.

While the old man was busy storing away the dry fish they had carried down from the lake, Kootenay undressed and walked down to the hot pool naked, only his bearskin hanging around his shoulders. The hot pool was the one luxury he had missed at Fish Lake, on the Top of the World, and at White Swan Lake. Now he enjoyed sitting in the warm water and counting stars in the dark sky above, and he would enjoy this luxury all winter long.

Kootenay was dreaming of floating in a hot pool when the old man shook him awake, and pulled the bearskin from his naked shoulders, and said, "We've got to be moving. I told you we have to go to the camp at the lower lakes to retrieve some of the duck eggs, and I would like to find out if the bailiff has been there looking for you."

The old man shook Kootenay again. This time he was wide awake, and within a few minutes they were moving.

There was snow only as far as the cliff. Below the rock-wall, the snow had all melted. That was good since they wouldn't leave any footprints that could give away the location of their mountain retreat. The old man had always been very cautious not to leave any signs of his whereabouts, often taking long detours through difficult rocks and scree when he could see smoke from campfires down in the valley.

They crossed the river of the Kootenay with hardly any water in it. It was so easy to cross compared to the wild ride in the canoe in the spring. They crossed the swampy area at the end of the lake without difficulty. Then, just a little uphill, there was their camp.

Summer had done no damage to the reed-roof. The old man walked around the camp inspecting everything, including the firepit. There were droppings of wolf and bear, but he paid no attention to that. He poked around in the firepit, lifted out some charred fragments of bones, and dropped them back in. Then he inspected the inside of their old teepee.

When he came out, he said, "There were two or three in the party. Could have been a hunting party from the Nlak-Pamux. There are more fishbones in the firepit than any other bones. The Shushwap like to eat fish. But if they were Kootenay they must have surmised that you perished during the last winter, and as a result, they stopped looking for you and left in order to take the message home to their elders."

With that, he walked away, up the hill, toward the cache where their harvest of duck eggs was stored. The cache had been found by somebody. The stones had been rolled away from the pit. Only people or a bear could have moved those stones. The old man moved around the site, carefully, looking at everything. There were no footprints of bears or humans, all had been washed away by summer rains.

Then he said, "Here's what happened. The cache was discovered by the party just shortly after we left. Since the eggs were still fresh when they found them in the spring, they took what they could carry, but left the pit open. When the bear found the rotting eggs, he ate them shells and all. He in turn was then chased away by somebody else. That is the reason why we found no eggshells.

"I assume that it was well-armed people who chased the bear because nothing else could possibly convince a bear to leave the place where he is feeding. What happened after that is that a rainstorm washed a thick layer of loose soil over the last layer of eggs, those would be the eggs we stored in the still frozen soil. I'm certain there are still some eggs in that pit."

That brought Kootenay into action because he liked eggs the way the old man cooked them. Bending down on his knees, he reached down and started digging, and soon his knife lifted out egg after egg, and the eggs were still good. They feasted on stale, but still edible, eggs until they were stuffed. The rest of the eggs were loaded on Keeno's back. Then they disappeared in the tall reeds of the fen.

When they reappeared, Kootenay and the old man carried a huge load of reeds. He had instructed Kootenay that, for the long winter nights, when they went into a state of semi-hibernation, they needed something warm and soft to sleep on. There was nothing better than reed-grass, and together with the soft hay they already had, they would be warm and comfortable.

Both of them wandering over the hills they looked like moving haystacks. The huge burdens made them look unwieldy, but there was very little weight, so they made good time until they arrived at the cliff below their winter camp. There they had to tie their burdens into smaller bundles to allow them through the tight chimney on the top. All in all, things went far better than they had thought, even Keeno learned to climb shifting scree after his paws had developed the necessary calluses.

At their winter camp, there was a trace of fresh snow, reminding them that any day now, after a snowstorm, they would be cut off from the rest of the world. The old man and Kootenay reverted easily to their comfortable winter routine of sleeping late into the day, or at least until the golden rays of the sun lit up the entrance to the cave.

The old man had built them both thick, comfortable resting places from reeds and moss and mountain hay. Kootenay's bed was the most luxurious he had ever slept in. In the middle of his bed, a bowl-shaped hollow had formed. When he rolled into that and pulled his bear robe over the top of himself and his dog, he could think of nothing more restful while the winter storms howled outside and blew huge snowdrifts across the entrance of the cave. The only work Kootenay had to do was clear the snowdrift in front of the cave and a path to the firepit where he rekindled the fire from the previous day. Then he beat a path to the hot pool below, where he would relax until the cold stars appeared in the sky. When it got very cold, he found that his wet hair, which he carried in two braids, would freeze solid, like two horns. The old man found that very amusing when the boy came home.

As it was his habit, the old man would sit in front of the cave, between cave and entrance, not far from the firepit, and work on a pair of moccasins or mukluks, with his fleece hanging around his shoulders to keep warm. There were times when Kootenay thought that the old man was asleep, but his hands were moving. Then he spoke as if he were talking to himself, but his narrative was always directed toward Kootenay and never had anything to do with what he was doing.

"It is within the nature of the universe, and its task, to move everything from here to there, and to transform, to eliminate one and create another from the same substance. All things are just variables of what they were before. All things remain the same only as long as it takes to change them. So everything you see came to its present form by continuous change. There is no need to be frightened about that. All of it is quite familiar, even the dispensation of destiny is all the same. Everything will be as nature wants it to be."

151

The old man sat there as if he was listening inside of himself and not to the world around him. The only thing the old man was missing this winter was a pipe full of tobacco. And the only way to trade for tobacco was with the Sa-haptin or with White voyagers. There would be no chance for that this winter.

There would be times when the old man spoke after Kootenay had fallen asleep. He would keep talking unobtrusively, as he always did when he knew only the dog Keeno was listening. "And remember that nothing will happen to you that is not your fate; just like nothing can happen to a stone that is not the stone's destiny. Therefore, it should be reassuring to you that nothing can befall you that is not pre-destined to befall you."

Then he was quiet. His eyelids fell down, and he was asleep in his half-sitting position, as if he was waiting for somebody or something that he was prepared to receive.

After the first heavy snowfall, when the snow had settled, Kootenay and his dog were out hunting rabbits. He discovered that rabbits liked to establish their warrens at the edge of the forest, not too far from open meadows where the wind blew the snow away from the dry grass. There they could disappear into the protecting underbrush where wolves and coyotes and owls couldn't follow. Where the rabbits had left a well-marked trail, they would sit and wait for the intended quarry. If Kootenay's spear missed, Keeno was there cutting off the planned retreat.

Roasted rabbit was always a welcome change from their fish diet, especially when it was brazed over hot embers with salt and dried sorrel. The rabbit pelts were dried and stored. The old man later used them for trade.

Kootenay found it hard work when he went on a deer hunt in deep snow, even when he wore a pair of snowshoes. They were hand-me-downs from the old man. The next time snow conditions were more favorable, the snow had frozen to a hard crust and he could walk on it without snowshoes and move a lot faster, he came home with a young buck. A deer would feed them for many days, and life became an easy, drowsy half-sleep between eating and sleeping. For Kootenay, there was always the hot pool and the ice-cold rubdown in the snow.

In later years, when Kootenay's name had become Running Rain and he was an old man, while many of his grandchildren were playing around his lodge, he would think of these long-past, quiet winter days, when he owned nothing but a faithful dog and had no responsibilities, as the best days of his life. *But that was so many summers ago,* he would think when he was the elder chief of the Kootenays and many White people came from midday, out of the hot sun, on horses and wearing leather suits. In their wagons, they carried firewater, which they sold for furs and squaws and land.

During council assembly with the elders of the nation, he would try to explain, particularly to the younger members, that it was within nobody's power to sell the ground they walk upon, that nobody had the right to sell the land that gave them life and fed them and would feed future generations.

His vehement appeal would fall on deaf ears, and he would retire from his duties and walk into the wilderness where only he knew where he was going, never to be seen again.

But, for now, the long winter slowly passed. Kootenay perfected his deer-hunting skills with much advice from the old man, so much that they never went hungry. On some days, when the old man and Kootenay were walking to the hot spring, it seemed to Kootenay as if the old man had rejuvenated; his frame had filled out and a certain bounce had returned to his step. That this was due to the company

153

he provided and the abundance of good food he and his dog carried home was something he never became aware of.

Kootenay, in the meantime, never lost his desire to travel the secret trails of the Kootenay across the Shining Mountains, into the lands of the Na-Koda, the Sik-Sika and Tsuut'ina, and further on to the Cree, where a sea of grass stretched to the far limitless horizons, and Tsuut'ina are the first nations in Alberta.

He asked the old man to explain the passes through the Shining Mountains to him. So far the old man had refused, and a great wave of sadness would overcome him. At the same time, the old man knew that he wouldn't be able to stop Kootenay once he had made up his mind. He knew that one rainy morning, when water dripped from the trees, Kootenay would be gone, silently and unannounced, just like he had arrived.

The thought of losing his young companion was unbearable to him, but in the end, he could do nothing about it. He also knew when the time had arrived. He had his eyes in the sky for the first flock of birds.

He called to Kootenay, "Come, I will show you how to find the pass through the Shining Mountains." In his right hand he held a sharp rock, which he had used to scratch certain markings on a flat piece of slate. He now laid that piece of slate in front of Kootenay. Without pause, he continued, "The river of the Kootenay comes from midnight, and flows toward the noon sun. You travel from here to the Lake of the White Swans and wait at the lake until the swans arrive. You must not leave until the swans have left, as only the swans know when it is safe to return to the land of the midnight sun. Only then the ice has melted on the lakes and they can find food.

"From the outlet of the lake, you travel to the confluence with the river of the Kootenay. Don't cross the river, stay on the side toward sunrise. From here, you travel toward midnight until you arrive at the next major river. Before you get to the river, there is a small creek entering the river; you will have to cross that, but don't follow it. It leads to ice-covered mountains so high that they are always in the clouds.

"You will recognize the river by the large pool before its confluence with the River of the Kootenay. I know you will want to spend some time there and swim in the pool. There are many fish. Don't get tempted to follow any other river; that will lead you to mountains which the Nenii-Yawak call Kana-Naskis. There is no road through those mountains; many hunting parties have perished there when they were swept down by avalanches, never to be seen again.

"This river you must follow until you get to the Great Divide; you will know when you are there. From there all rivers flow toward sunrise, first through a sea of grass. After many miles, they will flow into an ocean, which we don't know; only the White people know that ocean. They come from there."

Then there was silence. The old man sat there staring into the fire, and the silence was filled with sadness that was felt by both men. Kootenay knew that he had to go and find the trail, and by so doing find himself, and his way, and the old trails of his people. The old man knew that the trail of his life was fast coming to an end, and that he had to find the "way" to close the circle of his stay in this wonderful world.

From this point on, there was a great silence in the camp. Kootenay continued his preparations in complete secrecy. He stored all the equipment he would need for his travels in a safe place. The old man knew that one morning, when the honking sound of geese was in the fog-shrouded valley, Kootenay and his dog would be gone. His snowshoes had disappeared a few days ago. He knew that Kootenay, like himself, could understand the language of geese, and that it would be the birds who told him when to be on the trail.

So the inevitable happened. One rainy morning, when water dripped from the trees, Kootenay and his dog were gone.

Second Book

20

A slim, tall man was walking on a narrow trail through the dripping forest. His steady spring-like gait and outward bearing was that of an experienced woodsman and pathfinder. He was dressed from top to bottom in tanned deerhide. His new moccasins had been impregnated with bear grease to make them waterproof, and they left no visible mark on the ground where the man walked. He carried his bundle by two leather straps slung around his shoulders. Protruding from his pack, above his head, were two implements; one a harpoon with a bone tip, the other his hunting spear with a razor-sharp, iron blade. Attached to his pack with leather thongs was a pair of snowshoes and a pair of mukluks fashioned from strong moosehide.

A dog with the winter fur of a gray wolf and the heavier profile of a malamute walked ahead of the man. Only the wet nose of the dog, which sniffed nervously down the trail, indicated that the animal was fully aware of all the dangers that lurked behind every turn. That the animal had only one ear and that the one, single ear was diligently scanning the forest trail ahead for unusual sounds, was not immediately apparent from the position where his master walked, as the head of the animal was hidden behind a bulky bear robe, the master's sleeping gear. Besides the sleeping robe of his master, which the dog also used when he needed to, the dog carried smoked venison, victual for a few days, and some smoked fish, which the dog knew he would eat.

Kootenay and his dog were happy when they arrived at the camp with a dry lodge where they could dry out from the long walk in the heavy rain. Kootenay first made a fire in the lodge. He found that the habit of the old man to leave a store of dry firewood and woodshavings in the lodge ready for a warm fire was a good one. As soon he struck his flint, the warm glow from a crackling fire flooded the teepee. While the dog stretched out next to the warming fire, Kootenay ordered Keeno to stay.

He went out again to see if the ice on the lake had gone so he could fish while they waited for the swans to arrive. He found that there was still some ice on the lake; only the shoreline was completely ice free. When he got to the other side of the peninsula he found that the shallows to the outlet of the White River and parts of the lake where the spring sun hit were ice free. He knew then that the fishing would be good while he was waiting for the swans.

He walked back to his teepee. He first fed his dog. Then he undressed and ate some smoked venison. For awhile he lay under his robe and listened to the gentle drumming of the rain. When Keeno put his head between his paws, Kootenay knew that all was well, and he fell asleep.

The boy, now turned man, awoke to the sound of geese chattering above. As it was still dark outside, he listened in order to figure out that they were saying. He couldn't. All he knew was that they were cruising toward midnight under the cover of darkness. When he looked outside he found that the sky was full of stars. It had stopped raining while he was asleep, and the flocks of geese were cruising by the stars. That was the only way it was possible since they couldn't see the ground.

He went back to sleep and slept soundly until a bright shaft of sunlight, coming through a slit in the top of the teepee, warmed up the lodge and he heard the buzzing of a fly above him. When he pushed back the branches at the entrance of the teepee, he looked into a bright, warm spring day. There wasn't a cloud in the sky.

As his moccasins and leggings were still wet from the day before, he hung them high in the branches of a tree for drying. He pulled his harpoon from his bag, and after securing the entrance to his teepee, he walked, naked as he was, halfway around the lake where he knew a creek was running into the lake. There the fishing would be good. He speared many fish there, not too far from his camp.

The first trout he caught from the ice cold water he ate raw, after slicing the meat off at the head, and then pulling the filets off the bones. The rest of the fish went to Keeno, who was sitting there waiting for the morsels.

For several days, he fished here and filled his larder. While at the camp, he had his smoke-pit going. When he found the fresh, new sprouts of sorrel next to the creek where the ground was moist, he picked as much as he could, eating some of it fresh and drying some of it for later use. At the same time, he had his ears and eyes glued to the sky, where he hoped those graceful, white birds would appear. So far, he had only heard the sound of geese and ducks. They seemed to be cruising further toward sunset along the river of the Kootenay on the windward side of the mountains, where they could catch the updrift of the wind currents to propel them higher and higher until they could cross the highest passes of the Shining Mountains. Then, from the Great Divide, they would try to hitch a fast ride on the down-rushing wind as it became katabatic, called chinook by the Indian people.

The temptation to pack up his gear and follow the birds was great, but he paid heed to the old man's advice and waited for the swans to arrive and to leave when they left. Later on, at the end of summer, he knew it was good advice. When he crossed the mountains, there was still deep snow lingering in the passes. So he fished and waited and had his eyes glued to the sky.

One golden evening, he heard the familiar honking sound of the lead birds. The ice was now almost gone from the lake; only on the shady side small icefloes persisted. This time there was no wind, so the two lead birds drifted down in graceful, tight circles until they touched down on the water. Right behind them came the tired formations, flock after flock, until much of the lake was covered.

Kootenay sat there and watched, struck with awe at this wonder of nature. Watching the birds, he had lost track of time. He walked to his teepee in total darkness, not realizing that he was privileged to watch one of the great wonders of this world.

On the following morning, he packed his gear in order to be ready to travel as soon as the birds left. However, the birds didn't oblige. They were quite content to stick around for another day and rest.

The following morning, while it was still dark outside and only the snow-covered peaks of the mountains across the valley showed a golden touch of early light, Kootenay heard the rushing sound of wings. The swans were taking off. He jumped up from under his cover and ran outside, carrying only his bearskin, Keeno behind him. He walked to the peninsula from where he could look out across the lake. From there he watched the swans lifting gracefully into the early morning sky, flock by flock, and forming that familiar V-formation. He watched them cruising high above the valley of the White River toward the Valley of the Kootenay. Just when he thought he had lost the first flock from his sight, the birds had reached the heights where the golden rays of the morning sun touched them, and flock after flock turned to gold. He could see them until they melted into the golden haze of the morning sky.

Kootenay and Keeno left their familiar teepee, Keeno would never see it again, but the memory of the golden swans stayed with Kootenay all his life. They found the game trail on the morning side of the White River. The trail showed signs that it was used by all kinds of animals. They crossed creeks in spring flood with melted snow. They had to detour where giant, fallen trees blocked their advance. They crossed avalanche slopes still plugged with hard snow from last winter. When they made camp it was a hastily erected lean-to from branches, and the hard forest floor was their bed.

Kootenay never failed to make a campfire. Within the crackling light of the fire, he felt safe. It was as if he knew the skill of making fire gave him dominion over all other creatures. Even when wolves howled around them and they could see their hungry, green eyes staring at them, Kootenay knew they wouldn't dare to come any closer to this team of man and dog. They knew a man swinging a hot fire-brand was deadly, and they left them well alone.

After a few days of travel in the forest, Kootenay had lost track of time. He had become one of the lucky ones for whom time has no meaning. The only thing he knew was that he had to have the sun on his back to travel toward midnight, and that they did.

They had long left the White River behind and were now following the river of the Kootenay on the morning side. They had seen the river rise in spring flood, and when the thunder rolled up the valley and shook the trees, the downpoor made the waters rise even more. Later in the summer, the river was low and they walked on flat banks of gravel and sand. This was easy going compared to the forest along the White River.

One afternoon, they crossed a creek in shallow water, and not long after the creek there flowed a mighty river still muddy in spring flood. This had to be the river the old man had mentioned, the one that led to the pass across the Shining Mountains. The river had the color of milk where it flowed into the River of the Kootenay, while the Kootenay had the same color as the Kokanee ice, which he could see from the summer camp of his people. But where the old man had said a large pool had to be, there was no pool. A torrential flood, coming down the river from the ice fields in the mountains, had changed the landscape and the flow of the river completely. Both rivers combined had sliced a new channel for a new riverbed through the forest. However, when water levels receded to a more normal summertime flow of the river, a few separate pools had formed. With no outlet to the river, they had been cut off by narrow strips of sand and gravel, and to Kootenay's good fortune, a school of fish found itself cut off from the main river in one of the pools.

They set up camp there, high above the river, where they could overlook the valley and the pools. There was so much deadfall in the forest Kootenay didn't have to do any cutting. Fallen trees formed the rear of the lean-to, which protected them from unwelcome intruders such as wolves and bears. The front of the shelter was open to the fire and the river as they had to watch the pool with all the fish in it. Along the riverbank, Kootenay had seen bear and wolf tracks, so he knew they were in the neighborhood just waiting for the water level to drop so they could get at the fish. Kootenay, of course, wasn't going to wait that long. He was tired of eating smelly, dried fish.

After he started a fire, Kootenay set up a smoking rack. Then he stood in the middle of a pool, completely naked, with his harpoon raised high in his right hand. A lightning-fast strike produced the first trout. He tossed the fish into the gravel where it kept on wiggling. Keeno walked around it, watching with great interest, but he didn't touch it. He liked the smelly, old fish just as much.

They camped there for many days. They fished and swam with Kootenay picking berries in the glades on the hillsides. Between Kootenay and Keeno, they managed to keep the bears away from their fish. The only animals they couldn't keep away from their fish were the eagles. The birds claimed their share early in the morning, when they came diving down out of the slanting sunlight and took what they needed before anybody could see them. When Kootenay jumped up to scare them away, it was too late every time. As far as Keeno was concerned, he made no effort, as he knew very well he couldn't do anything about it. As the pools were getting shallower, the water was also getting warmer, much warmer than the flowing water in the river. They went swimming; then they lay there stretched out in the warm sand to dry.

Kootenay would have forgotten his strong desire to travel the secret trail of the Kootenay had it not been for one cool morning when he found frozen dewdrops on the high grass. It had frozen into sparkling crystals of ice. As he walked through the frozen grass, it sparkled in all the colors of the rainbow, but it also reminded him that summer was coming to an end and that they must move on if they wanted to find the Sik-Sika and the Na-Koda people and spend the winter with them. Without their hospitality, he would not survive the winter.

The next morning, they moved on, following the river which seemed to flow directly out of the snow-covered mountains. For several days, they followed the river, always staying on that side of the river touched by the sun all day. The game trail he was following was also on this side of the river. The higher up the mountains they got, the more difficult it became to follow the trail along the river, and they were almost out of food.

Now, in a very difficult situation they lost the trail completely, but it seemed to continue on the other side of the river. They crossed and followed the faint trail all afternoon. Late in the day, they had left the forest below them and had entered a zone above the timberline. This was a strange world to Kootenay. In his home valley by the lake, he had never climbed so high, where no tree could grow, where the trees gave up the struggle against the harsh climate and only stunted dwarf trees and grass clung to the ground. Then there were only steep barren fields of shifting scree. Still there was a visible trail. What Kootenay couldn't know was that this trail was used only by the occasional bighorn ram who wanted to transfer into another valley for reasons unknown.

Over the next ridge, an awesome vista opened up. All the mountains were covered with ice and snow; glaciers flowed from the top of the mountains, out of the clouds, far below him, and emptied their ice into a blue lake. On his right, above where he was standing, a huge pillar of rock was pointing into the sky like a raised fist. He thought he knew this rock, but at the moment, he couldn't figure out how he could. Then a great wave of fear gripped him, the fear of the unknown. He turned around, and his hand touched his dog without looking at him. He stared at the raised fist of rock while his hand touched and fondled the dog. That comforted him; it felt good not to be alone. Then it came back to him while standing in shifting scree.

He was half asleep in the warm cave at their winter camp last winter. There was the voice of the old man from far away, "This place is called Waka-Nambe, where the Great Spirit pushes his warning hand into the sky, telling you not to continue across the pass of ice. This is not the secret trail of our people; too many came to harm here." As Kootenay didn't want to descend into the valley of ice and snow, he turned around and walked back toward the spot where he had crossed the river. They had wasted a lot of time climbing up to Waka-Nambe.

On the way down, they were overtaken by darkness. Going on was too dangerous; they had to try to make camp in the barren emptiness of high alpine tundra. The wind was icy cold and unrelenting. They pushed on downhill, toward the river, until they couldn't see any more. Behind a thicket of stunted trees, they found shelter from the wind and bedded down.

Kootenay found the last few chunks of smoked venison. It didn't still his hunger, but he felt better. Now he suffered from thirst; it was the worst. He laid his bear robe on barren rocks behind the trees and rolled into it; then he pulled the remainder of the robe over himself and the dog. As soon as his hands and feet had warmed up, Kootenay was asleep.

He slept soundly until he heard his dog barking. His dog stood on a large boulder and barked at a pile of stones from which a peeping sound came forth. Keeno had watched the tiny pika for quite a while. He was an expert on rabbits, and he considered himself a specialist in catching them. This little fellow was different; while it looked like a rabbit, it was no larger than a mouse. When he ran toward it, it disappeared in a pile of rocks, only to reappear in another spot making that peeping sound. Disgusted, he lay on a rock his head between his paws waiting for Kootenay to get ready.

All Kootenay had to do was get Keeno into his harness. The descent into the valley was easy now in the morning sun. Below them, the valley was obscured in swirling fog, and further into the distance was an endless layer of white clouds. Far in the distance, toward midnight, stood a high mountain all clad in ice and snow, the only mountain higher than the clouds. This mountain was to remain Kootenay's shining beacon of light as long as he traveled above the treeline.

On the steep trail they moved downhill until they were enveloped in the morning fog. Sometimes the sun would disappear. Then, when the fog got thinner, it floated in the sky like a white metal disc. They were on a good trail now, even though he couldn't see much of it.

They were close to the river they had left the day before. As they followed the river upstream, Kootenay found that it made a sharp turn, more toward midnight. He was certain of that because he had the warm sun on his back again, and as he had hoped, the well-traveled trail was there again. What had happened was the last flood, the same which had washed away the pool at the confluence with the Kootenay River, also washed away the trail up there for a stretch, so he mistook the poor trail that took them to Waka-Nambe for the secret trail of the Kootenay. He had been wrong. He had learned the hard way, and he would never forget.

As the day progressed, the sun burned off the fog. They traveled in bright sunshine. Kootenay was now very hungry. There were no signs of game in the dense forest; not even the fast-flowing river showed any sign of fish. So he thought that he would let Keeno roam ahead in the hope that he might catch a porcupine or a rabbit. For this purpose, he took the load off Keeno's back and carried it himself.

The going was slower, now that he had to carry his own bundle. Soon he became aware of something that bothered him even more than the extra load on his back; the fact that he had worn out the soles on his moccasins in the sharp rocks on Waka-Nambe. Now gravel on the trail pierced the soles of his feet and made walking very painful as he tried to catch up with Keeno. Finally, as he couldn't walk any longer, he changed his worn-out moccasins for the new mukluks that the old man had made for him. Now he walked easier.

After a long time, when Keeno didn't return, Kootenay thought the dog had struck out on his own to hunt for food.

Keeno stood in front of him. The first thing that struck him was the putrid smell of carrion Keeno had on him. Kootenay followed the dog to where he had been feeding, as it seemed to him the only reason why he had stayed away so long. In a clearing in the forest they found the kill. It was a wapiti, obviously a bear kill. The bear had dragged the carcass into the clearing in the forest, taken his fill, and then left to sleep it off. He had first ripped open the belly and fed on the soft entrails of his prey, then he left.

Kootenay knew that a bear would feed on his kill for days and would not take lightly to surrendering his prey to anybody except a strong pack of wolves. Kootenay now did what he had to do. He built a fire. With that, and the help of his dog, he would be able to keep the beast away until he found out if there was some meat left on the carcass. When the fire flared, he had a moment, and he found out what he wanted.

One of the hindquarters of the wapiti had been covered by the rest of the carcass, so flies and other insects had no chance to get at it. It even smelled better than the rest of the meat. He now moved fast as his sharp knife got into action. Kootenay had become very skilled in dressing game. First he peeled the skin off the meat; then he severed the quarter from the joint. This whole operation had taken only a few minutes. He had to move on fast since there was the possibility that the owner of the putrid carcass might return any moment for another feast. Kootenay knew that bears could be very quarrelsome when it comes to defending their food.

When they moved on, Keeno was carrying their food and Kootenay carried his own bundle. They moved fast to get as far away from the kill as they could. Kootenay had no misgivings about scavenging and sharing food with a bear. He could remember, as a boy, when bears raided their drying fish and destroyed the racks in the process; at least they gave him a chance to get even.

That night, they found shelter in a small cave, not too far from a waterfall. Kootenay had to be careful there, too, about bears, as the strong smell of the meat might give them away. In the shelter of the cave, they felt safe at last; nothing could approach from behind, and in front of them was a good fire with meat cooking on skewers. It felt good to have a tummy full of food. Sleep came easy after travel in rocks and stone. They stayed there for two nights. Kootenay found mushrooms and berries to supplement their diet.

The next day they traveled on in good weather. After two days, they arrived at a lake that had a lot of fish in it. Kootenay called it the "Lake of Many Fish." The mountain that rose into the sky not too far from the lake had a flat top with a cap of snow on it. So far, they had been very lucky that the weather had been good. There had been no snow, but that could change very fast.

At the Lake with Many Fish, Kootenay fished for a few days and cured and smoked fish. He had found out that fish were a lot easier to dry and smoke than meat. When he walked around the lake, he found a camp that had been used by many people for a long time. He also found that the lake had two outlets; only one flowed toward sunset. From his new camp he could see a spectacular mountain, but further to midnight, he saw a pass across the Shining Mountains.

The following morning, they were on the trail. Keeno had accepted the heavy load of dried fish with resignation. Kootenay was very happy that he had decided not to follow the marshy creekbed, which seemed to fill the valley as far as the eye could see. Instead he followed the high ground from the outlet of the lake. Then they disappeared in impenetrable forest for the rest of the day. When they reappeared, they were on a good goat trail leading up toward one of the most beautiful passes across the Shining Mountains. When he now turned around, he could see the lake where he had fished far below and the mountain with the snowcap almost below him.

Soon he reached a spot where all the creeks and rivulets of melting snow flowed toward sunset, but when he stepped across the ridge, all the waters flowed toward sunrise. Kootenay had no explanation for that. He had stepped across the Great Divide where on one side all waters flow toward the great ocean, and on the other side the waters flow toward the ocean from where the White people appeared out of the drifting fog.

But this great mystery didn't keep his attention for too long. He saw something that caught his eyes and held them. On the next ridge, on the side of the setting sun, he had seen a few white specks, like small patches of snow, pure and white. Was it possible that an animal had decided to challenge the hardship of this rarefied world of the Shining Mountains, and if they had, why would they stay here when there was so much more food down in the valley? How could he find out?

Kootenay set up camp behind a rocky ridge, where the wind whistled through the crags. His bearskin was placed on the ground on a soft patch of sweet-smelling mountain avens. A snowpatch not far away would provide them with the water they needed. For their small fire, they used the dry roots of juniper.

As the sun was setting, he watched the golden glow of the sunlight climb upward across snow and ice. When he turned around, he could see the mountain, which he thought was the highest mountain he had ever seen. It looked like the orange rays of the setting sun had set fire to the top of the mountain. It was ablaze with a bright glow as with a flame, while the valleys and forests below were covered by a blanket of darkness preparing the world for a night of rest. The earth below him was now a dark, level plane, and above that line, the highest mountains still glowed like hot iron. Slowly, the orange sky turned to red and then to purple and black. In the now-dark sky, the stars appeared.

One would think that it was easy to go to sleep after a day of hard travel and climbing to the Top of the World on steep trails. Not so. Kootenay found himself in a stangely different world. His dog was restless, too. Keeno drifted around the camp and howled like a wolf when a shooting star pierced the sky with a streak of light. He didn't know what to make of it, and he let out a whimpering sound like a puppy.

Kootenay lay on his bearskin on his back and looked at the countless stars in the black sky. Behind him, in the rocks, was the everlasting mountain wind. He had the feeling he was suspended from the highest point in the universe and the complete vault of heaven was revolving around him.

Unable to sleep he lay there for a long time. When all the light from the sunset had disappeared toward midnight, there was complete darkness in his world, but only for a short while. Now dancing shafts of light pierced the dark horizon. Kootenay had seen Northern Lights before, though he couldn't remember the explanation given to him at the time. These streamers of dancing light shifted and twisted higher until they met at the highest point under the vault where he lay, only to fall back to the source of cold darkness from whence they had appeared. Kootenay was bewildered; all of these dancing shafts of light had come from midnight, but midnight was a place of total darkness.

From complete exhaustion, he fell asleep with only his bear robe around his shoulders. But on this child of nature only the eyes had a need for sleep. His ears recorded all the sounds around him. He heard the rustling sound of the chinook wind in the dry grass; he felt his dog next to him, but he didn't wake up. His nose recorded a symphony of smells; the smell of his dog was reassuring. From far away came the scent of a forest fire. All around him his nose recorded the sweet perfume of dry grass and the fragrant patches of mountain avens.

When the first rays of the morning sun touched his face, Kootenay was awake, but his eyes were still closed. His right hand felt around in a half circle and touched his dog and his spear. Reassured that in his world everything was where it was supposed to be he fell asleep again, but not for long. He remembered that the day before he had made up his mind to follow the white goat.

He fed his dog, then told him to stay. He drifted across barren tundra and rocky ridges eating dried fish, in his right hand a ball of snow from which he sucked moisture to still his thirst. He was on the trail of the white goat, this denizen of great hights. All day, he walked the ridges and scrambled the steep scree where everything seemed in perpetual downhill motion. All day he heard the relentless rushing of the chinook wind as it rushed through the cracks in dangerous rock.

Every time he felt close enough for his spear to come into action, his prey moved on. They seemed to know the effective range of his deadly missile. Then he saw them just above, unperturbed, chewing cud and looking down on him with contempt. He sat down and ate a handful of snow to still his thirst while he watched these astonishing creatures. They had chosen to live in this hostile environment, and all they asked from the rest of the world was to leave them alone. They knew all there was to know about surviving in their world. He himself, as the intruder, knew much less. Did that give him a right to hunt them? He turned around once more

173

and saw them sitting on their thrones, gazing out over their domain. As he walked away, there was no feeling of disappointment. How could he attempt to kill such an animal?

For the first time in his life he felt good that his hunting skills fell far short of his desire to bag a white goat. As he walked on he became aware of talking to himself. He had the feeling there was another person walking beside him. Up to now, he had only talked to his dog, but now he felt as if he were talking to somebody who was powerful enough to judge him, a conscious conscience, a moral sense of right and wrong. He feels for the first time that words well spoken could be heard and become tangible, and these words could be discussed with himself as his conscience.

As the sun set behind the mountains, he struggled up the steep hill toward his camp. He saw his dog bounding down the hill happy that his master had returned. When dusk settled over their encampment after their frugal meal, Kootenay pulled his bearskin over his ears and fell asleep without watching shooting stars.

The next morning they slept late. Here the sun touched and warmed them when the valleys below were still in deep darkness. Kootenay felt that he was in alien territory. The dark valley below looked strange and dangerous to him, and when he rolled back his bearskin, the air felt colder than the air at the lake of the Kootenay. It had a bite of frost to it.

The sun stood at high noon when they finally moved on. From the barren mountain tundra, they slowly drifted down into stands of forest. Kootenay noticed that not only did the air feel colder there but also the trees were different. All the trees seem smaller; other trees were missing from there completely. Only the larches, where he could find them protected from the wind, seemed familiar, but much smaller. To his surprise, the larches had taken on the warm, golden color of late fall. It seemed early, but at this high elevation, the gold of fall returned much earlier than in his native valley by the lake.

Much of the afternoon he fed on berries and the yellow mushrooms he liked so much, while Keeno watched their possessions, or when he thought all was well, did some hunting on his own. While Kootenay was busy picking the tasty berries of black currants, he forgot that it was getting late in the day, and looking back where his belongings were, he noticed that his dog had disappeared.

Knowing that Keeno would return to the spot from where he had disappeared, Kootenay started setting up camp. It was a beautiful spot overlooking the forested valley ahead. Just as he had a fire going, Keeno reappeared carrying a ptarmigan, a bird in his white, winter plumage. It was Keeno's luck that the bird had changed into its snowy-white winter garb much too early, and the bird's undoing that he was white and not brown. Had he been sitting on a patch of snow, Keeno would not have seen him, and Kootenay and himself wouldn't have had roast chicken that evening. Keeno thought that he himself got the best part of the chicken before it was cooked. When Kootenay eviscerated the bird, he only ate the liver raw, and Keeno ate the rest before the fowl was on a skewer.

Ice fog unctuous, cold, and impenetrable drifted up the valley. When the frost on the bushes and grasses melted, it soaked them to their skin. They couldn't find their trail, and when they found it, they lost it. Kootenay decided to wait until the fog lifted. He built a fire to dry out. The thick forest became unreal; all sounds became muffled. Worse yet, there was no sound. All nearby trees took on the grotesque shapes of deadly monsters as they moved about in the swirling fog.

Then the ice fog lifted as fast as it had appeared. As it turned out, they had made their fire at the very edge of the forest. It was only a few steps until a wide, flat glacial flood plain lay in front of them. In the summer, when glacial ice melted, this would be a difficult place to cross. Now the rivulets of melted ice from the glacier, which filled the valley higher up, flowing through fields of gravel, were easy to cross.

When Kootenay stepped from the shade of the forest into the bright light of the flood plain, he had to close his eyes for a moment, not only from the bright sunlight but also from the reflected light from the shining ice of the glacier which flowed down through the valley in glittering waves and that blinded him.

After crossing the braided stream of icy runoff, they were received by dark forest with good game trails. They drifted along in the forest with the sound of the stream of melting ice and snow on their left. When they reached the valley bottom, they found a small lake muddy with glacial silt. Kootenay also found, to his consternation, that two new creeks started there; one flowing toward midnight, the other flowing toward the sun That was very confusing, as he had assumed that all rivers would flow toward sunrise. Toward sunrise there was a solid wall of gray rock reaching into the sky. Nobody would be able to walk through this precipitous rampart of barren stone.

21

Not knowing which way to turn, Kootenay set out to find a campsite. He picked a spot not too far from where an avalanche had brought down a huge pile of broken timber. He had learned by now that it was to his advantage to have a ready supply of dry firewood and material for building a shelter. There was a huge pile there, all he had to do was untangle it.

For a few days they were comfortable there. They had found shelter amongst the pile of splintered wood. Kootenay carried home piles of thick moss for warmth on the cold ground. But, they needed food! Fishing in the fast flowing creeks had no results. One of the creeks was so muddy from glacial silt it contained no fish. All day, he followed the game trails in all directions, but there was no sign of any game; it was as if all the animals had disappeared from the forest.

It was here, in this camp, in the Shining Mountains, that they felt for the first time the despair of hunger and cold. Kootenay found a few dry mushrooms and red rosehips that stilled his hunger a little bit, but there was no food that he could live on. When the first snowstorm of the early fall hit the valley, berries and mushrooms disappeared under a blanket of snow in front of his eyes. Now that this last source of food was gone he was desperate.

For the first time in his life, Kootenay was homesick for the lake in the valley where the water never froze, where he could go fishing all year. But, worst of all, for the first time in his life, he felt lonely for the warm hands of his mother. During the long night, when the storm howled around their shelter and hunger pains gnawed in his gut, he could hear himself say the word "mother." Then he remembered the great sense of shelter he had felt embraced by her soft, warm body.

It snowed for several days. Our pilgrims, in the meantime, did the only right thing, they slept through it all. In front of their snow cave was a crackling fire. Kootenay had rolled a heavy log over the fire, and it burned for a long time.

The snowstorm ended as suddenly as it had started. They awoke into a bright, sunny day with hard frost. The whole world sparkled as if it were covered with diamonds. Klotenay, however, had no eyes for all this beauty. He was much too hungry for that. All his thoughts were centered around food.

From somewhere in the distant back of his mind came the horrible thought again that he could eat his dog if he had to. But, when he looked at Keeno and saw his trusting eyes, he felt bad, and he pushed the thought as he could out of his mind. He put on his mukluks; he had already filled the bottoms with dry grass to keep his feet warm and dry. Then he attached the snowshoes the old man had made for him. After taking the sheath off his sharp spear, they were out in the deep snow. While the break in the bitter winter weather was welcome to Kootenay, it did not bring any relief form hunger. It was as if all the animals had disappeared from the face of the earth. There were no tracks of any game. All animals had moved deep into the forest, where they spent their time resting and preserving their strength for the long winter ahead.

Late in the day, when they were on the way to their lodge, they found the tracks from a pack of wolves. From the tracks, it was clear that even the wolves had a hard time getting around, as their feet sank deep into the snow and their bellies were dragging deep in the snowdrifts. The tracks led directly to their lodge. That had Kootenay worried a lot. If the wolves had gotten into their den, they would have ripped apart his bear robe, and without that, he would have great difficulty surviving through the cold nights. They rushed on found that it was the smoldering fire that had kept the wolves out.

A pack of hungry wolves could be desperate and very dangerous. So Kootenay decided to move on, but not before he had built himself a travois for his dog. He found himself two very flexible willow poles, just like he had seen the braves of his tribe use them when they were on a hunting party. That way he had his hands free for his spear in case the wolves attacked while they were traveling.

After he attached the ends of his travois to the harness over Keeno's shoulders, they were on the road. Kootenay, wearing his snowshoes, blazed a trail in the deep snow. Keeno followed pulling the travois willingly. Traveling along, they could hear the small stream on their left under the ice. When a bright moon came floating over the ridges, they kept on traveling through the night by the cold moonlight. Sometimes they heard the wolves howling at the moon, but they were never close enough to worry about them. The wolves may have known that you don't mess around with a hungry human being accompanied by a hungry dog. It was as if Kootenay had known that if he now sat down for a rest he would go to sleep and never wake up. Then the wolves would come and kill Keeno and then they would eat him, too. Kootenay feared being eaten by wolves.

All through the night they staggered on in the deep snow. On some steep hills, Kootenay had to help Keeno pull the travois. He could see that the strength of his dog was waning fast. Pretty soon he would refuse to go and the desire to break out of his harness would overpower his learned obedience, and his wolf ancestry would take over and force him to strike out on his own for a chance to survive.

During the second night out, when they were sliding down a treeless hill, one of the great natural wonders of the eastern slopes of the Shining Mountains took place. A chinook wind came blowing down from the snowy heights of the mountains. Kootenay, of course, had experienced this kind of wind before in the hills above the river of the Kootenay, but this was different. As this katabatic wind flowed down-slope on the prairie side of the Shining Mountains it picked up speed, and as it descended it warmed up by many degrees in a short time.

First they heard the shrieking sound in the treetops; then it became a steady roar blowing through the valley. It was as if a big fan had been turned on. At the same time, the wind became much warmer. The trees in the forest shed their burden of wet snow and stood bare in stark contrast to the morning sky. From the higher mountains came the thunder of avalanches.

When the wet, melting snow started rolling downhill, it swept everything in its path into the valleys below. In the forest they had reached, they were safe; the only thing they had to watch was the falling snow from the trees. On the wings of the warm wind traveled all the fragrant scents from a faraway ocean to the cedar forests of the Land of the Kootenays. In young Kootenay, the soft, caressing wind had the effect of an elixir of life. He forgot how hungry he was for the moment and walked on with renewed vigour.

They were now beside a river that flowed in a straight line deep in a valley between two mountain ranges. The chinook was eating the snow so fast that Kootenay noticed the trail they were on was almost bare of snow. To make things easier for Keeno, he freed him from the travois and loaded his bundle on his old harness. As they reached the valley bottom in the afternoon, they heard the thundering sound of a waterfall. In the distance, they could see spray blown high in the air by the thundering waters. The river they had followed ended abruptly when it joined the larger river below the waterfall.

Kootenay now climbed up a steep cliff in order to see if it was possible to cross the river there. From the top of the rocks, the view he got to see was awesome. He could see the full height of the waterfall and the swirling pool it thundered into. Further down where the river they had followed flowed into the river he could now see, there was no chance to cross the river, swollen as it was from the melting snow. Climbing down from the cliff, he decided to follow the river upstream; that meant that he would have to find an opening through the rocks over which the river tumbled.

That Kootenay had made the right choice which may have saved his life we will see. The going there was easier, as it looked as if the game trail they followed turned away from the river and wound its way through a field of boulders and a sparse stand of pine trees. Up there the valley looked all different. While the river below the falls was a raging torrent swollen by the melting snow, the river up there widened out as it flowed through a flat valley of boggy meadows before it narrowed and cascaded over the cliffs. They followed the game trail through the bogs on the sunset side of the valley.

From where they were now, they could, when they turned around, see part of the valley from where they had come. All the hills around them were heavily forested, only straight ahead were there some rock outcrops or cliffs. Over one of the rocks stood an almost invisible wisp of smoke or steam, or it could have been some fog rising from the wet forest.

As every traveler must, in order to survive in this world, be keenly aware of everything that goes on around him, may that be sight, sound, smell, or feeling. Kootenay now sniffed the air but could detect nothing. If there had been a fire, it had been out for a long time; therefore, it wouldn't do him any good. But there was the moist nose of his dog; it moved back and forth as if there was more to be sniffed at than just smoke from a fire. Kootenay noticed it and let him go. He followed, his spear unsheathed ready for a fast strike. They were now on a sparsely treed uphill slope with the dog leading. With every step, they got closer to the cliff and Kootenay noticed that Keeno got more nervous. He could smell something that his master could neither see nor smell.

Then, without warning, there was the fragile voice of an old man. It came from a slightly raised location higher up in the rocks and made them stop in their tracks. Still, they couldn't see anybody. Then the voice said, "From whence art thou?—And whither art thou desirous to go, Pilgrim?"

Then there was silence. Nobody could be seen. The voice obviously expected an answer before exposing himself to a stranger. The old-fashioned words and accent and pronounciation sounded so funny to Kootenay that he couldn't help laughing, even though he could understand what the old voice said.

When Kootenay didn't answer right away, the old man's voice came down again from his hide-out. "What might your name be, young fellow, and what brings you hither?"

Now Kootenay thought of the first question, and he said, "Kootenay."

There was a long pause, as if the old voice had to figure things out first. Then he heard the voice again. "Did you say Koo-Denay?"

"Yes, I said Kootenay. That's my name and the name of my people!"

He heard the old voice again saying, "Oh, Koo-Denay, of course. It's been a long time!"

What happened next was nothing less than miraculous. The figure of an old man appeared dressed in pure white goatskins. He floated down from his cave in ethereal weightlessness on natural steps in the rock, moving toward a good-sized basin in the ground. The basin was large enough to swim in. As Kootenay stepped closer, he could see warm water bubble up from the sandy bottom of the waterhole and a thin mist rising from the warm water. What he had thought to be a waterhole in the swampy ground was a warm pool fed by underground springs. The pool receded into the shadows of the overhanging rocks.

When Kootenay looked up, he saw the man walking toward him, drifting like a white cloud. Only Keeno was confused; he had never seen an animal covered with so much white fur, and since he was so hungry, it might be good eating, too. At the moment, he was looking at Kootenay to see what he was going to do.

To his surprise, this white animal lifted his arms and hugged Kootenay and said, "Be welcome, my son, in my humble abode if you come from the Koo-Denay from across the Shining Mountains." Then he pointed ahead for Kootenay to follow. "Oh," he said in his fragile voice; that seemed to indicate he didn't want to be interrupted. "It's been a long time since I heard from the Koo-Denay; things have changed so much. My father used to tell me about your people. When they were on the trail of In-Ni in the sweet grass, sometimes, there were so many buffalo in a long line they couldn't be counted. When we ran them over the cliffs at the 'Head Smashed In,' there were so many butchered that we had food for the whole winter for many people. Now I hear not so many come any more. Too many are hunted by White people.

They say there is a powerful White chief who wants to take all the land from the people."

They had arrived at the entrance to the cave above the basin, when the old man turned around and said, "I hope you will find it convenient to take advantage of the hospitality of my abode. I see that you and your dog have gone hungry for many days. You will have to rebuild your strength afore you travel on. I have much food. It is not good to travel on an empty stomach. You will stay with me as an ambassador from the Koo-Denay Nation. I have had hunting parties here from the Na-Koda and Tsuut-ina people. They were on the trail of wapiti and moose; they have had much luck! They left me all the meat they couldn't carry in their canoes, so be my guest."

He went and got smoked meat and fish and different herbs and spices and salt. When he saw Kootenay wolfing down the precious food, he went to him and touched him on his shoulder from behind, and said, "Take your time, son. Nobody will take it from you. While you stay with me, you may eat as much as you like."

When Kootenay and Keeno had stilled their hunger, Kootenay crawled into a corner of the cave where there was a pile of marsh grass under layers of moss. He stretched out on top of that, and he was asleep before his head touched the soft cushions. He slept and ate for two days, while Keeno lay in front of Kootenay watching the old man.

A young man will recover fast from starvation and fatigue when given all the food and rest he needs. This was the case with Kootenay. After a few days of eating and sleeping, he had completely recovered. How long he slept, he didn't know. After he had a swim in the warm basin below the cave, he felt as strong as ever and he was ready to continue his journey to find the main camp of Na-Koda, Nenii-Yawak and Sik-Sika people. He mentioned his plan to find their camps and stay with the people who had once known the Kootenay before they moved across the Shining Mountains.

The old man explained, "Buffalo have been hard to find in the sweetgrass. Many braves are camped at a place called Yaha-Tinda. There are many wapiti and moose there at our winter camps. But you are very badly equipped for hunting moose. You will have to learn how to hunt with bow and arrow. I still have my hunting bow, which I will not need any more. You are welcome to have it. We will start your training tomorrow!"

He went to the dark end of the cave. From there he took down a bow, quiver, and steel-tipped arrows. In the Kootenay Valley, the Indian people lived mostly on fishing. As a result, Kootenay never had any instruction in the art of archery. The few braves who went into the mountains to hunt the woodland caribou preferred to use their spears when they laid in wait for the herds on their migration to their winter feeding grounds. On the narrow forest trails, the animals walked in single file and could easily be taken by experienced hunters equipped with spears.

The following day, Kootenay couldn't wait until he could hold the precious piece of wood that was the hunting bow. The old man carried all the equipment for the archery practice himself. They walked down from their cave above the valley floor toward a clearing in the forest. The old man walked ahead, with Kootenay and his dog behind. Not in a long time did the old man have such a feeling of importance. It made him walk more erect than he was used to. He could train a young man in the art of archery.

When he was a boy, they had to lay in wait behind bushes for a buffalo to come close before they could fire their arrows. To face a buffalo bull at close range was a frightening experience, and it required a considerable amount of courage and skill. For that reason several braves would work together as a team.

When they arrived at the place where the training was to take place, the old man began feverish activity. Against a steep embankment of an old riverbed, he piled branches and layers of moss. To that, he attached the pure white pelt of a snowshoe hare. When he returned to where Kootenay was standing, his manner of speaking changed completely.

Before the science of projectiles, where the performance of any given weight of projectile, under any given condition is known, the teaching and use of archery was an art or magic on its own. Only very few chosen individuals became masters in the art of archery, and with that achieved great respect in societies who depended on their skills for food.

The old man was fully aware that every word he spoke was now a command, and he made it clear that Kootenay understood it as such. He now took the bow, holding it in his left hand. The bow was not strung; the string was hanging loose. He began, "You never leave a bow strung unless you want to use it, remember that. Wood is a living thing; it gets tired and loses its power. Your life depends on the power of your bow. Don't forget, if you have a bow that breaks or is weak, you might be in trouble. In order to string your bow, you never push it into the ground; that applies all the force to the notched end, and you might break it and make your bow useless. Now watch! In order to string your bow properly, you do it like this."

He placed his legs apart slightly with his knees bent just a little. Now he held his bow in his left hand, with the bow protruding with the attached string hanging loose. The exact center of the bow now rested in the back of his bent knee. When he put pressure on the bow with his left hand from behind, the bow curved forward. It required all his strength to perform this task. When the bow was bent far enough, he slipped the looped end of the string over the notched end of the bow.

After he stepped out of the half-circle of the bow, he handed it to Kootenay. "Unstring it now," he said.

Kootenay tried, but as much as he tried he couldn't do it. The old man said, "You have to concentrate the full power of your mind to the bow. Only then will the wood give enough so you can bend it."

After a while, Kootenay tried again. He held the bow with his left hand and pushed the bow with all his strength, and with his right hand he pushed the string off the bow. While he did this, he could feel a mysterious vibration flowing from the tight bow through both his arms into his body.

He felt like he had become more powerful, like he could achieve dominion over everything he aimed his bow at, and he could extend the reach of his spear tenfold. From now on, he would never again go without a bow and a quiver full of arrows. When he now let go of the bowstring, he heard a vibrating sound coming from the bow as the tension of the wood relaxed.

For the rest of the day, the old man taught Kootenay concentration. He made him sit down with his legs folded. Then he told him to focus his eyes on an imaginary target within the range of his arrow.

"Now concentrate both your eyes and your mind on the target. And remember that it is the power of your mind that will guide your deadly missile to the target." Then he said, "And one of the most important things to remember is that you must control your breathing. Your mind and your eyes remain on the target. Now, when you exhale the air in your lungs, your hands and your body are completely relaxed. At this moment, when your eyes are focused and you are completely relaxed, it is the power of your will that will guide your arrow to the target, and only then will the game submit to the power of your will to sacrifice itself to still your hunger so you and your people may live.

"With all this power in your hands, the most important quality you must practice is humility. And always be aware: With great power comes great responsibility. Never take more than you need; never spoil anything out of greed."

For many days, Kootenay practiced concentration and breathing without firing an arrow at the white rabbitskin. Only then, when the old man thought he was ready, was Kootenay allowed to fire his first arrow at the target. The old man marked off five times ten paces, waved his hand at the target, and stepped aside. Kootenay leveled the bow and re-leased the bolt so fast that the old man didn't even see the arrow hit the target. When he walked away he knew that he had taught him well.

Kootenay became so good with bow and arrow he thought he could hit anything with it. One warm night, he looked at the yellow moon. He made up his mind that one day he would be able to hit the moon with one of his missiles.

For the next few days, Kootenay and his dog were out hunting the white wabasso. The fresh meat was a welcome change for the old man. The skins would be traded for to-bacco. Then they went upriver to hunt beaver before the river froze.

One day, Kootenay got itchy feet, and he asked the old man to tell him about the trail to the Na-Koda and the Nenii-Yawak people who were hunting in Yaha-Tinda country. The old man looked at Kootenay for a long time and said nothing. The truth was that he would have liked Kootenay to stay for the winter. He knew that once the young man had made up his mind he couldn't hold him and one fine morning he would be gone, silently, just like he had arrived. That was his way.

One evening when the campfire was crackling and a warm fog was drifting up from the basin below the old man spoke. "It is best that you wait for the rivers to freeze and before too much snow hides the trails. From here, after crossing the river on the ice, you go up the Minne-Wanka Gap, the trail will take you into Ghost River country. There is much timber and good hunting there. From the Ghost River, you have to turn toward midnight. In a few days, you will see burnt timber and much fallen timber along the rivers there. The next river you cross is the river of the Red Deer. It is between the Red Deer and the Clear Water rivers that you will find most of the braves of the Na-Koda and the Nenii-Yawak. They have good lodges made from buffalo hides, and they sleep under buffalo hides that keep them warm all winter.

"I smoked the pipe with a White man a few summers ago. He told me that he was going to travel all the way to the great ocean where the sun goes down behind the water. This man told me that there are fewer buffalo now in the sweetgrass than there used to be, and the people are going hungry.

"Across the ocean, where the White people come from, they have horses made from iron. Those horses run on trails of metal and make much noise and black smoke. He said that the White people will lay ribbons of steel from ocean to ocean, and the iron horse can run day and night and never stop."

Kootenay listened with great interest, even though he couldn't imagine what an iron horse looked like. He had seen horses of course. The Sa-Haptin people called them Appa-Loosa. The Kootenay people never had horses; they preferred to have dogs in the mountains and forests to pull their sleighs in the winter. Kootenay himself had owned a dog for as long as he could remember, and having Keeno as a traveling companion was part of him he would never change.

22

Kootenay left the old Na-Koda early in the morning, after he had finally fallen asleep under his buffalo robe. The old man had hoped to be awake when Kootenay left the cave for his trip to the Yaha-Tinda hunting grounds. The old man had gotten used to the humble, self-assured demeanor of this young man, who was so eager to learn everything that was new to him. In his generous hospitality and care, he had watched the half-starved skeleton of a boy recover completely and grow into the most deadly hunter. When he left, he walked like a mountain lion on the hunt. Now, the boy he had loved for only a few short weeks was gone.

Kootenay had crossed the frozen river just a short stretch above the waterfall, where the river was squeezed into a tight canyon before it tumbled over the precipice. He heard the thunder of the waterfall below as he was engulfed by drifting patches of ice-fog while he climbed the steep embankment on the far side of the river. When the sun rose over the mountain, he crossed a dry creek bed. From there he could make out what the old man called the Minne-Wanka Gap. As soon as he entered the steep canyon, he realized how right the old man had been when he said not to walk through the gap in deep snow. The game trail followed the canyon at the edge of a high cliff. Only the sound of the creek told him how deep it was to the bottom. When he came to a headwall, he had to take the load off Keeno's back and carry it himself over the top, and then help Keeno over the steepest part of the cliff. Above the headwall, the valley widened out and the going became much easier.

The bundle Kootenay carried consisted of a pair of snowshoes dangling from one side, his spear attached to the same side, securely fastened to the other side was his new hunting bow, which the old Na-Koda had given him along with a quiver full of precious steel-pointed arrows. Kootenay loved the hard work of the steep uphill climb; the deep, rhythmic breathing gave him great pleasure. Now he turned around to look back at the valley he had crossed during the day, the Valley of the Bow as he now called it. At the spot where he thought the waterfall had to be, thin puffs of mist rose from the water in the cold air.

As the trail steepened, he had to bend forward to adjust his pack. He saw his new moccasins, and he felt lucky. These moccasins had soles from strong buffalo hides; the inside he had stuffed with grass that kept his feet warm. The old man had said that soles from the backside of a buffalo hide never wear out. Later on, when the snow got deeper, he would wear a new pair of mukluks made for him by the old Na-Koda. He had watched the old man while he worked on them. He had used an old pair, as he was inclined not to throw anything away that could still be used. He pointed out that the old leggings were better than new ones, as they had been waterproofed with bear grease and were soft and pliable. They would cover Kootenay's legs up to his knees. Then the old man took the top grain leather from a buffalo hide and soaked it in water until he could stretch it to any shape. In this case, he shaped it to Kootenay's feet. He did this by pounding the wet leather into the hollow of a tree and the letting it dry. To attach the soles to the top, he used an awl made from a thin sliver of bone and very thin strands of leather. Once the soft leather dried, it formed a very strong bond.

Forgetting about his shoes, Kootenay looked up and found that they had reached the top of the pass. While they were still traveling in the valley, there was very little wind. Now, as they reached the height of the pass, the wind hit them with full force. After squeezing through a narrow rock crevice, they found a game trail which was used by white goats and bighorn sheep. On the lee-side of the wind, they found a camp spot that had been used by hunters and mountain walkers like themselves. In the valley they had left behind, there was still a little bit of golden daylight; while on their side of the valley. in the shade, it was getting dark. Behind the rocks and out of the wind, the temperature was dropping fast and the forest-covered foothills looked dark and far and threatening. Kootenay didn't know yet that he was about to enter a land of temperature extremes. While he couldn't remember if the lake of the Kootenay ever froze, the lakes on this side of the mountains were frozen solid.

They ate pemmican supplied by the old Na-Koda. A patch of snow served to quench their thirst. High above the foothill-forest, now shrouded by almost total darkness, Kootenay rolled into his bearskin, with his dog stretched out in front of him. In the fissures of the rocks above, the wind sang them a lullaby, and they were soon asleep.

Long before the sun tinted the far horizon in fiery orange, Keeno's good ear picked up the barking sound of a pack of timber wolves. He raised himself on his front legs, stretched, and looked into the darkness where the sound of his archenemies was coming from. Then he turned around and licked the face of his human companion in order to find out whether he was still alive.

Kootenay was so used to this habit of his dog that it allowed him to sleep so soundly that he didn't pay attention to his surroundings; all he did in his sleep was reach out from his warm cover and touch the animal to reassure him. Then he reached behind his head to make certain that his spear was in the right spot in case he needed it. While he did this, he was sound asleep.

Keeno himself, now reassured that everything was the way it should be, lay down on the little bit of bearskin that was left for him. Then there was silence, the great silence when the night is the darkest just before the sun prepares to rise above the horizon and man and beast like to catch some sleep. Even the pack of wolves down below in the dark forest had settled down to await the sunrise.

Even Keeno had gone to sleep it seemed when his good ear perked up and began to swivel about, his eyes still closed. Keeno's sensitive ears had picked up the rushing sound of wings. When he realized the sound came from a flock of migrating birds, Keeno lost interest since he knew he couldn't do anything about birds flying above him.

But now Kootenay's ears had picked up the sound of birds' wings, too. At the same time he opened his eyes and he was privileged to witness one of the great wonders of nature while he was still warm under his bearskin. The birds had started out the day before, when the lake where they had spent the summer and raised a batch of young swans began to freeze. The young birds had used up a long stretch of open water to get airborne, but once they were in the air, they found their wings very quickly and they followed the old, experienced birds to form the V-formation in which they would fly toward the sun to a lake where they would spend a night resting and waiting for the stragglers to arrive.

On this eventful morning, they had started out early, for they had to gain enough altitude to clear several passes across the Shining Mountains. A thousand birds were on the wing at the moment when Kootenay first heard them. The first formation approached in total darkness, and Kootenay couldn't see them. When they gained altitude, their wings flared up into a golden flame when the tangent rays of the morning sun hit them. The birds could see the rocky crags in the golden light of early morning. That's where they had to go, through the Minne-Wanka Gap. Kootenay watched as the V-formation changed to a single line as they cruised toward the opening in the mountains, as they had done for a million years.

Kootenay, as he listened and watched, didn't think that these birds were using the same road that had taken him months to travel, first crossing the Shining Mountains then following the river of the Kootenay and from there to White Swan Lake, all in one day. He didn't think that old man Kootenay might be watching, too. Kootenay watched as golden bird after golden bird crossed the mountains and disappeared in the haze over the Valley of the Bow. Further on, the birds would use the updrift of the chinook wind and fly along the snow-covered ridges of the Shining Mountains.

Kootenay's mind was filled with wonder as he lay there under his bear robe. He never thought that some of these bird might be the same as the ones he had watched last spring. This wonderful ebb and flow of life on the wing was still to continue uninterrupted for many years, until White people with their shotguns almost wiped out the swans from Kootenay's lands. When Kootenay, who was later known by his permanent name Running Rain moved to the hot springs and the lake, which is still called White Swan Lake today, in order to spend the last summers of his life there, the graceful flocks were beginning to thin out.

For now Kootenay was adjusting a load on Keeno's back, which the dog accepted without complaint because he seemed to know that they would be traveling down into rich hunting grounds. The droppings on the trail in the forested foothills told Kootenay and his dog that there was plenty of game in the hills down below.

23

The first river they crossed in the land of the Na-Koda people was almost dry. A few frozen pools had water in them, but Kootenay had to pound a hole through the ice to get their drinking water. The water tasted very good after drinking melted snow. Quite often, the frozen puddles would melt again during the day when it got warm. As a result of the very cold nights, Kootenay would change his traveling habit completely. Without even noticing it, he would sleep late under his bearskin until the sun was warm enough for comfort, and in order not to betray his presence to other hunters, he would always build a smokeless fire.

After a few days, they entered a river valley that had been devastated by a raging fire. The forest fire, started by lightning, had burned through the bone-dry timber with the speed of the katabatic wind that kept fanning the conflagration. The rain, which dropped from the clouds, never reached the ground as the air was so dry. It had left only those fire-blackened tree trunks pointing their dead fingers toward the ice-blue sky as a reminder of the awesome forces of nature.

While he stared at the grotesque skeletons of the once-living trees, he was reminded of what the old Na-Koda had told him, that he had to cross the Valley of the Burnt Timber. The old man had also told him about the Valley of the Fallen Timber. Kootenay had missed that, as it was further toward sunrise. Kootenay now knew that he had to keep traveling toward midnight to get to the Yaha-Tinda plains.

195

As Kootenay didn't know what he had to expect, he was in no haste to travel on. The trail had become his destination. That would only change much later when he found that a snug teepee made from buffalo hide could be very cozy. For now Kootenay was looking across the frozen Burnt Timber River and watching how dry seeds of fireweed were drifting across the valley on the wings of a cool, autumn wind.

On the other side of the creek, the seeds were picked up by an invisible thermal updrift; that was a spot where the bright sun had heated the grass-covered ground. Now that pocket of warm air was drifting upward, high into the sky, and taking the pure white seeds with it. The shining seeds were taken high enough that they would drift as far as the next valley, where they would descend and in time sprout and grow into more fireweed.

While Kootenay was looking into the sky and up a barren hill, he noticed some movement at the edge of the forest, just above the dry meadow, where a bull wapiti appeared out of the forest followed by a smaller bull. There were no cows around, so the bulls were feeding peacefully. Kootenay knew that this time of the year was the rutting season, when all eligible bulls of the herd settled their claims for the available cows by locking horns. He watched the bulls for a while; they were feeding peacefully. That meant there were no cows around watching. They had to be in the forest above, and they would appear out of the forest for feeding around sunset.

He checked the wind; it was not in his favor. He had to circle around and approach from behind, but how? If he walked across the open meadow, the bulls would see him and they would disappear and warn the cows. He also had second thoughts about facing a rutting wapiti bull all by himself. He had to find out if there were some cows around.

There was the frozen creek bed; it was the answer of course because he couldn't be seen from the meadow above.

As it turned out, there was very little water in the creek so high in the mountains at this time of the year. The only thing he had to watch was that the ice on the pools was strong enough to carry them. When he thought they had gone far enough, they climbed up through the steep gravel of the bank. Now they had to stalk their quarry in the hope that Kootenay could get within the range of his deadly arrows. The sun was setting behind billowing clouds when they settled down within a clump of young trees. Then he took the heavy burden off Keeno to prepare him for the chase.

He pulled an arrow out of his quiver and strung his bow exactly the way the old Na-Koda had instructed him. His dog Keeno was shivering with excitement in anticipation of the chase; Kootenay had to settle him down so he wouldn't give them away in his excitement. Out on the clearing, Kootenay could hear the sparring sound of clanking antlers when the first cow appeared on the meadow in the last light of the day. Still, they were all too far for a good shot. Kootenay realized it could cost him one of his precious arrows. From behind them came a crashing sound out of the forest, as a wapiti cow came thundering down the steep meadow behind last spring's calf. They had been scared in the forest by something unknown, and they were hoping to find safety within the herd out on the meadow.

When the cow got the scent of Kootenay and his dog, she stopped in her tracks, her calf behind her. Kootenay was ready, his arrowhead poised, string pulled back until his right thumb rested on his cheek. Then he heard the air escaping from his lungs as he exhaled. There was the singing sound of the bowstring as he released his deadly projectile. His eyes couldn't see any longer, but the power of his mind was focused on his target, below the shoulder blades of the calf. As the arrow penetrated the body of the calf, it leaped straight into the air, and then it ran as if it could run away from the piercing pain in its side.

Keeno, who had waited for this moment, was in hot pursuit. The calf ran only a few steps before its front legs collapsed, and it slowly settled on its side. At that same moment, Keeno was there, and he held fast, just in case the quarry jumped again.

When they both bolted from their hiding place, the herd had scattered in panic and disappeared in the forest. Now there was a great silence on the wind-swept hillside; only the rustling of the everlasting wind stirred the dry grass. As Kootenay bent over his quarry and he touched the still warm body of the cow, at this very moment, for the first time in his life, he became fully aware that he had to kill in order to live. For the first time in his life, he became aware, and he had to face the age-old dilemma of all of mankind, kill or perish, head on, and with it the burden of the awesome responsibility he carried in his hands. With a fish he never had that feeling.

When he looked down at his dog, who was hungry, too, he pulled his knife out of his mukluk; with it the thought disappeared. What remained forever in his mind was a consciousness of conscience. The faculty of the human brain which determines the dividing line between right and wrong and good and evil.

The eyes of the hunter adjusted fast to the darkness. With skilled hands, his knife bled the game and opened the cavity below the chest. He reached in and pulled out the still warm liver; he ate it still warm. Then he fed his dog from the quarry.

They sat there for a long time watching the moon rise over the mountains and listening to the sounds of the night. In the pale light of the moon, they walked back down to the creek where they bedded down for the night. Kootenay left the entrails of the game where he had dressed the animal in the hope that if a pack of wolves or coyotes was close by they would claim that instead of coming after the carcass he had laid in front of them on the ice. With full tummies, they slept well; only Keeno had heard a bunch of coyotes quarrel over the intestines they had left on the top of the hill.

Now, with their food supply assured, they traveled toward midnight, crossing frozen bogs and creeks with ease. After a few days, they found themselves on the banks of a larger river; this had to be the River of the Red Deer. The fast-flowing water of this river hadn't frozen completely, a crossing would be difficult. Kootenay decided to travel upstream toward the Shining Mountains on a wide flood plain.

They crossed the river higher up on a beaver dam. Kootenay set up camp there. During the night some snow had fallen, and the tracks of game became visible. He had chosen the site carefully, as he didn't know what to expect. Young braves might take him for an enemy. Kootenay felt safe there at the edge of a dense forest, where he could retreat into the woods and there was plenty of dry wood for a smokeless fire. He built a lean-to which was open to the warm noon sun.

At first, Kootenay had thought of making a fire. Then he changed his mind. He ate some of the tenderloin meat with a little bit of salt; to drink, they went to the river. The following morning, Kootenay heard the thundering sound of horses' hoofs for the first time in his life. His caution with setting up his camp and not making a fire had paid off; the riders hadn't seen them.

When they went down to the river to drink, Kootenay found the strange hoofprints in the snow. They had forded the river there in the fast-flowing ripples where it wasn't frozen and the water wasn't very deep. Their tracks continued on this side of the river into the mountains.

Kootenay and his dog followed the trail of the horses all day, staying close to the forest, where they could disappear at any moment if they had to. All day, they crossed dry creekbeds and gravel fields until late in the evening when, after they had climbed a grassy knoll, Kootenay smelled smoke. He couldn't see where the smoke came from, but a thin layer drifted over the wide valley, indicating there had to be many lodges. Kootenay was puzzled.

They walked on toward the river for a while. Then the river disappeared underground in the gravel, and they stood in front of a rock wall that seemed to block the trail. The horses droppings led them along the wall to a canyon with steep walls and overhanging rocks. Kootenay stepped on a rock and looked inside of the canyon. It was almost dark inside, water was dripping from the walls, and to his surprise the water in the creek bed had reappeared. The riders had obviously dismounted and walked through the canyon; there was enough room for that. Since he didn't want to get his feet wet, he stepped back from the rock he had been standing on in order to figure out how to proceed.

With the help of Keeno's nose, they found the trail through the rocks. From the barren top an amazing view opened up in front of their eyes. Below their feet lay a wide, flat basin, forming a grassy plain irrigated by the meandering creek. At one time, long before people made their home there, this hollow had been filled with glacial ice. When the ice melted, it had first laid down a layer of rich soil, and then the rushing water had cut the canyon through the rock-spur through which the remaining creek now flowed.

As the sun was setting behind snow-covered mountains, Kootenay could see in the golden sunlight many teepees. From the opening on the top of each teepee, a wisp of smoke was rising into the still air above the peaceful scene. Along the meandering creek, poplars still carried their golden leaves of fall, as the valley was well-protected from the strong chinook wind. The golden patina created by the mild afternoon sun and the thin layer of smoke lent the whole picture an inviting aspect. This was a place where human beings had decided to make their home with all the clutter involved in their activities. He could see horses and dogs and children running, and he felt like walking down the hill and presenting himself to the elders of the community. At the same time, he realized this could be very dangerous. He was an intruder, nobody knew him. He didn't even know whether they would understand his language.

So he proceeded with great care and hesitation down the hill, using the stunted pines as cover where he could. When he arrived on the flat below, next to the creek, the dogs around the first teepee got wind of him and reported their presence to the occupants. At the same time, the angry pack came charging toward them. Then two braves appeared from one of the teepees and mounted their horses and came charging after their dogs. The pack of dogs in the meantime were not interested in Kootenay; they charged at Keeno in a mad rush in order to find out what was under the bearskin which Keeno was carrying. Keeno, knowing that he was well-protected by the burden he was carrying, bared his mighty wolf fangs and let out a bloodcurdling snarl.

Keeno must have been an impressive sight with only one ear, the remains of the other a reminder of past violent altercations years before. When the hackles rose on his neck, the pack realized that this dog, which looked like a bear but acted like a wolf, had to be reckoned with and stayed well out of his reach. Kootenay talked to Keeno quietly, and the dog settled down, reassured that the situation was well under control.

In the meantime, two riders approached at a full gallop, riding around them in circles. Kootenay could see that they were unarmed; that meant that they had peaceful intentions, or they were much surprised by the unexpected appearance of a stranger in their midst when they had thought that their camp there in the mountains was completely safe. There had been stories that a party of White traders with an Indian guide had traveled through their country further toward midnight.

In the meantime, the circles the two horsemen were riding in kept getting tighter. Kootenay was perplexed; he had known for a long time of his own intentions to visit the people of the Na-Koda and Sik-Sika and Tsuut'ina, but now that the moment he had been looking forward to had arrived, he was tongue-tied and didn't know what to say. He had nothing to offer them as a gift. He had watched visitors from other nations at home, but they always carried gifts. He had nothing.

In his despair, he bent down and pulled out the fresh pelt of the wapiti; it was a good winter pelt. His arms stretched out in front carrying the pelt. He walked toward the riders and said, "I'm Kootenay." He stopped, and since he couldn't think of anything better than the place where he was given his hunting bow he continued, "I come with greetings from the old Na-Koda at the River of the Bow!"

The two riders stopped and looked at each other; they didn't understand. Now, that they were certain he had come with good intentions, they waved to him to follow. Not too far away he saw a man standing in front of a teepee all dressed in tanned deer hides. Kootenay was waved toward him. He saw that the person he was looking at was much older than the riders he had met first.

It was clear he was the man in charge of this hunting camp. Kootenay walked to him still carrying his fresh wapiti pelt as if it were a gift. This time, he knew what to say, and what to do.

"I'm Kootenay," he said clearly. "I come with greetings from the old Na-Koda who lives at the River of the Bow in the cave above the basin where the warm waters flow."

Now he took his bundle and untied his hunting bow and quiver and laid all down on the wapiti pelt as a sign that he had no intention of ever using his arms against the people.

He watched how the old man nodded when he said old Na-Koda. "I have never met the man. You are very fortunate to have met him and received from his wisdom. He was one of the great hunters, his reputation is that of a wise man. When he was a young man, nobody ever went hungry. The bows and arrows he made were magic. There were stories around that he guided his bolts to the target by will power alone." He continued, "And you are Koo-Dene? When I was a young man I heard the story that the Koo-Dene people moved across the Shining Mountains and they were lost at a place called Waka-Nambe, where the snow never melts. They were never seen again. I am happy to see that not all Koo-Dene people perished at Waka-Nambe.

"I welcome you at the camp of the Sik-Sika people in the hope that you will accept, and take part in, what we have to offer you as long as it is convenient to you as an ambassador of the people of the Koo-Dene."

Kootenay, realizing that he was being received in great honor, now reached for his precious bow and the quiver full of arrows and handed it to the man. As the old man touched the bow while Kootenay still held it in his hand, he felt like the magic power of the bow was transferred from him to the old man. Kootenay didn't know that the handing over of one's most valued possession into the custody of a man of superior authority would be taken as a sign of submission, and that he was willing to surrender his personal freedom to the laws of the Sik-sika Nation while he remained in their domain. It also meant that the older man had adopted him and Kootenay was now in his custody and under his protection. On the other hand, Kootenay knew he could expect to receive his gift back at the appropriate time.

Kootenay had done exactly the right thing, which was for a young man of his age, a very wise thing to do since it stirred pride in the older man who didn't have a son of the superior outward appearance of this Kootenay boy. Who, as he could see, had traveled in the wilderness and survived and thrived with only a half-wolf as a companion. On the other hand, he had a daughter a few summers younger than the young man who stood in front of him.

Kootenay watched as the man rubbed his hand along the silky grain of the bow and said, "Not everybody can own a bow as valuable as this one. I was told that the old Na-Koda would only take the wood from an old mountain ash high in the Shining Mountains. The tree is supposed to be hundreds of summers old. The wood in this bow is a living substance; it has the song of the chinook wind and the thunder of lightning and the crackling sound of frost of hundreds of visitors in all its fibers."

He now took bow and quiver and the wapiti pelt and walked ahead of Kootenay, toward a teepee covered with buffalo hides. He pointed toward the teepee. "This will be your lodge as long as you are disposed to accept our hospitality. You are free to come and go as you please. I will send you somebody who will look after your comfort as soon as I can find her." With that the man walked away carrying the bow and arrows.

As soon as Kootenay tied the flap back on his teepee and stepped into the almost dark interior of his new abode, he knew that he would like it. In the center of the teepee was a large firepit. The rest of the floor was covered with thick buffalo furs. He had never seen anything like it, so he bent down and touched the thick fur under his feet. After he crawled over and pulled the flap across the opening, he lay down and pulled his bearskin over himself. He fell asleep, his dog Keeno beside him.

Kootenay and his dog hadn't slept in anything as comfortable as this teepee since they had stayed with old Kootenay in his cave, and since the thick buffalo hides muffled all sounds, they slept late into the next morning. Now, in a warm teepee, Kootenay had reverted back to his old habit of sleeping completely naked. Not expecting anybody close to his teepee, he pulled away the flap and bent down to step outside into the bright sunshine bare naked, as it was his custom when he stayed in his mother's lodge. As he heard the giggle behind him, he turned around and stood face to face with a beautiful young girl.

She was almost as tall as himself. Her hair, tied behind in one single knot, was as black and as shining as her eyes, and sparkled with a bluish tint. Kootenay didn't know anything about girls, and about women he only knew his mother, who was by no means an old woman. As long as he lived with the Kootenay, he had lived with his mother. He had never known another woman.

The only time she could remember when boys and girls mixed naked was when they went swimming in the lake in the summer. She had never seen a young man like this Kootenay before. The challenges, hardships, loneliness, and deprivation had made him a man in body and good to look at, though in his mind he was still a boy.

He didn't know what to do with a girl. She giggled. That was nothing to worry about; girls always giggled. What was she doing here? The man hadn't told him that he was sending his daughter to look after him. He needn't have worried; she knew exactly what to do. She had orders from her father to look after all his needs. Of course, Kootenay didn't know that it was the custom of the tribe to loan a squaw to an important visitor.

When it finally dawned on Kootenay to get dressed, she had already built a fire. When he grabbed his clothing, she told him that he couldn't have it; it had to be cleaned. That was something new to him; nobody had ever told him that there was something he couldn't have. He was alarmed. For the first time, he felt like he was vis-à-vis with a power which he couldn't overcome. He watched her clean his leather shirt and stockings with dry snow.

She replaced the layer of grass in his mukluks with a layer of dry grass. She prepared his food. He wasn't used to that; he was used to looking after himself, so was his dog Keeno. He went around with his tail between his legs. But it doesn't take long to get used to the better things in life.

When the first real snowstorm of the winter arrived one night and blanketed their world with layers of deep snow, life in the camp became slow and torpid; while it snowed, nobody moved. Then, when it stopped snowing, it turned very cold and the camp became almost lifeless. For the moment, as long as there was enough food; there was no need to do anything. The only signs of life in the camp were the thin plumes of smoke rising almost motionless above the lodges and into the azure-blue sky.

Then one morning, he found his mukluks, snowshoes, and bow and arrows inside his teepee. He knew what that meant. He would now have to prove that he was a qualified member of the tribe. He would now be given the opportunity to prove his skills as a hunter and provider of food for the community into which he had been accepted without prior conditions, where he lived in great comfort, and where he was cared for when he was at home. As he was fully aware of the unwritten rules of reciprocity his acceptance of the responsibility as a provider was self-evident. He hadn't known anything different; all his young life he had been prepared for that, and he was ready.

He stepped out of his teepee. The air was warm and felt soft, like deerhide. It carried all the smells from faraway, unknown oceans to the spicy resin of the pines of the hills. Meltwater was dripping from bushes and trees, and gobs of heavy, wet snow fell to the ground. It felt good after long days of hard frost.

The plan was that two contingent teams of hunters, six in each team, would move higher into the mountains on separate trails, thus covering a larger territory. Then they would turn toward midnight and fan out and cross the Clearwater River, where scouts had reported a large herd of wapiti to be wintering at or near the Wabasso River. The two teams would communicate by prearranged smoke signals. Travel would be on foot since the steepness of the mountain terrain would be difficult and food for horses would be hard to find in the deep snow.

Early next morning, the two teams were on the move. Right from the start, Kootenay discovered that he had several advantages. His snowshoes were of a better design. Old Kootenay, living in Kootenay country where there is always more snow, simply built a better snowshoe for deeper snow than the people on this side of the Shining Mountains, but his greatest advantage was Keeno. Early in the morning, as soon as he realized they were off on a hunt, he jumped around like a puppy, and he accepted the burden of Kootenay's sleeping robe and their food while Kootenay carried his hunting gear and blazed a trail.

As soon as they were on the road, they reverted to their proven routine of Keeno walking behind in Kootenay's packed footprints. They moved toward sunset, along the river all morning, where the river made a bend toward midday, they made a turn until they had the sun in their backs.

At this time of the year, the sun stood low over the horizon. It barely touched the jagged outline of the treetops on the other side of the valley. Making camp along a steep riverbank, where the last snowstorm had piled up a deep snowdrift with an overhanging cornice, all they had to do was dig into the snowdrift, remove the snow, and cover the cold ground with pine boughs and they had a warm sleeping place deep in the snow cave. When they saw a plume of smoke rising from the next valley, they knew they were right on target.

Early the next morning, when the first rays of the sun hit their snow shelter, they sent the promised signal, and they were on the move. During the cold, clear night, the top layer of the snow had frozen to a hard crust, which carried the hunters and made walking easy, but during the day, where it was exposed to the warm sun, it became soft. While it carried Kootenay, Keeno broke through the soft crust, and the dog slowed them down.

Around midday, they crossed the frozen Clearwater River and found many game tracks. So Kootenay's contingent decided to stay and hunt along the Clearwater instead, while the other moved on to the Wabasso. While two men built the camp, the rest of the contingent fanned out to scout the surrounding hills for game. In the meantime, no fire was made in order to not warn the herd of their presence.

The scouts covered much country, up over a forested ridge where the terrain drops down toward the Ram River. They stayed on this side when they found a box canyon with steep, open meadows on each side with patches of thick forest. Many tracks led into the forest where the herd retreated during the day when it was warm. They would come out in the evening to scratch through the deep snow to the dry grass to feed.

Much time was spent in the hunting camp scouting or waiting. When a herd was located an attempt was made to move them in a certain direction where certain individuals were separated from the main herd. When the hunters thought culling was needed, they would usually target the oldest bull. Only when there was a shortage of food and the people went hungry would they take a cow with calf.

That Kootenay had become a loner was evident when he went scouting on his own. Between him and his dog, there was a deep understanding. The dog seemed to know when they were on the trail of game, as they were this afternoon.

They were heading up a creek in deep snow when Kootenay spotted a bull elk higher up in the valley. The animal had just arrived at timberline, and he was still climbing. Kootenay could see him clearly now. The antlers on this bull counted at least twelve points, maybe fourteen. He was enormous, and he was still heading uphill across a very dangerous scree slope deep in snow. What was he up to? Was he trying to draw all the attention of the hunters away from his herd and toward himself by going up a snow-covered avalanche slope, where he could be killed by a slide? Or was he just scouting out a safe escape for his herd, who would follow his trail under cover of darkness? Or maybe the smart devil thought that all the hunters would follow him and miss the main herd while he climbed into the next valley.

Kootenay was still trying to figure him out when the bull changed his itinerary and traversed around to the left across the slope toward a rock outcrop, very smart. The rock would protect him from above, and by that time, he would be more than halfway across the most dangerous part of the slope. One thing was certain; that under all this dangerous-looking snow there had to be a safe trail that the bull knew about. Now Kootenay knew what to do. He moved across the creek and climbed up through the forest, Keeno right behind. On the ridge, he turned right and followed an exposed col in the deep snow, where he hoped he would find the bull's trail.

Kootenay was now the mighty hunter. He didn't think that he would have to spend a long night in the cold forest, and that he might have to build a big fire in the forest to stay alive. Kootenay knew that he had an advantage over the bull; while he could eat on the run, the bull had to rest and chew his cud. While he on his snowshoes didn't sink in very much, the bull was very slow in the deep snow and hindered in his movements. But still, Kootenay was not aware that the bull had lured him into a very dangerous situation.

They pushed on. It was almost dark when Kootenay found the track of the bull. Up here it was much colder than down in the valley; the top layer of the snow, which had melted during the day, had now frozen to form a hard crust. This crust was strong enough to carry Keeno and Kootenay, but not the heavy bull.

When Keeno froze in his tracks and pointed downhill, Kootenay knew they couldn't be too far from their quarry. It was now impossible to hold Keeno back while Kootenay rushed after him. What he saw when he arrived at the spot where the bull had decided to bed down for the night was the beginning of a drama which would take hours to reach its climax. When the bull saw the dog coming after him, he decided to make a stand, not knowing that the mightiest hunter of all was right behind.

When he lowered his mighty head in order to skewer the dog with the needle-sharp ends of his spreading antlers, Keeno realizing that the bull, hemmed-in as he was, had only limited room to maneuver, stayed out of his reach. When he had a chance, he sank his fangs into the great tendon of his right hind leg, determined not to let go. With this, Keeno showed his wolf ancestry, as a pack of wolves will always try to hamstring a large animal and slow it down before they move in for the kill. The bull now trying as he would to reach the troublesome Keeno with his antlers couldn't.

A fully grown wapiti bull is an awesome sight at any distance, and a fearsome opponent at close range. Now Kootenay saw the mighty hulk in front of him, and with his rank smell in his nose, he heard the rasping sound of his breath. Now Kootenay did everything the way he had learned it. He reached back for his arrow, set the notch to the string, pulled back until his hand rested against his cheek, then heard himself exhaling at the same moment as he heard the sound of the arrow penetrating through the shaggy fur deep into the rib cage of the monster.

The beast just stood there shaking himself, as if he could shake off the penetrating pain in his chest. The bull had lowered his head; his full attention was now on the man who was far more dangerous to him than the dog, who slowed him down but couldn't kill him. Kootenay, realizing that one single arrow might not be enough to kill the mighty beast, stood in front of him ready to jump out of the way in case the antlers moved toward him. There was enough dim light reflected from the snow that he could see hate burning in those eyes that he, the supreme ruler of the range, he who had roared his challenge to the four corners of his known world, now had no takers for his challenge. Now he was facing a superior power of the will in this lithe man, who stood there eye to eye while he was bleeding and weakening, his strength fading away.

Kootenay, knowing there would be no fast end to this struggle, unless he could deliver a decisive coup de grace, worked his way around to the exposed side of the beast while he pulled out his spear. There was one short moment when the bull, swinging his antlers back toward Keeno, who was still hanging on to his hind leg, exposed his ribcage. There, below the shoulder bone, Kootenay thrust his spear deep into

211

the innards of his quarry. At the same time he jumped back, out of the way of the antlers, while he pulled his hunting knife from its sheath. There was still enough anger in the beast to throw his antlers and skewer this deadly man if he could. When Keeno realized his quarry giving up the struggle, he let go and watched how the hind legs of the bull slowly collapsed, as if he were bedding down to rest. At the same time, his crown of antlers settled down slowly into the deep snow.

Kootenay did now what he had to do. He pushed his dagger deep into the neck of the bull, and with a sharp slice, he severed the main artery of the fallen giant. Then Kootenay and his dog drank the still warm blood, which gushed from the open wound, until they were sated.

While Kootenay was trying to recover his spear and arrow, he lay down on the warm carcass of his quarry and fell into a deep, dreamless sleep in total exhaustion, as a consequence of the extreme overexertion during the chase and the ensuing duel. Keeno bedded down at the feet of his master; he didn't sleep at all. He heard the faraway howls of a pack of wolves. That kept him awake during the night.

Early the next morning, when Kootenay felt cold on one side and warm on the other, he woke. Above him, the tree-tops were turning to gold from the slanting rays of the sun while he recovered his spear and arrow. Then he built a fire to warm himself and to signal his teammates to come and recover the prize.

When the rest of the team arrived, a great feast was held! All the entrails were divided equally among the party and eaten raw, while still warm. Then the quarry was skinned. The valuable pelt was taken to the camp, where it was later tanned by the squaws and made into clothing. Nothing was wasted, even the mighty antlers of the bull, the only real proof of what a mighty hunter Kootenay was, were taken.

The meat was cut into equal loads right there in the snow, even Keeno had to carry his part. When all the work was done, the most expert man in smoke signals took Kootenay to the highest point on the ridge, where they built a fire. It was there that Kootenay learned the secret language of smoke signals, and how to build the proper fire.

The first part of the fire was allowed to burn down completely. While this took place, they collected green pine boughs, which wouldn't burn but instead made lots of dense smoke. The best smoke was achieved by placing green boughs on hot embers. Then a blanket was used, held by two men, to manipulate the upward flow of the smoke. Kootenay found that it was possible to have quite a conversation over long distances.

That done, they put out their own fire and waited. It wasn't long before they saw a plume of smoke rising from the forest where the headwaters of the Wabasso River had to be. The message was clear, "Good hunting, much meat, will make cache, will leave for camp tomorrow."

Down at the spot where they had butchered the wapiti, everybody was ready; they shouldered their loads and moved down into the valley where their camp was waiting for them. Kootenay was looking forward to sleeping in a warm snow shelter under his bearskin. The trip home to the Yaha-Tinda was much easier because they could use their old trail. There was great rejoicing in the camp when the men returned, loaded heavy with meat.

When the women found out who had brought down the bull, Kootenay's status in the community rose, and he was accepted as a full member of the tribe. The women of the camp took over making pemmican or dried and froze the meat. After the second hunting party arrived back from the Wabasso River, loaded with venison, they had enough of their basic food to last them for the winter.

At about the time when the sun couldn't drop any lower toward the horizon, a terrible blizzard hit the valley during the night. The fearsome wind had blown across the icefields in the Shining Mountains, where it picked up more cold. When it, during the night, descended into the Valley of the Red Deer, it hit the teepees like a flowing mass of liquid ice mixed with needle-sharp ice pellets. It was impossible to stay outside for any length of time. All Kootenay could do was secure the smoke-flap, which had been left open for the smoke from the fire to drift off. After he closed the flap over the door, he crawled over to the firepit. The fire was out, but the rocks around the pit and the ground were still hot. The rocks would stay warm, so would the ground around the pit. It was warm in the teepee. He felt good to be in a comfortable lodge.

The girl, Shiny Locks, he called her that because she had the most beautiful, shining hair, had been sleeping with him on the far side of the lodge ever since her father had given her to him. Kootenay, not knowing what to do with a girl since he still hadn't lost his natural shyness toward girls, slept on the other side.

The girl, of course, while she knew that Kootenay was shy, felt no such inhibitions. He touched Shiny Locks, who had moved to his side of the teepee while he was outside closing the flap. It was the first time he had touched her, and he felt the softness of her body and had the sweet scent of her velvety skin in his nose. It was during this stormy, winter night that a communion between these two human beings took place and was consummated.

The fierce winter storms continued for many days, only to be followed by hard frost. It got so cold that even the oldest people couldn't remember it ever having been that cold before. A thick ice fog, mixed with the smoke from the tee-pees, hung over the camp like an unctuous breath of death.

214

Many animals who got stuck in the deep snow froze to death. Hunters later found them standing in their own snowy graves where they had frozen to death! For our Indian people in their warm teepees, life slowed down to a torpor. In Kootenay's teepee, all Shiny Locks had to do was keep the fire going; for Kootenay life became tranquil and pleasant.

Only once during the winter, when a herd of deer drifted into the camp looking for protection from a pack of hungry wolves, did he use his bow and arrow. They always had a need of fresh meat. Then it was back to sleep again.

The sun started rising higher over the rocky ridges on the far side of the valley. Still the cold did not abate, and life went on comfortably and without haste. Then one night a warm wind came rushing down from the snowy heights. It shook the snow from the trees and howled around the teepees, scaring the people out of their sleep. When Shiny Locks looked out of their teepee, she said, "Chinook."

Within a few days, all the snow had melted in the valley as if by magic. The horses who had been scraping in the snow for dry grass now found more food along the river, where the willows were growing. When the people ventured outside of their teepees, they heard the thunder of avalanches going down higher in the valleys. The mountains were shaking their burden of snow from their rocky shoulders.

With the thunder of snowslides came the hope that it would be spring again. Life had become very comfortable for Kootenay. For the time being he had no intentions of moving on.

The following summer, Kootenay, with three young braves from the Na-Koda people, was hunting white goats in the wilderness of the Shining Mountains. They had loaded their horses with buffalo hides for teepees. Then they traveled toward midnight into the far reaches of the Clearwater River.

215

The river was in spring flood from the melting snow in the mountains. So they set up camp to wait for the higher water to drop. When they thought the water level had dropped enough, they traveled upstream before they found a spot where they could risk a crossing. When they found good grazing for their horses, they decided to make camp there at the upper reaches of the Clearwater. It was a smart move since the next large river was the Sakatchewan.

This river rose in the everlasting ice of the Shining Mountains, and as far as the Na-Koda people knew, no Indian people had ever penetrated into this land where the ice never melts. But a few summers ago, a White man with an Indian guide had traveled up the river and found a pass across the mountains. He came to a place where all rivers flow toward sunset, and from there to the great ocean. When Kootenay heard this story, it became clear to him that this White man could have been the same man the old Kootenay had met at the Lake of the Kootenay.

They sent out one scout on horseback to find out if it was possible to cross the Saskatchewan. When the man returned, he confirmed that it would be impossible to cross the river with horses. So they decided to hunt for white goats in the upper reaches of the Clearwater.

The white goat chose to live only in the most remote regions of that part of the world which the Sik-Sika, Na-Koda, and Kootenay people called their home. They were hunted mainly for the great value of their pure white fur. White traders would give anything for the pelts of white goats, and the Indian people could ask for much tobacco or flints or knifes. That's why they were there.

It didn't take Kootenay very long to find out that his companions didn't know very much about climbing the barren ridges and sheer rocks where the white goat was at home. He didn't tell his friends that he considered the white goat a

216

sacred animal. In the meantime, they lived on bighorn sheep taken from the rocks and ridges in the barren mountains. Kootenay found that quite often a wounded bighorn sheep would climb into inaccessible rocks to prevent being taken by the hunter. It was here that Kootenay used his rock climbing experience in order to recover their game.

For the young hunters, it was a summer of great fun and games, interrupted only by short, violent thunderstorms. After the first snowfall, they moved down into the valley where it took them several days to round up their hobbled horses. The horses, now left to their own devices, had wandered far and wide in search of the best forage. The hunters found that their mounts had completely recovered from the starvation of the winter before.

After the first untimely snowfall, the weather in the foothills of the Shining Mountains turned into what the White people would later call "Indian Summer," when all the elements of sky and air had made peace with each other. Even the everlasting wind had freed itself from the rest of the elements, while all other living creatures fell into the most comfortable attitude of well-being and do-nothing. The sun floated like a golden fireball through the transparent sky and left the eye to wander into the most distant remoteness of the universe.

Had there been an observer to this peaceful scene, he would have found our four companions prone and stark naked in the warm sand next to a crystal pool, absorbing what could be the least warm rays of the sun of the short summer. Once in a while, one might dive into the cool water for a refreshing dip, only to reclaim his spot in the warm sand. Evenings by their campfire there were tales to be told of their people, stories so old that nobody could count that far back.

It was during one of those dreamy nights under the stars when Kootenay was warm under his bearskin that he felt for the first time the desire to be home. Kootenay was suffering from homesickness! How was his mother doing? Was she looking at the same stars as he? Was she still alive? There was pain inside of him, but it wasn't pain like one cut with a knife. He had experienced that many times. This was different! This was something deep inside that made one cry with pain. He was glad that it was dark and his companions couldn't see his tears. He, the great hunter, crying?

On the way home to their winter camp, somebody noticed that Kootenay was listless. When asked, he said nothing. What could he say; there was no recognized disease called homesickness.

Home again in his lodge, Shiny Locks looked after him as best she could, but his mood didn't change. Only after he started making plans to leave the Na-Koda did he feel his purpose in life return and his mood changed.

One day, Shiny Locks presented him with a new anorak. She had made it herself from the same wapiti pelt he had given to the camp elder when he arrived. She had tanned the hide and then chewed it until it was soft and pliable. It was indeed the finest of chamois she had ever produced. Kootenay wore it very proudly. For a time his mood changed back to his happy-go-lucky ways.

During the winter, his pain of homesickness never left him, and he made plans to move as soon as the snow melted. Only once during the winter did he mention his plan to return to his home by the lake to somebody, and that was during a sweetgrass ceremony when he, after smoking the pipe, transcended into that sweet feeling of euphoria that one feels after fasting for two days. Then the sweat lodge and then sweetgrass and the pipe let the body free itself from all gravitational forces and float above all earthly limitations, and he told a brave he could trust.

He told this man of his desire to return home to his people at the lake of the Kootenay. The brave understood very well and promised to tell nobody. He told Kootenay about the trails and passes through the Shining Mountains, trails that would be easier than the trails Kootenay had used to come there.

This is what he said. "From here, you travel toward midday, where the sun is at the highest. In the morning, when you start out, you have to have the rising sun at your left. When you make camp, you have to have the setting sun at your right. After a few days, you come to a lake which the Na-Koda call the Lake of the Broken Leg. There is a good camp there with very good fishing and good hunting. Here you will need a few days of rest for yourself and your dog. When you travel on you come to the river which you call the River of the Bow; it is the same river where you were given your bow by the old Na-Koda. The river will be in spring flood when you get there.

"I understand that the Na-Koda have a raft there that you can use to cross the river. Remember, in the morning, you still have to have the sun at your left. If the river is too high and there is no raft, follow the river upstream until you come to a steep rockwall, which is called Yam-Nuska. You will find the river there very shallow, but very wide and very cold. You will think your feet are freezing off, so if you think you must cross here do it fast. From here you travel toward the midday sun. Across the wide flood plain of the river, you will see the mountain pass which will take you into a valley with good hunting and good fishing in the creeks.

"Toward the setting sun, there is a steep ridge which is snow-covered most of the year and is so steep that it cannot be climbed. This ridge is called Ni-Ha-Hi. You follow this ridge to the end. There are good game trails here, and you will be tempted to make camp and stay and follow the scent of deer and elk and enjoy the pleasures of the hunt.

"If you travel on, the best place to start from is at the confluence of two rivers that come from the mountains. You follow the river closest to the sun; the old game trail along the river will take you first to a small lake. From here a trail leads you down into the most wonderful valley in the world; it is called Kana-Naskis. From the Kana-Naskis, there are several passes that will take you where you want to go, to the Kootenay."

Kootenay had listened very carefully to every word. Every name was etched in his mind. Later, he would recognize every feature of the landscape as it had been described to him when he got to it.

As winter turned into spring, he would lay there and listen during the night when he couldn't sleep. At first it was only the wind, or it was a short, violent blizzard that roared through the valley and left a lot of wet snow. There were lots of times when he thought that this winter would never end. But then came one day when the chinook wind moved through the forest warm and moist and melted all the snow. The trees stood bare in stark contrast to the bright blue sky.

One morning, there was a different sound in the sky. It was the sound of birds' wings. As we know, Kootenay could understand the language of geese. He would sit there by himself and listened to what they had to say. First he heard orders given by the lead bird not to break formation. It was the only safe way to fly. Then he heard the story how they had used the updrift of the chinook wind to clear the ice-encrusted ridges of the mountains, and now they could use the tailwind to cruise fast into the land of the midnight sun, where they had left. There they would find the lake they called home. Still, Kootenay kept on listening for the right sound; until he heard it, he knew it wasn't time yet to move.

Then came the morning. After he had lain sleepless all night, there was the sound of the golden wings of the swans. He lifted the flap of the teepee and looked out. While the camp deep in the valley was still in deep darkness, the wings of the swans were lit by the golden, morning sun shining like precious metal. The birds were cruising on the invisible waves of the wind. Then he heard the trumpet sound of the lead bird, who told the following birds to stay the course; it wouldn't be too long to the lake where they could sleep and rest for a night, before they took to their wings again to the lake where they had received the precious gift of life.

24

He hadn't told her anything about his plan to find his way back home to the warm waters of the Lake of the Kootenay. But, if he thought that she didn't know about his plan to leave her, he was wrong. She knew when his heart beat faster than normal or he talked more about his mother than he usually did that there was a plan in his mind to leave her, but she didn't say anything. Like all women, she carried her lot quietly doing her work as she always had without asking or complaining. She didn't even tell him that she was with child, his child.

Then one morning, when the thunder rolled through the valley and rain drummed on the teepee, he and his dog were gone. He had arrived unannounced, and he left quietly. She heard him leave, but she remained silent, knowing that when the trail called he would be gone. She carried her great suffering uncomplaining until a few months later she bore him a son who would much later be called "Many Names."

On the way out, he avoided the canyon, as it was full of water. In driving rain, he found the crossing of the river, and from there on he was in familiar territory until, after crossing the Burnt Timber, he looked up to the steep canyon of the Minne-Wanka Gap. He knew he had travel toward the midday sun. Further to the sun he knew he was in Na-Koda territory. He avoided contact with all hunters. His campfires were small and smokeless. Where he traveled he left no trace of his passing; the visible signs of his moccasins were washed away with the next rain.

After passing through the Ghost River Wilderness, he found the lake his companion had called the Lake of the Broken Legs. When he first approached it, he found the shoreline very swampy. From this side it was impossible to get close to the water. On the other he found the land rising as a gentle meadow upward to the foothills and from there to the snow-covered mountains. At the end of the lake, where a creek drained the lake, he found a logjam and the only place on the lake where there was good fishing.

The fish in this lake were small, but there were many. He used a net which the girl with the Shiny Hair had made from horse hair. Not too far from the lake were the remains of an old fishing camp not used for many summers. All the lodgepoles were there, leaning against trees. Drying and smoking racks were broken down there. He repaired them and set up a teepee for shelter. Then he went fishing. Kootenay and his dog ate their first fish raw; the rest they dried or smoked.

There were long days of early summer sun and wind and easy living. During the short white nights, he would lay there in the grass and watch the stars, and he thought that nobody would ever be able to count them. He would lay there and look at the moon and dream that one day he would aim one of his arrows at the moon and hit it with one of his bolts.

When Kootenay thought that they had enough provisions of smoked fish, they traveled on, following the only creek from the lake. During the day, the creek, which had started meandering through flowering meadows, became a deep canyon, and the trail they were following was pushed into dense forest. At the end of the day, they arrived at the banks of a fast-flowing river.

This had to be the River of the Bow. Kootenay wondered if the old Na-Koda might still be around, and wondered if he would visit him. He pushed it out of his mind since he didn't know how far it was to the old man's cave. Besides he was on his way home.

When he saw the fast-flowing Bow River, swollen with run-off from melting snow, he knew that he couldn't cross the river even with a raft. He decided to make camp and the next day follow the river upstream to where the shallow ford had to be.

In the setting sun, he could see the vertical rock wall his companion had called Yam-Nuska. The following day it took him all day to reach the Yam-Nuska Wall and ford the river. His dog Keeno had to swim most of the time while Kootenay had to carry all their food and gear. He was dead tired when he crawled under his bearskin that evening, in the high grass on the other side of the river.

Keeno, as if he knew that his master had done all the work that day, kept guard all night. He heard the bear who prowled around the camp all night, but it never bothered the camp. The pack of coyotes who got a scent of their fish in their noses decided to stay clear when they got a scent of Keeno and his master; they knew that it was bad medicine to tackle with this man and dog team, and left them alone.

As they didn't have to worry about food, Kootenay headed toward the rising sun and the wide flood plain of the river. From there he could see the pass through the heavily forested foothills.

On pleasant forest trails, they entered into another valley of verdant meadows and murmuring brooks with pools full of fish. This pleasant landscape of green hills and bubbling streams invited them to linger. They lived on fish and spruce grouse. Keeno learned how to catch birds, and Kootenay had a lot of fun shooting them with arrows.

Further toward the sun, Kootenay saw the snow-covered ramparts of the Ni-Ha-Hi. It took them a full day to travel the length of this ridge. The Sik-Sika brave had been right, it was impossible to climb across this ridge with a dog. They marched on to the spot where the ridge dropped down toward the valley, where a crystal-clear stream came rushing out of the mountains.

But where was the other stream? His companion had been talking about the confluence of two rivers! Where was the second river? He seemed to be stuck in this thick forest with a river in front of him and nowhere to go. There was only one thing to do; he had to climb the ridge to above timberline to orient himself. But how? The forest was so dense and finding a way through seemed impossible.

He made his way along the river to the spot where the esker of the Ni-Ha-Hi dropped steep into the river. He had to walk along the very edge of this dangerous cliff to gain any elevation. Only a very thin cover of vegetation kept the gravel from sliding into the river below. Where the trees thinned out he could see where the valley widened and where he thought another valley started. That made him decide to turn around and follow to where he hoped would be the meeting of the two rivers.

Bushwhacking along a river with washed-out riverbanks is never easy, so when he found a spot where the river widened he decided to ford the river.

He found the tracks of deer, wapiti, and moose. This was reassuring. That he was on the right trail he found out after he crossed a swampy piece of land and he saw the river wild and clear.

Pleasant days of travel were had in this valley. As soon as he had walked for a while, he felt as if the climate was milder, or was it just because the sun shone into this valley all day long? Sleeping under the bearskin by pools full of fish and only the stars for a roof over his head made him forget the hardships of winter.

After the third day along this river, he saw a high mountain covered with ice and snow. He thought that it was the highest mountain he had seen in a long time. The river he followed had become a small creek before he had to cross another creek that came tumbling down from the glacier on the top of the mountain. On the other side of the valley, he saw herds of wapiti grazing peacefully, a sure sign that nobody had been up there to hunt. At this time, Kootenay had no interest in wapiti; he wouldn't disturb them as long as he had fish. While he was thinking that, he stood at the shore of a small lake. In the shallows, barely above where he had just crossed the creek, he could see countless small trout; so many he saw that he thought the sandy bottom was covered with them.

Immediately he started looking for a camping spot. On the side of the lake, he had to cross a wide field of scree. He had to walk all around the lake to the other side before he found a small meadow where he built a lean-to from fallen trees and covered it carefully with branches. In front of the open side of his shelter, where it was always in his view, he built his smoking rack.

From there the meadow sloped gently down to the lake. Even now, in the middle of summer, part of the meadow was covered with bright yellow glacier lilies. Kootenay and his dog stayed here for quite a few days until a big bear, who liked to eat the bulbs of lilies, came close to their shelter.

Early the next morning, they moved on since Kootenay expected the bear to return to dig up more of his favored food. If he discovered their fish, he would have made life miserable for them. It wasn't far from the lake to the height of the pass, and from there to a green meadow and a wide open ridge was only a very short climb. From this barren ridge Kootenay had his first view of what the Na-Koda people had called Kana-Naskis.

He stood in awe. He had never seen anything as beautiful as that. Beneath his moccasins stretched a wide valley covered with dense, verdant forests, with rivers and lakes and waterfalls. On the far side, a gigantic wall of ice and rock touched the blue sky as far as the eye could see. Then what he saw made him wonder if it was real. Out of a wall of glittering ice a black tower of rock pointed toward the sky. Had he not seen that warning tower of rock before? Only from this side it was leaning slightly.

It had been a few summers when he stood beneath this mighty tower of stone. He was afraid. At this moment of recognition, he shouted in defiance, "Waka-Nambe." An echo brought him the answer, "Waka-Nambe."

At this time of the day, huge, puffy white clouds were rising above the ice fields and drifted across this landscape adorned with natural wonders. The same clouds that had formed above the ice dissolved and disappeared as mysteriously as they had formed over the next mountain range. The clouds, puffy and white, looked like they were ripped to shreds by powers unseen and unknown. Of course that what he was watching were the same forces that caused the snow-eater wind that could make the snow melt within hours.

It is easy to forget time when you are reclining in a flowering meadow and the larks are singing above and around you is the buzzing of bees. That he had been privileged to get a glimpse of Shangri-La he would realize many years later when the White people came.

They built fences across the land and made it their own. Many times he would tell his people about the sacred trail of the Kootenay, and it was him who encouraged the young people to walk the trail, to suffer hardship and privation, but also enjoy the gifts of plenty to invoke the spirits of their fathers.

It was late in the day when Kootenay and his dog traveled on. It didn't matter how far or how fast the sun sets behind the mountains. When he reached the height of the pass, he found himself on open alpine meadows and the mountain range on his right still stretched as far as the eye could see. The flaming sky from the setting sun left one side of the mountains in total darkness, while on his left the golden glow crept up over the rocky crags until it lost itself in outer space.

They found the protecting branches of a stunted tree good shelter for the night. The next morning when the slanting rays of the rising sun touched the mountaintops, they walked down into another valley. Kootenay had noted that he had crossed another watershed. This time one stream flowed toward midnight. The creek, next to the trail he was on now, flowed toward the midday sun. That confused Kootenay. Up to now most rivers on this side of the Shining Mountains flowed toward the rising sun; this one didn't.

Kootenay had been following the small river all day when the puzzle of the river that flowed in the wrong direction was solved. It was there that the river made a sharp left turn. At this point, the river had found an outlet from its mountain-fastness by chewing through a mountain range and flowing where it was supposed to flow, toward the rising sun. Kootenay crossed the river there and kept on walking toward the noonday sun. From there the land began to rise as he followed a dry creekbed.

All day long he was on a steady uphill climb. Slowly the trees became shorter until only stunted bushes remained from what used to be a dense pine forest lower down. When he finally reached a flat plateau where all trees had given up the struggle against the unforgiving elements, he found the ground covered by sweet-smelling mountain avens. Under his moccasins it felt like walking on soft cushions.

When he turned around, he could see the sharp outline of the Shining Mountains, which he knew he had to cross to go to his home by the lake of the Kootenay. He realized that somewhere he had gone wrong.

Now, completely out in the open, on top of a barren plateau, he was hit by strong gusts of wind. It was getting dark, while behind him the sky still glowed in a golden sunset. He had to find shelter fast. But up there, exposed to the wind, there was no shelter to be found, no rock or tree to hide behind, nothing. With the wind in his back, he walked toward what he thought was the edge of a cliff until he found a spot where he could step down onto a sloping bench covered with dry grass. He had to be careful there. Only after his eyes had adjusted to the darkness could he see that the plateau dropped off sharply, he couldn't see the bottom.

How large the spot was, he didn't know, but he managed to sit down his back against the rock wall and stretch his legs. When he managed to pull his bear robe over himself and his dog, he knew he would be warm and survive the night, a night full of monstrous dreams and fitful sleep.

Once he dreamed his dog had fallen over the cliff. When he looked down, he could see his dog falling, falling, falling. When he woke up, drenched in cold sweat, he turned around and reached to his side. There was his dog licking his hand. For a short while, he went back to sleep. It wasn't a deep sleep like he was used to when he was in a comfortable teepee with the Sik-Sika. He heard when the wind stopped, and now he could hear all kinds of things. He heard when falling rocks rattled over the cliffs below him. He heard when a pack of coyotes above him went about their nocturnal errand. It was one of those nights when morning didn't want to come. When it finally came he was wide awake.

As a traveler in these parts, Kootenay already knew that one must expect unforeseen perils or, on the other side, unexpected pleasures on the trails one has to travel. That the spot where he and his dog were spending the night, which he had chosen unwittingly and out of desperation, would offer him a view of an ocean of grass at sunrise, what he had come there to see in the first place, he couldn't know when he sat down in almost total darkness.

Long before the sun rose above the flat horizon, shafts of orange light danced far into the still dark sky only to fall back to the celestial source from whence they had come. Then the whole horizon of the celestial hemisphere began to burn in a smokeless fire, which intensified at the very spot where the new day was born out of a sea of dry grass. At the very moment when the sun rose above the horizon, Kootenay had to close his eyes, as they were still used to the darkness of the night. When he opened his eyes again, the walls of the sky had moved far away to such unimaginable distances that he couldn't believe the world was that big. Above him the golden dome of the sky began to pale into a gentle blue of day.

As the golden sun began to warm him, he stretched his legs. Then he looked around and realized how precarious and exposed the perch he had chosen for the night really was. He lay down and looked over the cliff. When he saw the dark forest below a band of gravel, he pulled back and retreated to safer ground with his dog.

While Kootenay was organizing his bundle, Keeno ran away. When Kootenay looked up, he saw him chasing ptarmigan. The birds, still in their summer feathers, were almost invisible when they sat still on the ground. Kootenay found out that the birds were so convinced of their disguise they didn't fly until he almost stepped on them, but once he knew what they looked like, he had no problem getting close enough to hit them with his arrows. Right after he shot one, Keeno returned carrying a bird, too. Now that Kootenay knew where to get fresh fowl, he decided to stick around and hunt ptarmigan.

Before they could set up camp, they needed water. For that, they had to move down the mountain, below the treeline, where they found a dry creekbed. In this region, most creeks dried up fast after the winter snow melted. Further down, where they found stagnant pools of water. Kootenay decided to set up camp. The water, pure and clean, stilled their thirst. Kootenay had become an experienced backwoodsman in his travels in the wilderness, and to him, the forest provided everything within easy reach. There was enough fallen timber for a lean-to and soft moss for a warm bed. Not too far away, he found the rocks for his firepit.

Then came a few days in sun and wind. Kootenay and his dog walked the high ground far above treeline hunting ptarmigan. The morning was the best hunting. The birds seemed lethargic from the cold night. At first, Kootenay wondered why Keeno could see the birds so far away. Then he realized that his dog got the scent of the birds long before he could see them. Every time Keeno crouched down, he had the smell of a bird in his nose. Now Keeno moved very slowly and without making a sound. With lightning speed, he pounced upon the invisible bird, sometimes knocking him out of flight.

The next day they hunted as a team, Kootenay and Keeno walking side by side. Once the dog knew what Kootenay was up to, he stood still and pointed. Kootenay was lucky enough to experience the thrills and delights of hunting with bow and arrow and to have the privilege of the companionship of a good dog. Whether he carried home a full bag or just a romp and wander, to Kootenay and his dog, it was all the same. At this time, Kootenay couldn't know yet how valuable such seemingly unimportant incidents would be in his later life, when responsibilities for his people burdened him down with worries.

One night, Kootenay and Keeno were resting stretched out on a patch of dry mountain avens in total darkness. The sky was filled with billions of stars and a golden moon. That night, Kootenay renewed his thought that one day he would shoot one of his arrows all the way to the moon, and he would hit it, too. I know that nobody will believe that it was an Indian boy who first had the idea of sending one of his missiles to the moon, but then, nobody knows what Kootenay was thinking about during that night. To him goes the honor of having first thought of sending one of his missiles to the moon.

It was also during that night that Kootenay's travel plans were changed for one summer. It was during that mild night, while they were sitting on a rock on top of a mountain watching the play of Northern Lights toward midnight, when far out there in the sweetgrass, Kootenay saw the twinkle of lights. That those lights were campfires of Na-Koda, Sik-Sika and Tsuut'ina people he couldn't know, nor could he know that the lights were set among a range of hills where there was good water and good grass. Only the following day, after he had decided that he would go and investigate, did he realize that what he had thought to be the haze of a warm day was the smoke of the many lodges and fires.

They walked along the cliff until it narrowed into a rock band and was easy to climb through. From there a barren, windswept ridge pointed to a green valley below. Keeno carried a heavy load, including a string of birds dangling from his bundle, so did Kootenay. While they were climbing through the rock band, Kootenay hadn't noticed dark, threatening thunder clouds building up behind them. Under those threatening clouds, they descended down the barren ridge into a green valley expecting to be drenched by rain at any moment, but it didn't rain. Kootenay watched the clouds drifting far out into the sweetgrass, with lightning flashing from the clouds and streaks of rain hanging below those clouds. No drop of rain ever touched the earth where he was, or as far out into the parched plain as he could see.

Kootenay, of course, had never seen anything like that. It rained and no moisture came down to the earth. When he later told his people about the thunder that didn't bring rain, he called it "Running Rain," but the people didn't believe him because they didn't think that it was possible that rain, walking across the land, could evaporate so fast in the dry air that it couldn't reach the ground. That the air on the other side of the Shining Mountains could be so dry that rain would sometimes disappear before it reached the parched earth they would not believe, but the name Running Rain stuck to him. He was to be known by that name for the rest of his long life. But, at the moment, Kootenay and his dog were walking down a barren ridge with many skeletons of dead trees sticking their ghost-like trunks into the dry air like hands begging for rain. For days, they walked over grassy hills where only low bushes could survive in the harsh wind and dry air.

Only along creek beds, where there was some moisture left on the ground from melting snow, rows of poplars could be seen. After the first frost, the leaves had turned into that translucent gold that made the world shine with warmth.

One day, Kootenay heard the thunder of horses' hoofs on the other side of a hill, but the riders didn't see him, as they were passing in a fast gallop and Kootenay and Keeno were hiding under some rosebushes. It was the following day that Kootenay first saw the encampment of Na-Koda, Sik-Sika, and Nara-Wak peoples along a creek among the willows. He was well hidden on a hill in some Saskatoon bushes that still had some dry berries on them. The dry berries tasted sweet and made him feel good after eating nothing but ptarmigan and rosehips. The first thing he noticed was that these people had many horses; most of them were hobbled and feeding on dry grass. Only mares with foals seemed to be allowed to roam free. No braves were visible; only squaws and children were running around and doing chores.

Kootenay knew that he had to approach with great caution. He didn't pay any attention to the squaws; it was the young braves he had to worry about. If they were riding a horse, they could easily run him down. He decided to wait until the sun was setting before approaching the camp. In the meantime, he was eating Saskatoon berries.

When the sun went down behind the Shining Mountains, Kootenay appeared out of the bushes and walked toward the closest teepee. Not a soul was stirring until he walked out from behind some willows. Then a young squaw appeared. He startled her. She made an attempt to run, but he held her and so stopped her from running away.

He said to her, in the dialect he had learned from the Sik-Sika at the Yaha-Tinda, "I come in peace. I am Kootenay from across the Shining Mountains, but I am bringing greetings from the Sik-Sika who are hunting at the Yaha-Tinda." Then he handed her the last two birds he had dangling on a string. She stood there for a moment not knowing what to do, holding the two birds. Then she said, "Come," and walked ahead of him to a teepee that stood separate from the rest and was covered with buffalo hides.

She bent down and opened a leather flap and said a few words he couldn't understand. An old man with snow-white hair appeared from under the flap, hanging around his shoulders was a buffalo robe that seemed to bend the old man down even more than he was. The girl now laid down the two ptarmigan in front of the old man, turned around, and walked away. When she was gone, the old man turned slowly toward Kootenay. It seemed to Kootenay that it was time to speak.

He now said, "I am Kootenay, and I come from the country across the Shining Mountains."

The man spoke in a different dialect, but Kootenay could make out what he was saying. But, to make things worse, the old man seemed puzzled and said, "If you are the great hunter who stayed with our people at the Yaha-Tinda I have heard about you. You have helped to feed the people up there, and you are welcome in my lodge."

Kootenay now said, "I am the same. I stayed at the Yaha-Tinda and at the River of the Red Deer. I was on my way home when I lost my trail. Then, one night, I saw the many fires of your people. Now I'm here hoping I could take advantage of your hospitality and ask for directions."

"You are very lucky, my son. Come, we will smoke the pipe, and you can tell me about your people."

They went inside the teepee and sat down. It was warm inside. The fire had burned down. Only the glow from the dying embers spread a wholesome warmth.

They smoked the pipe silently, and then Kootenay became drowsy. When, after a long time, the squaw appeared with the two ptarmigan she had roasted on skewers. They ate and drank water from a leather pouch. When Kootenay took the rest of the birds out to his dog, the old man was sound asleep. The old man hadn't allowed Kootenay to bring his dog inside since he didn't know the close relationship between Kootenay and Keeno.

During his stay in the camp, Kootenay took part in one of the last buffalo jumps ever to take place in Chinook country, at Head Smashed In. After that no In-Ni would return to feed in the dry sweetgrass of Chinook country, and the people would go hungry. Many starved.

Kootenay learned a lot during the days of the buffalo hunt. It was while the sun was setting behind the Shining Mountains that Kootenay had helped to set the fires that would force the herd over the cliffs. Braves on horseback rounded up the In-Ni. When he heard the thunder of many hooves coming toward him out of the sunset, he noticed a mighty bull trying to break through the ring of fire. The hooves of the primordial beast shook the earth under Kootenay's feet when he saw the shaggy beast approaching out of the smoke to where he stood. There seemed to be nothing he could do to force the beast to follow the rest of the herd. His bow and arrows seemed puny against this earthquake of muscle and horns. How many arrows would it take to kill a beast like this? His arrows wouldn't even penetrate through his shaggy mane.

All he saw at that moment was two mighty horns and the hot breath of the bull. He knew he had no time left before he was trampled to death by the monster's hooves and those to follow. And still he stood his ground. When he had the rancid stench of the gargantuous beast in his nose, at that very moment of desperation, he had the answer. In those split seconds of despair, when he thought his life would end there in the sweetgrass, in the setting sun of Chinook country, he held a bundle of dry grass in his hand and set it on fire. When the bull was almost on top of him, he shoved the flaming blaze into the monster's nose. It was the power of the will of the young human being, a man who had learned to hold fire in his hands for a split second, that made the mighty beast change direction. Then there was the smell of singed mane and burning flesh and the beast was gone, over the cliff. There was the thunder of horses' hooves when the mounted braves forced the last In-Ni over the cliff. Then there was great silence.

Kootenay was seen sitting there by himself licking his burned hands, smelling the wind and the sweetgrass and watching the last fire of the setting sun behind the Shining Mountains where he would be going soon. During the coming days, there was great rejoicing in the camp. Many squaws came from all over sweetgrass country to prepare the meat and claim their share. During the coming winter, the people would have enough to eat. At night there was hard frost so no meat spoiled. When the hunters finally left, the remaining offal was cleaned up by wolves and coyotes and ravens.

25

After the first hard frost and a two-day snowfall, the weather cleared and turned into the most beautiful Indian summer. Before reaching the high ridges of the foothills, Kootenay and his dog walked along the creeks under golden poplars during the warm fall days. Kootenay thought that if he traveled fast he could still make it across the Shining Mountains on the trails explained to him by the old man. He had listened very carefully to the old man but, as it turned out, not carefully enough. He traveled toward midnight, and when he saw the first creek flowing out of the Shining Mountains, he thought that there would be a pass through the sheer rocks right there. He had to cross a very fast-flowing creek. He thought it would be difficult until he found a beaver dam. In the end, it allowed him to get across with dry feet. Then he followed a well-worn game trail, which brought him to one of the most beautiful lakes on the sunrise-side of the Shining Mountains, but there was no pass through the wall of stone that rose up until the snow touched the sky.

The lake wasn't large. On one side it was very shallow; on the other side a gravel field flowed from the rock wall into the lake. In the deep, blue-green water, there were many fish, little fish so high in the mountains, but with his dipnet, he would be able to feed himself for a long time. Now he raised his eyes from the water and looked back down into the valley from where he had come; he saw a mountain crowned by a layer of drifting mist. Kootenay decided to build his camp there and stay for a while.

Only a few steps from the lake he noticed a huge boulder. The boulder had obviously rolled down from the mountain when the spot where it came to rest was still under water and part of the lake. When the glacier ice melted, it deposited the fertile soil, which formed the level ground, and Kootenay now found it covered by flowering asters and yellow buttercups. When he got close to the rock, he found that it formed a shallow cave, which had been used by deer, sheep, and goats for shelter, as the ground was covered by all kinds of droppings.

It would also serve as shelter for Kootenay and his dog. During his travels, Kootenay had learned to build a lean-to, which suited him best for his sense of security and maximum protection from the elements. The lean-to would have an opening in the front where he built his firepit. The opening could be closed off by pulling a few branches across, but while he had a good fire, he kept it open to enjoy the warmth of the fire. However, the best part of it was that it received the first warm rays of the morning sun. He wasted no time going about his task, using the skills of the experienced woodsman, getting the necessary firewood to his campsite. An armful of branches would make a fine bed for him and his dog.

Without realizing it, Kootenay had discovered a little bit of paradise; a spectacular penetrable forests on the other, surrounded the blue-green waters of this lake with the adjoining flowering meadows. Toward the rising sun, where the creek that drained the lake in the spring broke through the rocks, the mountains, which Kootenay named the Mountains of the Mist, revealed themselves to Kootenay every morning, and soon Kootenay felt at home there.

Had he known how close he was to Kootenay country and his home, he might have moved on, and who knows, this lake might have a different name that it has today. As it turned out, the following spring, when he looked at the same mountains from the other side, he realized no matter how close to your destination, there are times when a detour is needed to find your way home.

When, on the following morning, he started his fishing, he found that he needed a very long handle for his dipnet to get down to where the schools of fish were congregating. He found the right willow pole on the other side of the lake.

During the fall, while Kootenay stayed at the lake, the weather remained nice and warm, and Kootenay forgot all about time. Even when the sun couldn't sink any lower and touched his camp only for a while at midday, he felt no desire to move on.

Even during the night, only a thin sheet of ice formed on the lake, and he had no problem keeping his fishing hole open.

Then one night the inevitable snowstorm hit the valley with a fury, and it snowed and stormed for days. After Kootenay dug himself out, he found that while he slept and rested, he had been snowed under and his camp was completely isolated and cut off from the rest of the world. For Kootenay, there was no panic; he had smoked enough fish to last him for a long time. To get around in the deep snow, he still had his old snowshoes. The only work he had to do was keeping his fishing hole open in the lake if he wanted fresh fish. Even his camp spot was well chosen, he found out during the next snowstorm, when he heard the hissing sound of snowslides coming down from the mountains. No slide ever came close to the spot where he slept safely under the snow.

While he could hold out until the snow settled, wapiti and deer suffered many privations. As long as they could dig through the snow on the wind-swept ridges, they stayed away from his camp. Now they lost their fear of the human and his dog. It was starvation that forced them down from the high meadows to lakeshore and the creek where the willows were the only food they could find. One day, Kootenay watched the animals feed all day on willow buds. When he approached them, they didn't walk away; only during the night did they disappear into the warmer forest.

The presence of a large herd of animals in the valley, not far from his camp, also attracted a mountain lion, and later Kootenay found the tracks of a pack of wolves. That caused him to keep a campfire going day and night. With the fire, he felt safe.

Even the longest winter had to come to an end. The sun rose higher above the horizon. Down there by the lake, it became very warm on sunny days, and the snow began to melt. Then one day, slides of heavy, wet snow came thundering down from the mountains. Sometimes the thunder was so loud it scared Kootenay. On the following day, a monstrous avalanche came thundering down from the cliffs; a whole mountain had shaken the complete burden of snow from its shoulders.

The debris from the slide, together with rocks and stone, covered part of the lake and filled in his fishing hole in the ice before it stopped. Luckily for Kootenay and his dog, they were on the other side of the lake at the logjam fishing, where there was some open water, and they had watched the occurrence from a safe distance. Kootenay watched how the thundering mass of snow formed a huge unstoppable snowball that ripped rock and stone from their foundations. A stand of trees was swept aside like with a mighty broom, and all was swept downhill. Only a short while after the slide stopped came the thunder and then a wave of compressed air that almost swept Kootenay off the log he was standing upon.

The masses of sliding snow had only just stopped when another catastrophe approached. This one walked on four legs, was black, and expressed its discontent in angry grunts like a wild bear. It was a wild bear! Part of the same den, where the black bear spent every winter in hibernation, had been torn away by the avalanche, and Mr. Bruin had been rudely disturbed in his slumber. Now he came charging down the tightly packed snow looking for somebody to vent his indignation upon. Since he was a local resident of some ill repute, due to the fact that he was always in a bad mood when he came out of hibernation, he had no good reputation to defend. He was mad, and he was hungry. So he headed for the spot where he knew the big rock was supposed to be. There was always somebody there trying to find shelter. This time it was Kootenay who had found shelter with his dog Keeno. This also had to be the worst spot to be in when facing a grumpy bear. Since he couldn't see too well, he used his nose to find the rock, which was still covered with snow and was also Kootenay's food cache, where he stored his fish under the snow.

The hungry bear stopped in his tracks when he got wind of the fish. So far Kootenay had watched all this with the greatest equanimity, but now that he saw his food supply in danger, he made a big mistake, which would have disastrous consequences for himself and his dog. He forgot that you never interfered with a hungry bear while he was feeding. Keeno, who had had the bear in his nose for a long time, charged toward the bear. Kootenay tried to call him back, but this time Keeno wouldn't stop in his rage to sink his fangs into the monster.

Kootenay grabbed his spear, leaving his net and the fish he had caught behind, and charged toward the bear. Maybe between Keeno and himself they might be able to scare the beast away from his food. In the meantime, the bear, having found the fish under the snow, was munching away at their provisions when Keeno charged him from behind, sinking his fangs into its neck without result. The winter fur of the beast was so thick, his teeth couldn't penetrate deep enough. The bear, now annoyed at the pesky dog on his back, shook him off like a mere puppy.

Kootenay arrived at the scene in time to watch the sad end of this bloody encounter before he could even strike a blow with his spear. The bear, while shaking off the dog, had turned around and now, with his back against the rock, was sitting on his haunches. Keeno, who at first didn't want to let go, fell right between the paws of the monster. Now the bear brought his right paw down on Keeno with one swiping blow.

The blow pulled the hide and shoulder off Keeno's body, broke his back, and killed him instantly. Kootenay, knowing that his chances to overcome this gigantic beast without the help of Keeno were not good, stood there facing the bear, but he stood his ground with the bear's eyes on him. What the bear could see in those human eyes went past fear; it was a limitless determination to prevail.

Now a true miracle took place, which may have saved Kootenay's life. While Kootenay stood there, his spear ready to strike, his eyes on the beast, the bear, who had no quarrel with Kootenay, looked like all the anger had gone out of him when he saw Keeno lying there dead. Only the upper part of the bear swayed back and forth, as if he were deciding what to do. Then he turned sideways, away from Kootenay, and ambled up the hill from where he had come after the avalanche destroyed his den. Whether it was the fact that he wasn't hungry any more that he changed his mind or the power of the will of the human with the deadly spear, we will never know.

Now, with the danger of the bear gone for the moment, Kootenay felt an urge to run away as fast as he could. After a few steps, he turned around and kneeled down next to the dead body of Keeno, whose fur was still warm, touched the stump of the ear which had been bitten off by wolves many years before, and cried. For the first time in his life, with the death of his faithful companion, he was aware of the mortality of all life, even his own. How long he sat there sobbing and tears running down his cheeks he didn't know. Then, when he realized that the bear would come back to look for more fish when he got hungry again and would find the dead dog and eat him, too, he took the body of his dead dog and carried him to the top of the remains of the avalanche, dug a hole in the snow, put his dog in, and covered it first with rocks and then with snow. He hoped that the bear wouldn't find Keeno, and later, when the snow melted, the remains would disappear in the lake, where he would remain forever.

Kootenay, fully realizing that he couldn't remain there any longer with a hungry bear out of hiberation, found all his gear intact under the rock. All the fish had been eaten by the bear. He walked to the other side of the lake, where he found the fish he had caught not far from the logjam. His snowshoes and fishing net were there, too. He took his gear and crossed the logjam. On the other side, he strapped on his snowshoes; the snow was still deep there. He found a trail that pointed straight to the river he had crossed in the fall of the beaver dam.

26

The river followed a straight line along the same mountains he had to cross, toward midnight. He found going on the frozen river easier than in the forest. He walked day and night. During the night, the snow that was soft and tacky during the day froze to a hard crust, which carried him and was easy to walk on. When the moon came out and illuminated the valley with a pale, mellow light, he found walking much easier than during the day. He pushed on during the night, even when the riverbed ended, as if it was possible to walk away from his newfound realization of mortality. Why was it that this animal, which he had fed when it was still a puppy, had to die? Was he part of the same process? He walked until he couldn't walk any more. At daybreak, he dug himself deep into a snowbank, ate one of the fish he still had from the lake raw, and fell asleep. How long he slept he didn't know.

He woke up when the warm rays of the afternoon sun touched his face. His right hand reached around him; he found his spear but not his dog. That's why his feet were getting cold; he didn't have his dog any longer. He was overcome by the realization that he now was all alone in the world. Inside of him was a deep hurt, an emptiness that caused him much pain; this pain, unknown to him up to now, was different than any other pain he had suffered in his young life. He had suffered the pain of hunger, of thirst, of cold and heat, but this was different. It made him feel that life as he had known it wasn't worth living any longer.

When he pushed on, he realized that the frozen creek he was walking on was on a slight downhill slope. During the night, he had crossed another continental divide unnoticed. The landscape was familiar to him; he had traveled up here before. In his pain he hadn't seen it. The going got more dangerous when he had to cross the scattered debris of avalanches, which had piled up during the winter in the creekbed. When the narrow valley widened, he realized that he was back at the place the people here called Kana-Naskis. Then he knew he was on the right track; he wouldn't make the same mistake twice. Later in the day, when he saw the dark fist of Waka-Nambe in ice and snow lit up by the setting sun, he knew where he had to go.

The following day it was gut-wrenching hunger that made him forget the lonesome misery of his existence. He was now in a dense forest. The snow was deep here; without his snowshoes he wouldn't have been able to move.

He needed food badly. He saw the tracks of wabasso. The white rabbits were almost impossible to see in the forest when they sat still, but when they moved, Kootenay could see them. He also found the tracks of them, and the tracks of the wolves who hunted them. As the rabbits had never seen a human being, they remained sitting when he fired his deadly arrows. He hunted rabbits for a few days while he walked along forested mountains, crossed creek beds and open spaces where forest fires had burned large tracts of timber; only the thin trunks of scorched trees were left standing like dead skeletons. On the open meadows of the pass, he hunted ptarmigan. Here he missed his dog Keeno, who was so good at catching the birds. In beautiful sunshine, he crossed the Great Divide, which he realized when he found that the river he saw flowed toward the midday sun. The source of the river he now followed was two lakes, one of which was still frozen. While one of the lakes was open along the shoreline, it made good fishing, and he did like his people had always done when they found good fishing. An old campsite that hadn't been used for many summers was there. A circle of stones told him that here had stood a teepee at one time; the old lodge poles had rotted away in the grass. The snow had melted there in the warm sun. On a steep hillside, close by, a meadow full of yellow glacier-lillies made the day seem brighter.

After stocking up with fish, he traveled on along the trail, which followed the river towards the midday sun. One of the first things he discovered was that he was now on the warm side of the Shining Mountains. Indeed it was a lot warmer there.

Later he became aware that the sheer mountains, which he now had at sunrise, were the same mountains he had left at the lake which would later be called Running Rain Lake. Not more than a day's travel later, where a fast-flowing creek joined the river, he made a right turn because the landscape felt familiar. He followed a creek, which was in full flood with spring runoff. The going was slow there. In the heavily timbered valley, there was much dead-fall and snow. The only reason why he made any headway at all was the fact that he had a pair of good snowshnoes. Kootenay had discovered the "Pass in the Clouds." When he turned around at the height of the pass, he could see a mountain range so high the peaks were in the clouds. Many mountains carried glacial ice. These were the mountains on which the heavens rested.

Kootenay had seen them from the side where the sun rises, and the people called them Kana-Naskis. From every snowfield, waterfalls rushed toward the swollen rivers below, and the sound of the falling waters was everywhere. From the Pass in the Clouds he could look along a river valley. Far away in the milky haze of the warm day he saw a group of mountains; he thought it looked like the Top of the World.

247

Of course, he couldn't be certain. Going down on the other side from the Pass in the Clouds was much easier. After he walked across a frozen lake, he could take his snowshoes off. Walking became faster and easier on a good game trail.

The next river he came to was muddy with spring runoff. He knew there would be no fishing there. Had Kootenay known that this was the same river he had started from on his odyssey to find the secret trail of the Kootenay, he would have been very happy because he would have known that he was only a few days away from seeing his friend Old Kootenay. In the meantime, the only things that reminded him that he was close to home were the shimmering mountains below the midday sun.

On one morning, he heard the honking sound of white swans. Looking up into the blue, he saw a pair of white swans cruising toward midnight. Then he knew that the Lake of the White Swans was close.

Where the river turns toward midnight, he crossed the rushing waters. It was a difficult undertaking to cross there, but he knew the trail along the lake continued on the other side of the river; it would take him to the campsite at White Swan Lake.

The lake was free of ice; the willows along the shore were heavy with flowering pussy willows, and with the summer voices of the bees came the sweet smell of honey. The familiar camp looked like it had been used recently, even the birchbark of the roof was still intact. After he built a fire, he stored his gear in the teepee. Then he was out fishing.

It seemed easy to him to catch fish there; he never thought that he was a lot more experienced now that he was when he left this place a few summers ago. He caught enough fish to carry a big load down to the camp of Old Kootenay. He was going to go down tomorrow; even with a heavy load he could do it easily in one day. Being home he slept soundly.

He didn't hear the howling of the wolves. They had the smell of his fish in their noses, but there was also the smell of fire. They didn't dare.

Out of the soundless quiet of the morning, he heard the faint sound of countless wings. Kootenay rushed out into the open. At first the world seemed empty when he sat down on the rock by the lake, but then out of the purple dawn above the horizon they came, the white swans. By the thousands they came, and Kootenay sat there and watched how the early morning sun broke through their silver wings when they settled down on the placid waters.

Kootenay didn't leave for Old Kootenay's camp the next day, he knew the birds would rest and feed there for at least one day before they took off again to follow the River of the Kootenay. Then, after a long flight they would gain enough altitude to cross the Shining Mountains, the same road he had traveled which had taken him a whole summer to do, the secret trail of the Kootenay.

The next morning, again he watched the birds. Every one making the same maneuver, treading water, turning into the wind, gaining enough speed, and lifting off. Then the flapping sound of the mighty wings was heard as the birds gained altitude and formed a flexible V-formation.

Up in the sky above him, two birds were cruising in great circles and giving instructions to the birds ready for takeoff. Kootenay listened for a long time and watched the birds. Then, on this magic morning, he learned to understand the language of the white swans.

The trip from the camp at White Swan Lake to Old Kootenay's camp wasn't very far, but Kootenay carried a heavy load of food and his own bundle. He traveled a little slower than normal. He knew he had to leave the main trail and climb down the steep riverbank to the spot where the river made the bend Kootenay stopped often. He hesitated; he doesn't know why. Something was very wrong.

Around any camp where there was activity, there was a certain something, a certain smell. It took a while for him to realize there was no smell of smoke; there hadn't been a fire there for a long time. He dropped his bundle and started running now that he knew there was something wrong. When he got to the firepit, he found everything overgrown with small bushes and grass. The ashes that should have been there in the firepit had long since washed into the river by the rain; only the bleached bones of rabbits and deer remained among the rocks, telling that people had lived there.

There was no sign of Old Kootenay. But where did Old Kootenay go, and how long ago did he leave? How many summers was it since he had walked out on Old Kootenay? He couldn't remember. Kootenay walked the few steps up to the cave where the old man had slept when he stayed there. The curtain the old man had used to close off the entrance had fallen apart; the inside of the cave was devastated by a pack of wolves. The wolves had ripped everything apart that had the smell of human being on it. Only a few lumps of moss and some dry grass remained of the warm bed that Old Kootenay had rested on when he stayed there.

But where could he have gone? He had always told him that he would never leave this place; that he would spend his remaining days there. Could he have gone to the Top of the World and terminated his life there? Not easily; he was too old to go there by himself. He had difficulties when Kootenay went up there with him.

Up in the rocks, where Old Kootenay stored his food, the young man found the old man's pipe, which he used only on special occasions, and a pouch full of tobacco. Then there was the hot pool; he found the trail, but the trail hadn't been used for a long time. Much of it was washed out by rain and melting snow, gravel slides covered much of it. The going was difficult there; he couldn't afford to slip and fall into the swollen river. There were no footprints. The pool itself hadn't been used for a long time; a lot of rotting leaves had collected on the sandy bottom. The pool felt as inviting as ever. He felt the spot where the hot spring bubbled out of the ground while cleaning out the bottom of the pool. He decided to come back later but first he had to set up his camp.

Collecting firewood was no problem. There were so many broken-down branches and dead trees there that told him the old man hadn't been around for a long time. He would have used up all the firewood so close to the camp. Then Kootenay stored his fish in the old man's food cache in the rocks.

For the moment, he had forgotten about the old man. As he was walking toward the hot pool, there he undressed completely. All winter long, during his stay at Running Rain lake, he had been looking forward to that, to the utter luxury of lolling without desires or destination in the hot mineral water as long as he wanted to in order to absorb the mysterious healing powers of the center of the universe, of which he felt he was part. When he walked back to the cave, there were the stars in the sky and, around him, the wild sounds of the forest. In his cave, completely relaxed and dead tired and restored in mind and body, he fell down under his bearskin and slept.

He was up early the next morning, long before the sun rose above the forest and touched his cave. He walked down to the pool on this early summer morning for a last dip in the hot water. Then he was on the trail. He hoped to find the spot where he had hidden his canoe in the willows so many summers ago before it became too hot.

Since he didn't have Keeno with him any longer, Kootenay decided to climb down through the most difficult part of the rock wall, where the cliff was the steepest. The trail hadn't been used since he left there, and much rolling gravel had collected. Kootenay knew he was prepared for that. As soon as he stepped into the loose gravel, it started moving. To Kootenay, that was nothing to worry about; he traveled with the sliding scree to the spot where the slide narrowed like a funnel and dropped over a cliff. There he had to jump out of the moving mass of stones and hang on to the rock wall until the slide ran its course. Below him, he heard the thunder as the slide went over the cliff, then there was the dust and the smell of sulphur, and then there was quiet.

The rest of the descent was easy as he lowered himself down a few feet to a steep, grassy meadow, where he had lowered his gear before. There he rested for a while and looked out over the familiar landscape. In the morning fog, he saw the end of the lake where he knew his old camp would be.

Before he swung his pack over his shoulder, he stood back in order to have another look at the cliff that had given him so much trouble when he climbed it for the first time. Not far below him now was the thunder of the waterfall, while he still looked at the rock wall high above. There was one spot above what he thought was a narrow ledge to which his eyes returned time and time again. Something was protruding from above that ledge that looked like a shelf-like projection from the sheer rock wall.

It could have been a piece of weather-beaten root from a tree that had grown up there at one time. But, when he thought of it, it didn't look like that. His curiosity aroused, he looked at the rock wall again to see if there was a possibility for him to climb to the spot where he could see that mysterious object hanging from the rocks. After a while of studying the rock wall, he decided that to climb through this wall to the spot would be impossible for him; the only way it could be done was to lower himself down from the top of the spot, if he had enough leather thongs.

From the top, it wasn't even that far, but to do this, he had to climb back up through the scree, which was hard work. He thought he had to do it because an awesome thought was torturing his mind. He would have to use all the leather thongs from his bundle and from his snowshoes to get a rope long enough to get to the spot where this thing was hanging from the rocks.

The day was getting hot when he climbed back up through the scree; now that the sun had come around to this side of the mountain, it was hiting the dark rocks with blazing heat. On the top, where the ledge would be below him, there was a spot of level ground, almost like a small meadow with a few stunted trees managing to survive in the thin, dry soil. Kootenay tied his rope to the closest tree and tried it first to see if it would hold. He thought that it would hold if he lay flat on the steep rocks and slid down until his feet could touch the ledge; then most of the weight would be off the rope anyway. He moved very slowly, using every handhold his fingers could find. Then, finally, his feet touched solid rock. Looking down between his knees, he saw his feet but not what he was looking for. He had to move sideways.

To his surprise, a shallow cave opened up in the rocks; he reached inside, and his hand found a crack to allow him to pull himself into the opening if he kneeled down. What he first saw was the legbones of a human being, still attached to the rest of a skeleton. To get further into the cave he had to lie down. Only after his eyes had adjusted to the dark shade could he see the remains of a complete human skeleton. He could feel his heart stopping for a moment. With a dry, rasping throat, he heard himself stammer, "Old Kootenay."

After he pulled the remains into the light, he could recognize Old Kootenay clearly. His eyes had been pecked out by birds; some of his long white hair was still attached to patches of mummified skin. All the rest of the flesh on his body had been eaten by ravens and crows and magpies and eagles and maybe some rodents who could get in there had done the rest.

It looked like the leg bones, still attached to the rest of Old Kootenay's remains, had been pulled to the cave opening by some bird, who had given up when he realized that the tendons were too strong and he couldn't pull the rest of skeleton out of the cave, but in this way he had exposed the earthly remains of Old Kootenay to the outside world and to the inquiring eyes of Kootenay. He now worked fast; he pushed the earthly remains of his old friend back into the cave, legs first, so that his now grotesque face with the empty eyesockets looked toward the mountains of the Top of the World and the rock spires across the valley. He could, as long as he remained in this position, watch when the golden rays of the morning sun touched the snowy mountains on the other side of his valley.

Now that Kootenay was ready to climb back up, there remained only one unanswered question. How had it been possible for Old Kootenay to get into this cave without leaving a sign as to how he got down the rock face? He looked around and found a knot made from the ends of two different leather thongs. The rest of the leather had been eaten by mice and squirrels over the years. This solved the puzzle. Old Kootenay had used a double rope of leather. When, after he lay down exhausted and ready to die, he couldn't undo the knot with his feeble hands, he cut the leather and pulled the rope down into the cave from where he would be able to watch sunrise and sunset for eternity from his grave, undisturbed.

Climbing up the rock face was easy, he hardly had to depend on the rope. He saw so many handholds. He found his bundle at the base of the cliff and he traveled on, down to the waterfall where he ate some dried fish and stilled his thirst.

He followed the river for two days, when at sunset on the second day he arrived at the confluence with the River of the Kootenay. The landscape there was familiar to him, but the river valley had changed. A spring flood from melting ice and snow had deposited fields of gravel and a tangle of driftwood on the lower flood plain. He found the rapids where the canoe should be. It wasn't there. Kootenay looked disorientated for a moment.

He had counted on his canoe, as he didn't feel like crossing the mountains on his way home to the Lake of the Kootenay. He knew the river flowed toward midnight, where it entered the lake. On the spot where he was standing, the river flowed to the sun, so there had to be a big bend. However, Kootenay didn't know how far the river flowed to the sun before it made the big bend toward where he knew the Kootenay people lived. Kootenay had made up his mind that he wanted to know the full extent of the domain of his people.

If he wanted to cruise the full length of the river, he had to have a canoe, but his canoe was gone. He sat down to see if he could remember what they did after shooting the rapid. They wouldn't have left the canoe so close to the river that it could be washed away; Old Kootenay was too smart for that. Then he remembered; they had climbed up a steep gravel bank where the same river thousands of summers before had formed another flood plain much wider than the one today. That was when the great ice sheets melted. Kootenay dropped everything and ran across gravel and sandbars and up to the higher level of the flood plain. There, overgrown by willows and small trees, well-hidden, was his canoe. Under it, exactly where he had placed it, was his paddle.

When Kootenay pulled the craft out of the bushes the next day, he found that it needed some repairs badly. Some of the crossribs had rotted and had to be replaced; on the outer hull, a few pieces of birchbark had disintegrated and needed replacing. Most of the materials he needed were close at hand, but it was a different story with the resin. He had to go a long way to find the pine trees that produced the pitch he needed. Kootenay worked hard for many days to get his boat shipshape, though he didn't mind.

After the fatigue of crossing the Shining Mountains through ice and snow, he had regained his former fitness. He walked around completely naked while he worked. In the evening, he went swimming in a pool at the river. Day by day, he noticed the water level in the river dropping. The next day, he would be on the move.

In the evening on that day, a fierce thunderstorm came rolling down the valley. First wind gusts shook the trees; then hail and heavy rain followed. He had to move fast, turning his canoe upside-down to find shelter. The downpour lasted all night, with Kootenay sleeping under the canoe. It was a good test for the seaworthiness of his craft. Kootenay had slept well, and he was satisfied.

The next day, on a sunny morning, he launched his newly refitted ship, after portaging it and his gear to a calm backwater with a sandy bottom. He knew that it was very easy to damage the hull on a birchbark canoe on the rocky shoreline of a fast-flowing river. He took proper care. Storing gear and food in a canoe was another job that needed a lot of care. Kootenay knew what he was doing; he had watched, and he had made his own experiences.

When he was ready, he jumped in and got right on his knees in order to keep the main ballast at the center of his boat secure and maintain stability. When he now steered his ship into the fast-flowing main channel of the river, he found that it took little effort to steer. He had time to pay more attention to the ever-changing landscape as he was floating by.

27

Kootenay was now embarked on the final leg of his odyssey, a trip which would take him all summer and would cover a total distance as far as he had traveled on foot crossing the Shining Mountains twice. He would get to know the lands of his people, Kootenay country.

After traveling during the day, he stopped every night. When it rained, he slept under his canoe; when the weather was good, he slept in the open. After a few days, the river widened and flowed lazily within its banks, and cruising down the river was easy. The boat steered itself.

One afternoon, he came to a spot where a fast-flowing river joined the Kootenay from sunrise. At this time of the year, this river carried more water than the River of the Kootenay, and the water felt colder. Above where this new river had washed out a deep pool, Kootenay noticed a backwater which had been left behind when the water level dropped. A few fast strokes with his paddle pushed his canoe into a bar of warm, white sand. The backwater was much warmer than the river, due to the fact that the water had been stagnant for some time. Fishing was good there, and Kootenay stayed for a few days. The fish seemed to congregate above the spot where the river, which carried a lot of silt, flowed into the pool. It looked like the fish were waiting for the river to clear, so they could swim upstream to their spawning grounds.

Kootenay washed his clothing by rubbing it with clean, white sand. He had watched his squaw at the Yaha-Tinda do that. Then he washed himself by rubbing himself with clean sand. Then he went swimming.

When Kootenay had enough dried fish, he jumped into his canoe and cruised on. One day, he saw smoke, which could have come from a campfire or from a forest fire. He slowed his canoe and held it close to the shore, where he could stop fast and disappear in the thick forest. He was now at the spot where the river was making a big bend, which he only knew from the fact that his canoe was facing into the sunset. That night, he was very careful; he was now certain that the smoke, mixed with the smell of smoking meat, came from a campfire.

Whether the people who had made the fire were friendly or not, he couldn't know, so he steered his canoe to the opposite shore from where the smoke was coming. There he floated under a strand of overhanging willows, making sure he would be invisible from the other side. He made no fire, and that night he slept in his canoe since he had everything he needed in his boat. If he had to, he could get away in complete silence. During the hours of darkness, he heard no sound except the wind in the willows and the lapping sound of the waves against the hull of the boat. He woke to the singing of birds and to the racket ducks made in the morning, when they engage in their noisiest activities. He stayed there under his bearskin listening, alert to even the sound of a woodpecker as the bird hammered away at a hollow tree. Kootenay had never paid much attention to the song of birds while he was traveling across the Shining Mountains, with the exception of swans and geese, but now that he was cruising down the river he had so little to do that he had time to listen. He was amazed how many different birds were singing and he could distinguish by just listening.

When he got up on his knees, he parted the willow branches in front of him and looked across the water to the other side of the river; there he saw several men looking toward him. Had they seen him? There was only one possibility. They had seen him coming down the river last night and disappear under the willows, but they hadn't seen him come out, so they had to think that he was still there. They seemed to be on foot, and from what he could see from there, they were dressed differently. They seemed to only wear what looked like a skirt; the rest of their body was bare. Whether or not they wore moccasins, he couldn't tell. Obviously they hadn't come by canoe; otherwise they would have come looking for him. To swim the river there was very risky since it was so swift and deep. So what was there for him to do?

Actually it was very simple. Since they didn't have a canoe, he could just push into fast water and float away, or if he had in mind meeting these people, he could steer across the river and meet them on their side. It was risky; he knew that.

On the other hand, there were five of them in the party, and they were all well equipped, so they would know they weren't in any danger when they saw him. The more he thought about it, the more it became clear to him that it was worth taking a chance. But he didn't have anything to give them as a welcome present. Then he realized he did; he had Old Kootenay's pipe and a leather pouch full of tobacco. They could smoke the pipe and he could leave them some tobacco; that would do it.

With his paddle, he pushed himself away from the shore. As soon as he was out from under the bushes, he was gripped by the current and forced into the fast water of midstream, and he found himself shooting downstream with fantastic speed. He wasn't prepared for that, and it wasn't what he had in mind.

In the meantime, the braves on the other shore had seen him and came running and waving their arms while he struggled with the fast current. He was quite a stretch downriver when he managed to force the bow of the canoe upstream into the current. As he was still in midstream, however, he didn't make any headway until he eased the canoe sideways to the other riverbank. Now that he was in slow water, he managed to move upstream to the spot where the braves were waiting. When they saw that he was out of breath, they helped him pull his boat ashore, to Kootenay that meant they were a friendly bunch.

After he had steadied himself, and with the canoe secure on the riverbank, he had a moment to look around. Their camp was set up close to the river; in the stonepit was a crackling fire. The hunters had obviously been sitting around the fire on tree trunks when they first saw him in his canoe. Now they were talking to him in a strange dialect.

As it was clear to Kootenay that they were asking who he was and where he had come from, he said, "I'm Kootenay, and I come with greetings from the Kootenay people."

At first there was no response; then the oldest of the group stood up from the log he had been sitting on and walked over to Kootenay. At first he spoke in a strange dialect which seemed to be directed toward his companions. Then he changed to a dialect which sounded more like the language his people spoke.

When he spoke slowly, Kootenay could understand most of what he said. "We are Sa-Haptin," he said. "We have been traveling in Kootenay country for many months, and we hope that you will share our food with us for a few days."

With that, he pointed toward the campfire and walked toward it. Kootenay himself walked to his canoe, where he found Old Kootenay's pipe and tobacco; he carried both to the fire and laid pipe and tobacco down in front of the man who had spoken to him. The man nodded with a smile, but didn't say anything. While they were eating, there was silence. The group had been very lucky in hunting; they had very good venison curing on the fire on skewers. They had rubbed salt on strips of meat before smoking and drying it. That made it taste better. Salt was the one thing he had forgotten to look for at Old Kootenay's camp.

When everybody was sated, the man in charge of the party stuffed the pipe. Then he picked a small piece of glowing ember with his bare hands and placed it on top of the tobacco. Soon the pleasant aroma of the fragrant tobacco wafted around the camp, and the good feeling of a full tummy and a good smoke loosened the tongues. Soon there was lively conversation going.

As this took place at the time of the year when the nights are short and warm, the men smoked and told the latest stories. As this was the only way the latest news was transmitted among the Indian people in those days, Kootenay listened carefully. What he heard from the man left him with the impression that his world would undergo traumatic changes in his lifetime.

The man said that he had met a group of White men; they called themselves "explorers," and they came with messages from the Great White Chief. They traded for horses with the Sa-Haptin since they had in mind crossing the White Mountains to the Great Ocean. They had with them a man with black skin. They couldn't believe there were people with black skin in the world, so they tried to rub it off, but the black color wouldn't come off.

"This story was told to me by a Shoshone; he also told me that whenever the White people send explorers, soon thereafter they come in great numbers and take over the land. They come on wagons on wheels, pulled by horses. They can carry everything with them.

"Their women have long, yellow hair, so have their children. All men carry thundersticks with which they can kill a deer at a great distance."

261

It was late when the braves crawled into their lean-to. Kootenay followed and rested under his bearskin. He slept soundly within the safety of the group. Only once during the night did he hear the songs of a pack of wolves from far away. Right after that, he heard the sound of an animal walking through the grass behind him. He thought it was a coyote, so he didn't pay any more attention to the sound. Then he heard the same animal making a crunching sound close to the firepit, as if the visitor was chewing a bone. Kootenay reached for his spear, got up, and placed a large chunk of wood on the fire. Then he went back to sleep. From then on all was quiet except for the soothing sound of the river.

When the morning sunlight came dancing through the branches, he got up and got all the fish he had stored in his canoe and rubbed them with salt and roasted them on skewers over the open fire for breakfast. When the rest of the hunters got the smell of roasting fish in their noses, they were up and feasted on fish.

Kootenay forgot all about the nocturnal visit of this denizen of the night, and during the next night, the same sound occurred; only this time the visitor consumed all the fishbones that had been left laying around the firepit. Kootenay started asking questions about whether his companions had heard it too? Yes, they knew about the animal. He had been following them and hanging around their camp all summer long. They thought he was the only survivor from a litter of whelps; the rest of the pups were killed by a male wolf who was jealous of the pups because while the mother of the pups was nursing them she couldn't come into heat. They had avoided feeding him in the hope that he would leave and try to find his mother, if she was still alive. In the meantime, he seemed to find enough food around their camp that he was thriving, and he seemed to enjoy this kind of life and the freedom and protection it allowed him due to the proximity of the human beings.

Nobody had ever seen him since he slept during the day; only during the night did he get active and clean up what fell under the table of the hunters. That was about to change, at least that was the plan of the young wolf. He noted that there was a newcomer to the camp, and since then, there was delicious fish on the menu.

One day, Kootenay was sitting in the sun, with his back against a tree trunk, eating fish, when he heard the same sound he had heard during the night. The sound came from behind. The young wolf, of course having made all kinds of experiences, knew that it was always better to approach a human being from behind; one could tell a lot from behind just by smell. Besides the smell of fresh fish was overpowering. Kootenay, having heard the sound behind, sat perfectly still. After a while, the sound disappeared, only to reappear all around him. During all this, the young wolf remained invisible. Then all sounds were gone. But when he looked straight ahead, a few blades of grass were moving in an unnatural way, there was no wind. Kootenay kept looking at the same spot; then he saw it. Two yellow eyes were watching him intensely. Kootenay knew now that the wolf pup was studying him. He moved without haste. He took a bite from a smoked fish; the rest he dropped somewhere between him and the pup.

The pup, knowing that a human being willing to share food would be willing to accept him in the pack, was still not committed. He could still get away easily. But that piece of fish lying there was a great temptation for a hungry, young wolf.

Kootenay sat perfectly still watching the two yellow eyes for a long time. Then they disappeared, and the pup was gone. Kootenay knew the pup was hungry, but he was also very cautious. He wouldn't accept food from him yet. He got up and walked over to his canoe to get another fish. When he came back, the food was gone. The pup had taken food from him but not in his presence. Kootenay knew that only after the pup had accepted food out of his hand would he trust him enough to follow him; only after he ate out of his hand would the pup be his dog.

One day Kootenay went upriver in the canoe to a quiet backwater to do some fishing, at a spot where a small waterfall splashed into a pool. There were lots of fish. Large trout came and swam around his canoe. It was good fishing with spear and dipnet. Spear-fishing required a lot of concentration and good aim. While Kootenay was totally absorbed in his activity, he hadn't noticed what was going on along the shoreline. When he looked up, there was the wolf pup looking at him with big, yellow eyes, hoping that he would be included in a feast of fresh fish. For a moment, Kootenay felt as if all the deep distrust that he had seen before had gone out of those eyes.

Kootenay threw him a fish. The pup went over where the fish had landed, put one of his front paws on it, and pulled it apart like an expert. Kootenay was certain now that if he took his time and didn't scare him off, he would be able to make a deal with the young wolf. For a share of his food, the wolf would help in hunting and provide company for the young human being.

It happened on a nice, warm afternoon when Kootenay was smoking the fish he would need when he traveled down the river. He was sitting in the shade of the same tree where he had met the pup for the first time. First he saw two ears where the grass was moving, then two yellow eyes. The pup came crawling toward him on his tummy. He was hungry, wolf pups are always hungry because they are growing so fast. At this moment, Kootenay knew that if he had in mind making the young wolf his dog he would have to try today. It was a beautiful day, the birds were singing in the trees, and the sun was warm in the clearing. The world was at peace. The stage was set for a drama which had taken place countless times before, and would take place again and again as long as two different beings of equal ferocity were making deals for symbiotic cooperation. This kind of contract may last for a lifetime, as Kootenay knew from Keeno when he sacrificed himself and, with that selfless act, may have saved Kootenay's life. In the meantime, Kootenay was sitting there eating, taking his time and not giving any food to the pup. He wanted him hungry in the hope that hunger might convince the pup to make a deal.

In the meantime, the pup was twisting his eyes around as if he was trying to get a better look at the morsels of food Kootenay was devouring, and at the same time moving closer and closer until Kootenay could touch him with outstretched hand. Slowly, ever so slowly, he moved his right hand toward the pup, while holding a fish in his left. Kootenay could see that the pup was uncomfortable in this situation, he looked sideways to see if the door was open so he could get away if he had to. But now, at the spur of the moment, the pup made an irrevocable decision. While Kootenay was scratching his back softly, the young wolf turned on his back and offered his soft underbelly, the most vulnerable part of his body, as a sign of total submission to him. Kootenay was so touched by the limitless trust this young animal put in him that he had tears in his eyes

A wolf can do no more. From this moment on, the pup was eating out of Kootenay's hand, and he was his dog. Only once did some doubt arise between Kootenay and his pup. That was on the morning after Kootenay decided to say goodbye to the hospitable Sa-Haptin.

265

28

His canoe was riding low at anchor, heavy with all his gear, fish, and venison. The latter being a contribution from the generous Sa-Haptin, who knew that Kootenay had a long way to go to the home of his people. When Kootenay was ready to weigh his anchor, the leader of the Sa-Haptin came to the shore and handed him Old Kootenay's pipe and the pouch with some tobacco. Then he said, "To thank the Great Chief of the Kootenay for allowing us to trespass and hunt on their land."

Kootenay, not knowing that he would be the new chief of the Kootenay when he returned home, just said that he would convey the message. When he noticed that he hadn't seen the wolf pup and he thought that he had the forsaken him in order to remain a camp follower of the hunters, the pup came running out of the forest, where he had spent the night in his den.

The young wolf stood there uncertain, not knowing what to do. This was indeed a new situation. He had been prepared to walk with his newfound master, but to go on a cruise was a different story. While he was running back and forth, he made a frightened, whimpering sound like a new-born puppy. While Kootenay was waiting on his knees in his canoe, he was at a loss as to what to do to entice the puppy into his canoe; he remembered how he had called his faithful companion Keeno, who had been killed by that ferocious bear, to come into his canoe. He blurted out, "Keeno!" The pup made the enormous jump from the shore into the boat, while the Sa-Haptin watched in awe about the great power this young Kootenay man had shown over a wild wolf.

With a few powerful strokes of his paddle, Kootenay maneuvered his canoe into the fast-flowing water of mid-stream and the boat was shooting down river with the speed of the wind. He hardly had enough time to wave back to the hospitable Sa-Haptin when the campsite disappeared behind the next bend in the river. As far as Kootenay's new companion was concerned, he looked like he enjoyed cruising down the river and watching the world go by. As far as Kootenay was concerned, he had put all privations of the last winter behind him.

In a few weeks of easy living, he had put all the weight he had lost back on. He had grown a little, and his shoulders had widened. He was looking forward, with great anticipation, to seeing his people. But Kootenay's greatest joy was when he looked at his newfound companion, Keeno the Wolf. Kootenay had, over the years, developed certain rules with Keeno. He fed him only once a day, but then he let him have his fill. In time he got used to that. For the time being they had enough food.

Then the fast-flowing river changed into a meandering stream that flowed lazily between its grass-covered banks. There were times when Kootenay thought this lazy river would never end. Life was easy; while Kootenay was hunting ducks, it didn't take young Keeno very long to develop a taste for young ducklings. As he became more successful in the hunt for such delicacies, he often stayed away from Kootenay's camp all day. It was during those warm, endless summer days that Keeno developed the habit of insisting on hunting on his own for long periods of time. He was, in this respect, totally different than Old Keeno, who never left Kootenay's side. The only time Kootenay could count on

Keeno's presence was when a pack of wolves was in the neighborhood. Then he would stay close to Kootenay, and during the night he would lay at Kootenay's feet like Old Keeno had done.

Perhaps he never forgot, nor forgave, the big, gray wolf for what he had done to his siblings. He, the runt, had only survived because the big wolf couldn't follow into the far end of the cave where he was hiding. Only after Keeno realized that a pack of wolves would never accept him, and the life of a lone wolf was short and sad, he became the reliable hunting partner old Keeno had been.

It was on a warm, late-summer evening when Kootenay's canoe was finally cruising into the tranquil waters of the Lake of the Kootenays. He thought that some time during the following day he would be within sight of his camp, the camp from which he had been taken by order of council of his people. His people couldn't know that he was still alive. How would they receive him? How many summers had gone by since his involuntary departure from the camp?

Was the man who was then chief of the tribe his father? The only time in his life he ever felt like having a father was during his stay with Old Kootenay. Only his mother knew who his father was, and only his mother he could trust.

It was at this moment that he made the decision to approach the camp from the morning side of the lake. He would have to find the sandy beach where the braves had left the canoe. But he didn't realize that he was blindfolded; he would never find the sandy bay without knowing what it looked like. All day he cruised along the lake; he looked at every sandy bay he found. Everywhere he looked, he found a green wall of impenetrable forest. It seemed to him as if all bushes and trees had joined branches to keep him out of their secret halls of green twilight, as if behind the impenetrable wall of green they were hiding all secrets of continuing creation.

For the first time in his life, now that he was so close to home, he really felt homesick. At the next protected bay with a wide, sandy beach he set up camp. For his fire there was dry driftwood. They would sleep under his canoe, in the soft sand. When the golden sun was setting behind the mountains on the other side of the lake, he watched for signs of smoke from the fires of his people. There was nothing. His people had disappeared from his childhood world, from the only world he had known. The only thing he could recognize and was familiar to him was the unchanging mountain panorama, which told him where the old campsite of his people had to be. Maybe that would give him a clue.

Crossing the lake the next morning, toward the spot where he thought the old Kootenay camp had to be, didn't take very long. He tied his canoe to a stand of willows and climbed up a steep embankment to where he thought the camp should be. On the first sight, the area where the camp had been was completely changed. The spot where he had played as a child, and where he now walked, was overgrown with small bushes and a new strand of poplar saplings.

In most cases, when the Indian people moved their camp, they left their lodge poles standing or leaning against a tree. When he found the ring of stones where he knew his mother's lodge had stood, all the poles were gone. Had they taken them when they moved? And where had they gone? They couldn't have gone upriver. He had come from there; he would have seen them. They had to be somewhere along the lake.

His campfire burned late that night as he sat there and stared across the lake. He didn't see it as the red sunlight climbed up to the mountaintop on the other side like a burning fire. He felt like crying, like a child, but there were no tears. His eyes remained dry, but inside of him there was something that tied his innards into a knot, as all his childhood memories came flooding through his mind. Everything he could remember from his childhood was connected to this piece of earth. He had felt the earth here with his bare feet. He had felt the cool, clear water when he went swimming. He knew the pools were full of fish to still his hunger, but best of all, when he didn't feel good, there were the soothing hands of his mother. When he finally crawled into his bearskin, he lay there sobbing because he couldn't cry. His wolfhound Keeno walked around their camp in great circles not knowing what to do; he had never seen his master like this. When all was quiet and Kootenay had gone to sleep, he went and laid at his master's feet.

For the next few days, they went fishing. Kootenay still remembering the fishing holes of his youth, Keeno had fun with a bunch of turtles. When he first saw them, they were sitting on a log in the sun. When he approached gingerly in order to catch one, they dropped in the water with a loud splash. When he sat still for a long time and didn't move, they reappeared and arranged themselves on the log as before in the warm sun. As soon as he made a move splash, they were gone. That went on all day, until Kootenay had enough fish to continue the journey.

They cruised toward midnight for many days. Unnoticed by Kootenay, summer had turned into autumn, and the poplars along the shoreline reflected their golden light in the dark waters of the lake.

One day, he came to a spot where the lake widened. At first it looked like a side arm of the lake, so Kootenay decided to cross it and continue on the other side along the shore. He was just about halfway across when he let his boat drift for a while. He noticed his boat drifting sideways, as if there was a strong current. With a powerful stroke of his paddle, he pointed the bow of his canoe into midstream, where he thought the current might be the strongest. He didn't feel any movement in his canoe. Only the fast-changing scenery along the shoreline told him he was moving at a good speed. Kootenay had, on his own, discovered the only outlet of the Lake of the Kootenay that would take him to the river that flowed into the Great Ocean. It was as if a power much greater than his own had pointed him in the right direction.

For one day Kootenay and his wolf drifted on the placid waters of the Kootenay River without seeing any sign of human habitation. Up high in the sky stood the silver sparkle of the Kokanee Glacier, which grew in intensity during the day until it reflected the brightness of the noon sun. During that day, Kootenay made up his mind that if he couldn't find his people he might drift across the Shining Mountains and look for the Na-Koda squaw who had shared the lodge with him at the Yaha-Tinda. Maybe he could convince her to follow him to the warm side of the Shining Mountains to a place where the warm waters flowed.

Kootenay hadn't only been drifting; he had been dreaming. When he woke up, he had the scent of fire in his nose. Immediately he was alert, his daydream forgotten for the time being. There was no smoke to be seen. Only high in the sky removed to its real distance by the midday haze, stood the blue ice of the Kokanee. But there was a blue haze; it had to be smoke. Then, in a sheltered bay, behind a row of golden poplars, he could see the many teepees of his people.

Slowly he drifted over to the shore where a gentle, sandy beach sloped upward to a green meadow. A little higher, safe above the high watermark, stood a row of lodges covered with birchbark, as it was the custom in a land of silver birches. As he cruised along in complete silence, the camp showed no sign of life at this time of the day.

The situation changed when the camp dogs heard the crunching sound as Kootenay pulled his canoe up on the sandy beach. A whole pack of them came charging down the hill in a grumpy mood for having been disturbed in their late afternoon nap. Behind the dogs came a horde of grubby children. The dogs, having found their target, came straight for Kootenay and his wolf companion Keeno. The situation didn't look good for Kootenay and Keeno. Keeno, during his months of travel with Kootenay, had outgrown his puppy stage and was now almost a full-grown wolf. Kootenay had trained him to stay by his side when there was danger so that they might form a common front toward any assumed assailant.

Kootenay now put his hand on the shoulder of Keeno to calm and reassure him of his presence. So Keeno stood his ground, hackles raised. As the dogs came closer, he showed his mighty fangs, and at the same time he let out a blood-curdling growl. That stopped the pack in their tracks. With the first charge averted, the pair had time to regroup, and the dogs knew that the two were a group to be reckoned with.

The problem solved itself as an old, white-haired man appeared from one of the lodges. His body was bent down and rested on a gnarled willow pole, which he shoved into the ground in front of him with his right hand, while his left was trying to keep a caribou pelt from sliding from his shoulders. After the old man had managed to keep everything hanging around and from him, and himself, from falling down, it looked to Kootenay like the old man had reached, at least for the moment, a certain temporary equilibrium. When a sharp command came forth from the shaking bundle of fur and human being, it was meant for the dogs. It sounded more like a voice used to issuing commands than the frail bundle of bones that stood in front of him.

The man, now pushing his body toward Kootenay with his cane, said in a very authoritative voice, "What might the purpose of your visit be, young man?" His voice was strong.

Kootenay said, "Just a moment, please," and he ran down the hill to this canoe, where he found pipe and tobacco. On the way back, he saw the dogs lying in the shade of a tree, not paying any attention to him, but keeping a keen eye on Keeno.

At the teepee, the old man waved Kootenay inside. Kootenay bent down and lifted the flap so the old man didn't have to bend down. Inside the lodge, the old man seated himself on a pile of soft moss while Kootenay placed a handful of kindling on the still-glowing embers of the fire. When the fire flared up and spread a warm glow over the scene, they smoked the pipe. Or so it seemed to Kootenay. The old man smoked the pipe. It looked like he hadn't smoked good tobacco like this stuff for a long time. He would take a deep drag and hold the smoke in his mouth. When Kootenay thought he would blow the smoke in the air, it was sucked up by his nostrils from where it disappeared into his lungs. He held it there for a long time for the full euphoric effect to take place. Then, when he exhaled with a deep sigh, it looked to Kootenay like smoke was issuing not only from his mouth and nose but also from his eyes and ears. He repeated the procedure until he handed the pipe to Kootenay. Now Kootenay smoked while the old man sat there with a satisfied grin on his face.

Kootenay now put the pipe aside, and noticing that the old man looked at him as if he expected an answer to the question he had asked, Kootenay said, "I am the boy whom you people sent into exile across the mountains to learn how to be afraid and how to be humble. Well, I have learned humility and fear on the secret trail of the Kootenay. I have suffered the hardships and deprivation you encounter when you travel across the Shining Mountains alone. I have hunted wapiti and the white goat with Na-Koda, Sik-sika, and Nara-Wak. I was at the Head Smashed In to hunt the In-Ni. It was not good when you are alone when you look at the stars. On the other side of the Shining Mountains, I watched the rain running across the Sea of Grass and never hit the ground.

"And, above all, Sir, I have prevailed against all the odds stacked against me in the natural world. I found the way. Now I am here to claim my proper place, and my due share of the amenities available to my people." He continued, "On the other side of the Shining Mountains I watched the rain running across the sea of grass and never hit the ground."

At this moment the old man seemed to wake from a deep slumber, when in fact he had been listening very carefully. He said to Kootenay, "Tell me more about this running rain."

"Yes," he said, "it happens often in the summer. Dark thunder clouds drifting across the sea of grass, you can see raindrops coming from the clouds, but no drop of rain hits the ground."

The man shook his head like he couldn't believe what Kootenay had said. The next question sounded like the old man was interrogating an impostor. "You say you are the boy we sent into the wilderness six summers ago to learn how to survive and to become humble?"

"Yes, Sir, I'm the same I have always been, even though in outward appearance I have changed. I'm still the son of my mother. She would recognize me; where is she?"

"All the women are in the hills picking berries, as long as the weather is good they will not return home."

"Where are all the men who were at the council meeting that decreed to send me into the wilderness? The man whom I consider my father was there, too!"

"The man, who at that time was chief of the tribe, was not your father, but he had adopted you when your real father disappeared under mysterious circumstances and was never seen again!"

Kootenay, who had been listening with great interest, now stared at the old man as an awesome thought rushed through his mind. Was it possible that the old man whom he called Old Kootenay, and with whom he had lived for two summers, and whose remains he had interred in a rock cave, was his father? He had developed a father/son relationship with him. Kootenay was silent. He never mentioned anything about this to anybody. The thought he had would be his secret forever.

There was great silence while Kootenay recharged the pipe and placed a glowing ember on top of the tobacco. He handed it to the old man who repeated the performance until the glow of euphoria appeared on his old face. Then he was ready to interrogate the young man in front of him further. Quite abruptly he said, "We sent out a posse to look for you the following spring. They couldn't find any evidence that you were still alive. Later we had word from a traveler who told us that you perished at a place called Waka-Nambe."

Kootenay stared at him and said, "Waka-Nambe? I was at Waka-Nambe. When I saw the ice and snow, I turned around and found the real secret trail of the Kootenay. So the man they found in the ice at Waka-Nambe wasn't me; it was somebody else."

When he looked at the old man, he found that he had gone to sleep. That night Kootenay and Keeno slept in the old man's lodge. It was a peaceful night; nothing stirred. He was up long before the sun rose above the mountaintops. Only the Kokanee ice glowed high above the valley in the light of the early dawn. He found the trail that would lead to the Hills of Many Berries, where he hoped to find his mother.

He walked along the riverside under golden poplars all morning when Keeno, who had been walking beside him, suddenly stopped and his ears perked up. Kootenay stopped and listened. The sound of singing children was in the air.

275

One of the senior ladies of the group didn't have a very good night in their comfortable lean-to. She was restless, had a bad dream, and couldn't sleep. That was unusual with her; she usually slept better than most of the women who were with her harvesting the sweet, ripe berries. Then last night, she had a vexing dream. A tall stranger was coming toward her through the forest. The stranger looked like her son, the same as the son who had perished in the wilderness after he was sent into exile. Now, in her dream, this son was coming toward her. He was dressed in handsome chamois and he walked with the gait of the traveling woodsmen of his people. Walking next to the hunter she saw a gray wolf. But how could it be her son if he was dead? He had been declared dead a few summers ago. With that the image disappeared, and she awoke in a cold sweat.

The following morning, the women were late going to the berry-patches because the grass was wet from the heavy dew during the cool night. They had slept late. Only the children were up playing games and singing.

After the women had formed a single line on the narrow, wet trail, Kootenay's mother, the lady with the bad dreams, turned around and walked away into the morning sun. One of the women whispered, "She's had her dream again." The last they saw of her, she was walking downhill in the bright sunlight. Running behind her was a little boy of about five carrying a basket half-full of berries.

When Kootenay saw the woman coming toward him, he knew it was his mother. She looked beautiful. Odd, he had never thought of his mother as being beautiful. She was only his mother. Her black hair sparkled in the sunlight. When she saw the tall hunter, she knew it was the same man who walked with the wolf in her many dreams, she had had all summer long. She ran toward him and fell down on her knees in front of him. Her hands dug into the grass while tears were running out of her eyes. The tears that had dried up when they took him from her now flowed again, but they were tears of happiness. She hugged the ground he walked on while she cried in silence.

It was the little boy with the basket who broke the silence when he asked the tall leather-clad stranger, "Who are you?"

Kootenay then spoke and said, "I'm your brother."

"I didn't know I had a brother!"

"Now you do!"

The man who walked with a wolf, his little brother, and his mother walked back to their camp in total silence. They knew that, for now, everything they could say would be too much. No spoken word was fitting for the moment could be found. In the evening, by a crackling campfire, while in the dark sky a pale harvest moon drifted through thin clouds and when all the women of the camp were sitting around the fire, Kootenay told the story of his travels; how he got lost at Waka-Nambe, how it felt to be overcome by fear. He told the story how the Na-Koda people ran the buffalo over a cliff because the beast was so big nobody could kill it with bow and arrow.

But the women were most impressed by the story he told about the running rain. That dark clouds would form and drift above the sea of grass with lightning and thunder and rain hanging below the clouds and no rain will touch the earth; the women, of course, wouldn't believe that. They looked at each other giggling, like women always do. They just couldn't believe that it was possible to walk under a cloud and not get wet.

The next night he told the story how the avalanche scared the hibernating bear out of his den and then it came walking down the hill and killed his dog. The women asked, "Was that the same dog that disappeared from the camp after you were taken away?"

277

"Yes, he was the same. He traveled with me all the summers until the bear got him last spring. My new dog is a young gray wolf. He was given to me by the Sa-Haptin people. He followed them half-dead after the rest of the litter had been killed by a male wolf. After that, he followed me. He has been walking with me ever since."

Kootenay stayed with the women while the good weather lasted. When they returned to their permanent camp with all their baskets full of berries. When they arrived, he was given his own teepee as a sign of his great importance in the community.

After telling the story of the running rain a few times, the children of the village called him Running Rain, as a nickname at first. Then the name stuck. From then on Running Rain became his proper name, and the children stopped teasing him with it, while all the other children were called Kootenay.

When, after the first heavy storm all the trails in the forest were deep in snow, all the braves returned from their fishing camp, their canoes riding low in the water with dried fish, there was great rejoicing. Nobody would go hungry for a long time. When he told his people the story of his travels across the Shining Mountains, they listened, and admiration and even respect for him grew.

The months of early winter were a slow and easy time in the camp. It was the time of story-telling. The young hunters would meet in the warm teepees and smoke the pipe and relate their stories of exploits, of success and failure in hunting.

Running Rain became the most popular speaker. He had to tell how he found the secret trail of his people across the Shining Mountains, where the warm chinook wind blew through the passes and sent avalanches thundering into the valleys. His best story was when he told about rain walking across the land and no drop hitting the ground. In a land where it rains a lot, this seemed hardly possible.

Later in the winter, after the snow settled and froze to a hard crust, the caribou could walk on top of the frozen snow. They came in long lines on their old trails. The braves would don their snowshoes and follow the herd for days. They took what they needed; the meat for food and their skins for parkas and moccasins and carried all home to their camp where the women waited.

29

When the first warm days of the new year arrived, Running Rain became restless; he had been on the trail for too long to sit still for any length of time. During the long nights of winter, when he lay sleepless under his bear robe, he developed a plan to explore the full extent of the land of his people, which was now called Kootenay country.

He was already familiar with the river that carried the name of his people. From its source in the Shining Mountains, he had traveled as far toward midday as it was possible when he met the Sa-Haptin. Now all that remained for him to do was travel by canoe toward midnight, until he arrived at the wall of rock and ice so wrapped in mystery, beyond which no human being dared to travel, as Old Kootenay had told him.

When Running Rain refurbished the three largest canoes in their fleet, nobody suspected that he had in mind a major expedition into the land of midnight since it was normal that equipment was repaired when not much else was to do. Then he made new paddles out of straight-grained cedar wood. He made the paddles a little longer, with a larger blade, more like the one he had used when cruising the river.

Kootenay had established a solid base as a claim for leadership in his own community. In his role as a hunter and provider, he hoped that he would be able to extend that role to all the communities along the lake. He had no problem finding the five young braves he needed to man the three canoes for the trip, two men to each canoe. That his yearning to be on the trail with a group of like-minded companions was just as strong as the desire to explore his realm he decided to mention to nobody.

So it was that three canoes manned by six strong oarsmen and one gray wolf pushed off the shore toward the Lake of the Kootenay. As it was a warm spring morning, all the women and children of the village had met at the beach to wave good-bye to their men until they disappeared around the next bend. Then there was quiet. Only the rhythmic slapping sound of the paddles was to be heard as the oarsmen strained to overcome the strong current out on the lake. They hugged the shoreline on the sunset side of the lake.

They made good time, as they now had the noon sun and the wind behind them. Where the next creek flowed into the lake they set up camp and fished, as they hadn't taken any food. They spent two days there; then the flotilla crossed the lake and continued on along the other shore, where they found that many streams came rushing down from the bugaboo, many more than they could count, all in spring flood from the melting snow in the dark impenetrable forest. One day, they spotted a herd of caribou feeding on the fresh green next to the lake, so they set up their first hunting camp, building a lean-to from driftwood they found along the shoreline. There they filled their canoes with dried meat, which should last them for a long trip.

On that evening, when they were sitting by their fire, Running Rain had a feeling as if there was a change in the weather in the air. Even though, at the moment he couldn't see anything, the wind, which had been blowing from midday, suddenly stopped and it became death-still. For a moment, nothing moved; even the waves on the lake were calm and the surface of the lake looked like molten lead. It was as if the world was holding its breath to prepare itself for the violence of the oncoming storm.

From midnight an angry-looking, dark cloud engulfed the mountains on the other side of the lake. This was the weather change Running Rain, with the age-old experience of his people, had felt long before he had seen it. Now things changed with lightning speed. From the black cloud, which had rolled across the mountains, gray tentacles reached through the valleys and toward the lake, where they formed a roll of white cloud. Within that cloud came the wind that rolled an angry tempest of water toward them.

They hardly had enough time to pull their canoes out of the water and lay them on top of their shelter when a wall of rain drowned out all other sounds around them. A lightning bolt tore the world apart when it hit a tree behind them and brought it crashing to the ground. Then there was only the soothing sound of the rain drumming on their canoes. Running Rain's old habit of building a solid shelter had paid off again. They spent the night warm and dry, even though it was impossible to keep a fire going.

It was the morning that brought the big surprise. The world was covered with thick, unctuous, impenetrable fog. They had a hard time making a fire after the rain had soaked all combustible material, so they slept all day in the hope that the fog might lift during the night.

The fog didn't lift for days; it was as if the world had been enveloped in an unmoveable shroud of silence. Even the waves on the lake were silent. Behind them, in the forest, the birds had stopped singing. Everywhere there was silence. When Running Rain got up, he lifted his hand in front of his eyes. When he couldn't see it, he turned around and rolled himself in his still-warm bearskin and went back to sleep. This involuntary hibernation was nothing unusual with our group of young Kootenays, as they had no concept of time. Their inability to imagine the passing of time left them free to observe the changing of the seasons.

One morning, Running Rain heard the fluting sound of a robin singing high above him in a tree. He got up and looked around. He couldn't see the singing bird; it seemed to be singing high above the fog on top of a tree. What he could see was the disk of the sun floating like a polished plate of metal through the invisible sky, while down here, where he was standing, the fog was still as thick as ever.

What Running Rain now observed seemed to him the same phenomenon in reverse that he had watched a few days before when the fog came flowing down from the mountains; only this time it was quiet. There was no thunder and no wind. The only visible motion was in the fog; it was as if by magic it flowed back to where it had come from. It rolled and billowed and twisted and flowed up the steep valleys and over the forested hills and rocky crags until only one white roll of cloud was left hanging in front of the high, glacier-clad mountains. Running Rain stood and looked at his world in bright sunshine.

All summer they cruised the lake. When they came to the river that fed the lake, they found that it was swollen from the recent rain and melting snow and ice. It was impossible to cruise their fragile ships against this raging torrent. They stored their canoes safely above the riverbank.

For many days they blazed a trail along the river toward midnight, until one day they stood in front of a wall of rock and ice and snow. As it was late in the day, the sun was setting behind the mountains on the other side of the river, while on their side the ice-clad mountains were bathed in golden sunlight. They watched in silent awe until it was dark in the valley where they stood and the last rays of the sun reflected shafts of light into the dark sky above.

Running Rain and his team had reached the end of their world again, like the Shining Mountains which Running Rain had crossed accompanied by his faithful dog Keeno. That night, by the flickering light of their warm campfire, he had to tell his companions how he lost his way and came to the place called Waka-Nambe, where ice and snow had stopped him from going on, where fear and the cold had taught him about humility in the face of the powers of nature. When his companions were asleep, he rolled into his bearskin.

The return to their canoes was easy on their newly blazed trail. Their canoes took them back to the other side of the lake when they crossed the deep, blue water. Fishing was good there. Soon they were busy drying and smoking fish.

On the way down to the lake, they had noticed another river entering the fast-flowing river they were on. This river carried no glacial silt, which left its water blue and clear but with a strong current, so they beached their canoes and followed a game trail. After four nights they came to a lake, and for the first time since they left their home camp, they smelled smoke. Since they hadn't made a fire, the smoke had to come from somebody else's campfire, or it was from a forest fire.

They moved on until they saw smoke drifting across the lake. Now they had to be careful, as they didn't know whether they were facing friend or foe. Steep, densely forested slopes dropped down to the lakeshore. On spots, where high water had washed out the shoreline, trees had fallen into the water or were leaning at all angles, or they were ready to fall with the next rain.

The moose trail they were following wound its way around dead trees, rotting tree trunks, and very dense vegetation. Busy with bushwhacking their way through dense vegetation, they stepped suddenly into a flat gravel-strewn creekbed. It seemed to be the only clearing in this endless forest, and to their surprise, this was the spot where the smoke from the campfire came from.

The men sitting around the campfire were as surprised as they were to be meeting up with a group of fully armed men. Running Rain now showed that he was the natural leader of his group of men with his experience of many summers of travel in the wilderness. He stepped forward a few steps, pulled his bow and quiver full of arrows from behind his back, and laid them down in front. Then he raised his spear and laid it down, too. He motioned his men to do the same while he watched.

He called out in a loud, clear voice, "I am Running Rain, leader of the Kootenay people. We come in peace. We have no quarrel with you. If you will allow us, we will share our food with you, and we will smoke the pipe of peace." Then he waited.

From the other side of the clearing came a voice in a strange dialect, but Running Rain could make out what was said. "We are Nlak-Pamux. We have traveled far and have crossed many rivers to come to your country. If you will allow us, we will gladly share the food which we have taken from your water with you."

Running Rain was surprised to hear that they thought they were in Kootenay territory, which he hadn't been fully aware of. Up till now, he had lived with the idea that the world, and all the riches in it, were there to be shared between all the people who lived in it. Apparently this wasn't so. Surprised as he was about the new dimension of his experiences, he kept this thought to himself. But the knowledge that he was the landlord there had another, amazing effect on him. He felt more powerful approaching strangers on his territory. He felt like his stature had been enhanced immeasurably when facing strangers in his own backyard.

All these feelings were new to him, but for the moment, he forgot all this while he picked up his gear and walked toward the camp of the Nlak-Pamux. As soon as they got there, they were offered food. Running Rain was quite interested how these people prepared fresh fish. They had built a fire over a large stone with a flat, smooth top. After the fire was burned down and the stone was hot, they brushed all the ashes off the top. Around the stone they kept a small fire going to keep it hot. They also had salt, which they sprinkled on the rock; on top of that, they laid their fish. They also had mixed salt with dried herbs.

While the men ate, there was complete silence. Then they drank the clean, sweet water from the lake which the Nlak-Pamux called Trout Lake. When the sweet smoke from their pipe wafted around the camp, there was a deep feeling of contentment mixed with a sensation of peace in Kootenay country. As always, when men have a full tummy, conversation flowed easily.

The Nlak-Pamux told Running Rain that many White people came in long wagon trains from ships across the Great Ocean. They called themselves prospectors. Each one carried a thunderstick and they brought with them machines and tools to dig up the earth looking for metals. When Running Rain asked whether an attempt was made to stop these people, their leader said the White man couldn't be stopped until he reached the end of the world.

Running Rain and his men stayed at the Trout Lake Camp with the Nlak-Pamux hunters for many days while the weather was good. Summer had turned into fall, and along the creekbeds, the poplars had turned to gold. On the steep, rocky hillsides, dwarf maples burned in flaming colors like hot fires. Life was good for them; long, warm nights by a crackling campfire and story-telling. Running Rain had a foreboding feeling after listening to the Nlak-Pamux tell about White people coming and taking their land. The Kootenay said good-bye to their friendly hosts. On the trail back to their canoes, which would take them home to their people, they couldn't realize that life as they knew it had ended. Sweet life in Shangri-La was gone forever, never to return.

30

When they arrived at their home camp at the Kootenay River, they found that their old chief had passed away. In an unanimous vote by the assembly of all eligible braves and elders of the Kootenay Nation, Running Rain was chosen to be the new leader of all the Kootenay people. His mandate was to keep the White people out of Kootenay country. As it turned out, this task against overwhelming odds was a mission impossible.

For a few years, while his mother was still alive, Running Rain and his people enjoyed their old way of life in tranquility, traveling to the many camps along the lake and up the Kootenay River. Then, when he was getting older, White men with wagons full of firewater and guns, pulled by animals he hadn't seen before, called mules, came out of the midday sun and sold them firewater. Behind them came men who drove sticks in the ground, as boundary markers they said.

Over the many years while Running Rain was chief of the Kootenay Nation, he had guided his people with wise decisions and sound leadership. He was much respected and revered by everybody, but when White traders sold firewater and guns to the braves, he lost control of his own people. First he lost his reputation as a great hunter because a brave with a rifle could kill more deer than the best archer with bow and arrow. But that by itself was not enough; he could have learned how to shoot a rifle. It was when the effects of firewater controlled his men and diseases were brought by White people.

But what finally convinced him to go away and spend the final days of his life as a recluse was when one day a steamboat came cruising up the lake, or was it a large canoe? White people had attached a wheel to the end of it. From the top was belching black smoke. When it cruised around a turn, it blew a whistle that scared him, and Running Rain knew that could be heard all along the lake. He realized that he had lost authority over his people, and with that, he lost the desire to lead them.

According to stories told at many campfires up and down the lake at the time, he was seen by a group of hunters in a canoe crossing the lake with a yellow dog by his side. This could be the end of the story of a man called Running Rain; however, the author wishes to add that he heard the story of the final years of Running Rain told at many campfires and on lonely mountain trails even today.

As the discourse about the main character in this story seems to be based mainly on conjecture, the author wishes to acknowledge that it might be unwise to form an irreversible opinion on incomplete information.

When Running Rain reached the shore on the other side of the lake, he took his bundle, bow, quiver, and spear, and followed the trail, which he had traveled before many years ago. For reassurance, he touched his new companion Yellow Dog. This time he didn't hide his canoe; he knew he wouldn't need it again. Where he traveled across the land, he traveled lightly. His moccasins left no footprints in the grass. He disturbed nothing.

When he was on the right trail, he could feel it through the soles of his moccasins, just like he did when he walked here blindfolded many years before. He traveled up in steep creekbeds, across snow-covered mountains. He crossed rivers and streams; he swam in sun-dappled pools. Where he walked in the sun, the light shining through his white hair gave him a halo.

When he arrived at the lake where he had built his first teepee, he found nothing; only a ring of stones was there to indicate that human beings had once found shelter there. As it was his desire to leave no visible trail behind, he walked through the reed and the swamp at the end of the lake; then he crossed the River of the Kootenay. He walked for two days toward that wisp of steam where he knew the warm waters flowed. He walked along the river past the waterfall. After he climbed through the rock wall, he looked up to the cave where he knew the remains of Old Kootenay were watching over the Top of the World and the Land of the Kootenay.

Running Rain lived there for many years, spending his summers at the Top of the World. After Yellow Dog was killed and eaten by a mountain lion, he found himself a new wolf pup, which remained his steady companion until the end of his days.

Late in the fall, he moved down to his camp amongst the golden poplars at the Lake of the White Swans. He stayed there and fished. He smoked and dried his fish and carried it down to his cave.

Every fall, when the poplars dropped their golden leaves, the white swans arrived. Running Rain would sit on the rock at the lakeshore and listen to the birds. The swans got so used to him and his wolf that they thought he was part of the rock. Over the years, Running Rain had learned to understand the language of the swans. He listened carefully when they told about cruising higher and higher in the chinook wind, until they were high enough they could glide over the icy crags down into the Valley of the Kootenay. But they also told stories of the many people with thundersticks in places where they spent their winter. Many of the young birds were murdered there and would never return to the lake where they were hatched and the sun shone all day and night.

The longer Running Rain lived, the fewer birds returned to the lake where he had first heard the "Song of the Swans." One spring, when the ice had melted on the lake and Running Rain was a very old man, no white swans returned. He left the place where he used to sit and listen; he knew now that the world had changed so much that he didn't want to live in it any longer. He called his wolf and took his bundle. His weak legs carried him toward the Top of the World. Whether he arrived at the Top of the World and perished there at the place he loved so much is not known, or if he with the last strength of his body walked back to his camp and lowered himself into the shallow cave, where he could join his friend Old Kootenay and watch over the Shining Mountains and the Top of the World, will forever remain a secret, unless, of course, the cave is found.

But, then again, if Running Rain felt strong enough to walk once more across the Pass in the Clouds and across the Shining Mountains, he had all summer to do it; he might have made it to the place where heaven and earth meet. The same place people now call Running Rain Lake. Whether the lake people now call Running Rain Lake was named after Running Rain or Running Rain after the lake will forever remain a mystery hidden behind the mist of days long past.

As for myself, whenever I walk on the trail to Running Rain Lake, I can hear the story of Running Rain told by the whispering pines, but one must be very quiet and walk silently, otherwise the story will not be heard. Is it possible that at the point where myth and fable and fact merge we might find the beginning of a fairy tale?

Let the end of this story then be the beginning of the tale that it was for the people who walked the secret trails, the same trails that are now overgrown or blocked by fallen timber. For those who are willing and able to find and walk the trails, the whispering wind in the pines still tells the old stories. As for those who travel on the highways at the speed limit, they will never hear the tale of times long past and miss it completely.